As Maryam's Tree Stood Witness

*"Choose carefully between Love and Death.
You will have Tolerance or War."*

By Ali Kasem

ISBN-13: 978-9948-34-056-0

Cover design by: Ebooklaunch.com

Dedication

Dedicated to the memory of the late Mahmoud Kasem, my beloved uncle, who served the Expatriates community in England as solicitor for five decades and whose stories gave me the inspiration for the setting of this book.

Table of Content

Introduction

Maryam's Tree was born out of a deep hurt that I often feel for the world. We seem to be bombarded with reports of conflict—often deadly—between nations, political opponents, and even families, the people with whom we should feel safest. This sad reality was the inspiration for my book. But in these divided times, the hurt is not the overriding message of my book. More than anything, I wrote the book with a sense of hope. It is a story of divisions but also one of overcoming—at least for one of the couple I'll introduce you to.

As the story opens, two would-be lovers meet by chance at a village well. It could be the start of something magical. Yet the end is tragic because of clans at war in Yemen, South Arabia where my narrative begins. Then we skip ahead in time and move the action of the story to Birmingham in England.

Another couple meets, and here's where the hope comes in. This time, love wins out—despite the differences in culture and religion between a newly arrived ex-pat and the girl he buys a drink for at a pub.

And so we have two stories that start out much the same, but end in different ways. For a young character named Maryam, the wonder of new love soon turns into agony as bullets rip through flesh and other acts of horror follow. (Some scenes are hard to write. But the job of fiction is to mirror truth, and the truth is sometimes hard to see.)

Maryam's brother Salem is only seven when she was murdered for honor killing. But the culture of hate that pervades his birthplace causes more upheaval for him later in his life. He must leave his home for England, fearful the opposing clan has marked him as the next to die.

The next to die for what? The terrified young man on the run isn't even sure. It was an incident that took place before he was even born. Yes, that is the way of "blood revenge," a practice that can leave families like Salem's terrorized and separated.

In England, he meets Mary, and this time when boy meets girl, love grows. Despite differences in culture, family background, and religion, they find a deep connection. They face all kinds of trouble as their lives unfold, but the key throughout, they find, is communication: listening carefully until they understand each other. That sounds simple, right? But in fact, it's not. We as humans have complicated beings with many layers that play a role in how we think and act.

Whether its world affairs or family troubles, listening to each other is the only way to peace. The answer is communication: nation to nation, a group to group, and a potential new friend to the person across from him at the table.

The power to overcome lies in dialogue, not force.

Increasingly, this idea is being turned into a movement, which is the reason for the sense of hope I mentioned earlier. In the United Arab Emirates, where I make my home, 2019 has declared as The Year of Tolerance. The focus will continue into the new year that is fast approaching. Through policies and legislation, leaders have been working toward a goal of openness among cultures and peaceful coexistence. A special emphasis is being placed on making sure that youth understand the importance of these values.

Recently completed here was the National Festival

of Tolerance and Human Fraternity, a nine-day event with cross-cultural opportunities for togetherness for people of all ages. With activities ranging from the intellectual to the artistic, the festival proved that tolerance is not only possible; it can be a joyful thing.

As the international community continues to face new challenges, the United Nations Educational, Scientific and Cultural Organization (UNESCO) is working to build peace through international cooperation in the areas listed in the name. Founded in response to the atrocities of World War Two, UNESCO continues its good work on a variety of fronts. Examples include the promotion of quality education for all independent media, and freedom of expression.

That is the reason for my hope. While the need is great, so are the fervent efforts and ingenuity of people across the world who are working hard toward peace and tolerance.

In the next Prologue, you will come to know about the tragedies of violence that still taking place in different parts of the world.

Prologue

Yemen, South Arabia
1950

For Mohsen, the day brought something even sweeter than the rainfall that had come at last, restoring life and greenness to the drought-filled valley.

Something in the girl's eyes made him stop and stare. And he knew that for as long as he lived, he would not forget the way she looked in this moment, balancing a heavy jar carefully on her head.

This day felt important. Something was about to change. Mohsen was certain of it. The perfume of the newly opened flowers and the music of the birds seemed to promise it was so.

The girl stopped by a well underneath an ancient palm, and he went to her. He held out his hand to take her heavy burden, and he filled the jar with water. And then for the first time, Mohsen saw the smile of his Maryam, whose name he had yet to learn, although he had dreamed of such a girl, hoped that such a girl existed somewhere in the world. Her features were delicate with an inner light that seemed to shine out through her smile. Her face was small and heart-shaped and her shoulders were elegant and slender.

Mohsen beamed back at her with a smile so wide it almost split his face in two.

As he handed the jar back, she looked into his eyes. It was as if she wished they could always be as close as they were in that moment. Then a weariness crept into her eyes as she turned to make her way back home. There was a sadness in her hazel eyes as well, as if she didn't want to leave this magical place beneath the palm.

"Wait. Don't go," said Mohsen. "Who are you? Who's your clan? And—please—tell me your name."

As she began to walk away, the palm fronds waved gently toward her in the breeze, as if to whisper, Stay!

The sun had begun to set, and the fading light sent shimmery bits of silver through the dark and silky tresses that the wind blew into her eyes.

"Where do you live?" asked Mohsen.

As if she were too tired to speak, she nodded toward a house off in the distance. Such a long way to walk, he thought. And such delicate (and shapely) ankles that must make the trip with the heavy jar of water. He knew what to do. He'd carry the jar for her. He would go with her!

They gazed at each other, speaking only with their eyes. Silently, he begged her to stay for a little longer. We've never met, and yet I know you. You're meant to belong to me.

But then a darkness filled her eyes, and she turned, hurrying away as Mohsen watched her, startled.

Then he soon saw the reason she'd been frightened; they were not alone. A man had appeared, and Mohsen knew the man. His gait, his very watchfulness, meant that trouble soon would follow. As it always did with Marouf.

Mohsen felt a chill. Marouf was a gatherer of other people's secrets, which he used as ammunition. To those secrets, the troublemaker always added lies to make the outcomes darker, more explosive.

The girl's figure grew smaller in the distance. She was walking as quickly as she could with the full jar on her head.

Mohsen watched, his longing and his joy having turned to anger, just as hers had turned to terror. Just like that, with one intruder, love had turned into fear.

The sun dipped further from the sky as the light turned into a somber gray. The changing colors seemed to mark the moment when hope was marred by evil, the moment that two people in the valley became three.

Arriving breathless at her house, Maryam spilled half the contents of her jar in her haste to set it down. Her tears and sweat mingled with the water puddled on the floor. Tears or water from the well?

Love, modesty, or fear? She couldn't tell the difference anymore.

Her mother Asmaa, noticed right away that there was something unfamiliar in her daughter's manner.
"Maryam, what's wrong?" She grabbed her daughter's hand.

But the girl just shook her head and wept.

"Did someone hurt you?" Asmaa tried again, smoothing back her daughter's hair.

Maryam shook her head once again, and then she threw herself into her mother's arms. Why she wept she wasn't sure. Fear? Or modesty? Maybe it was love. Only in that moment did she understand that with all the other boys who had caught her eye, she had only played at love; this time love was real. Love had come in with a force, taking her breath away. But would she see the man again?

The spilled water and the sweat dried, but not her tears. She could not stop weeping, lonely for a man she didn't know — but did know, the man who had touched her soul.

Part of her was right there in the kitchen, and part of her—the most important part—was back there at the well. Did he wait there still? She wondered where he was and what he was doing now.

She passed the next days in a stupor, her mind on just one thing. She was waiting for a knock, for him to come and find her. But when the knocks did come, the door was opened to an aunt or cousin—and not to the gentle smile and warm, expressive eyes that had come to haunt her dreams.

Her family murmured to each other. Was she ill, they wondered. Could she have been touched by jinn?

Then the third day came with a knock that sounded different—softer, more insistent. Behind the door was a woman whose eyes met Maryam's. Something about the smile felt warm and familiar to the girl. She recognized the woman, although they had never met. This was the woman who'd made him.

Maryam moved forward and touched the woman's hand. For the first time since she'd fled from the evil man, Maryam felt safe.

On entering the home, Umm Mohsen stood back to look carefully at this girl who had so entranced her son. Before, he had been her quiet one, ever practical, but now it was as if the boy had been touched by magic.

Then the woman turned her eyes to Asmaa, who had come into the hall to watch with her other daughters. The visitor announced her name and which family she belonged to. And there among the little group, wonder disappeared into confusion; the room was filled with fear. Fear! There it was again.

Maryam's mother understood that the visitor had come in an attempt to understand what was happening to her son. But Asmaa knew already. In that way that mothers recognize the deepest stirrings of their children's hearts, she had come to understand that her daughter had found love that day at the well. But between this woman's clan and hers was blood revenge—old debts that must be paid with the taking of a life.

Why was the woman here?

With a soft look in her eye, Umm Mohsen studied Maryam. An understanding seemed to pass between her and the girl: that a part of both their hearts was filled with love for the gentle boy who had come to the well.

Then the visitor turned her eyes to Asmaa. "My visit to the house? That must be our secret."

After that, the house felt heavy to Asmaa, as if it still held the mark of an unexpected guest. She worried for the future of her daughter, who had always been so easy and content, singing sweetly while she worked without complaining of her chores. This was the first time that Asmaa had looked into her daughter's eyes and seen the fire of desire, a wanting in her eyes.

◆◆◆

The next morning, Maryam felt a rush of warmth as she took hold of the jar to place it on her head. He had touched the jar; it was no longer just a source of water, one more chore in her long day. She had been awakened to a joy she never knew existed. As she went about her day, she dreamed of how his touch might feel. He was a stranger, really, but at the same time, she knew him well; she had read his soul when she glanced into his eyes.

But even as she thrilled in anticipation of seeing him again, Maryam was terrified. When the interloper had come upon the scene that day beneath the palm, she had felt his soul as well, and that soul was dark. So much so that her feet had stiffened and, for just a moment, she had lost the strength to walk.

She imagined how it might have been if the dark man hadn't come. Before fear came into the picture, something had seemed to draw her closer to the stranger at the well. She had longed to lay her head against his strong chest, where his warmth and his heartbeat could comfort her and thrill her.

Now, she was lost in thought as she headed once more to the valley. Then her heart skipped a beat as she got closer to the well. As if a picture from her dreams had sprung magically to life, underneath the palm tree was the tantalizing boy who had occupied her thoughts.

Although she shyly cast her eyes down, she could

feel his yearning pulling her toward him. Could it be that he dreamed at night of the same things that she did?

♦♦♦

Joy welled up in Mohsen. If she would only look at him! He let his eyes linger on the exquisite lines of her tiny shoulders and the soft skin of her neck, but he longed to see her face. He had not been able to forget her eyes. They'd made him think of how the Oryx, with a single look, could a make a hunter stops and lay down his gun. There was power in those eyes.

Finally, she looked up, her cheeks flushed with a desire that he longed to press his lips against. But for now, he could only look. With no words said between them, they shared in the hope that soon they would be wed. That had to be a reason, they supposed, for his mother's visit to the family.

But until that day could come, a sense of magic hovered in the space between a boy and a girl who couldn't touch—but who knew that all the pleasures of the other would soon be theirs to cherish. Maryam dreamed of a wedding that would be more special even than those she had heard about in Arabian Nights.

Then the scene went dark, just as it before. Like a snake scattering its poison, Marouf passed them at a distance but close enough for them to see. And the magic disappeared, blacked out by a terror that chilled Maryam to the core and ripped at Mohsen's heart.

◆◆◆

A few days later, it was sunset when Maryam awoke to the rapid boom of gunshots that came in quick succession. This was followed by a knock and—she could barely take it in—news of Mohsen's death. He'd been murdered near the well, under the palm tree. She poured her pain out in a wailing that could be heard across the valley. But although she cried throughout the night, the pain was not diminished by a fraction. The pain would be with her always, as much a part of Maryam as her legs and arms.

In the days that followed, she hovered near the well, longing to see him once again. Of course, she knew that he was gone! But she waited for him still. "Soon," she whispered to herself, "I'll hear the sound of footsteps." And perhaps she'd even dare to brush up against his arm. Why had she not touched him? She waited for the sense that her groom was just around the corner, his dark eyes lit up with eagerness to have her near.

Her days went on like that, partly in one world and partly in another. While her ears had heard the ugly truth, her heart still whispered no. In addition to grieving the loss of the boy she loved, she was filled with guilt as well. She felt it was because of her—and their meeting at the well—that his light had gone out of the world.

Her family stood by, brokenhearted and powerless to help. They couldn't stop the weeping in the night or keep her from hovering underneath the palm where love had blossomed with such promise not so long before. So they bound her in chains. That is how she passed her days, as her voice grew hoarse from hopeless pleadings to the universe to bring back her love.

Exhausted from a lack of sleep, Asmaa searched desperately for a way to ease her daughter's pain and to bring quiet back to the house and neighborhood. Life must, after all, go on.

And so it came to be that when three elderly women from the village appeared on Asmaa's doorstep, she didn't have to ask the reason for the visit. "Please step in," she said.

A woman by the name of Quadria was the first to speak. "Something must be done," she said to Asmaa gravely.

"When?" was all that Asmaa asked.

"Tonight, when the sun begins to set. That is when we start."

◆◆◆

As daylight began to fade, Maryam felt the presence of the women in her room. One of them stroked her arm in comfort as others entered and released her from her chains. Strong arms held her firmly as she flailed against them. She didn't want to interact with anyone but him. Then she felt herself being pulled into the center of the room, where an array of dates and herbs were spread. Then she could see nothing but the white cloth that was flung over her head and body. She trembled at the sound of frantic singing and the loud, incessant beating of a drum. After it was over, they returned her to her chains.

For two nights, this went on. "What do you want?" they asked her. Just the touch of one man whom I will never see again, she thought helplessly. She winced against the noise of the drumming and the wails (which she sometimes failed to understand were hers).

The question that they shouted grew more and more insistent. "What is it that you want?"

In a move to quiet them, she finally replied. And yet in her grief, she scarcely understood the words that escaped her mouth.

Finally, on the third night, a man came in with the crowd, leading a black goat. In the midst of the singing and the shrieking, someone pulled the sheet off Maryam to unveil the scene before her. And in the middle of the frenzied movements of the crowd, she watched, appalled, as Quadria drug a knife across the throat of the bleating animal. Maryam's plaintive moans grew even louder as a woman held her head, forcing her to drink the blood and watch the bleeding from the goat's neck as the blood spread across the sheet and onto her dress.

In the days that followed, she stayed as she had been: withdrawn into herself, interacting with no one.

Then there came a night when she sensed movement near her bed. Someone released her chains. Confused, she stumbled out of bed, rubbing at the sores left by the restraints. Through the fogginess of her sorrow, she understood that she could go. She could go to the palm tree. And to him.

With her family fast asleep, she quietly slipped out of the darkened house. Soon, she reached her destination. She breathed in the scent of flowers and listened for his footsteps. Soon, she thought. He'll be here soon. What a reunion it would be! She'd bury her face in his chest and weep; he'd soothe away her sorrow with his kisses and his strong but gentle hands.

Then she heard someone coming. Here he is. At

last. She'd known all along that what they'd told her wasn't true. As she took a deep breath and prepared to run to him—to fly! —the sound of gunshots rang out in the air.

Underneath the palm tree where once her heart had soared, her heart beat for the last time. She slumped to the ground, and Maryam lay still.

Chapter One

Looking for Home

Birmingham, England
1966

Life is a mystery gradually revealed as days fade into black and new days begin. Nature whispers hints to those who choose to listen, teasing as the colors of a new sun spread across the sky. Salem didn't like the way his own mystery had been playing out. He recently had fled from his home in Yemen as a likely target in a feud whose bitter roots predated Salem's birth. He'd left behind a young family, although the marriage between him and Yasmine had been wrong from the start. He had tried and she had tried. They had tried for years. But they'd been only children (he was fourteen; she was twelve) when their families had forced them to be wed. Had it been any wonder that her innocence and youth had made her shy about the marriage bed? Once they were man and wife, their parents had waited for a long time to see the blood of the new bride, proof she had been a virgin on their wedding night. But, despite her modesty, two boys came to them in time. Their sons were Ahmed and Omar.

It shouldn't be this way, thought Salem. A father should be with his sons. But a string of murders connected Salem's clan to another family. The two clans were also linked by a tragic love affair involving Salem's sister. And Salem's father thought the killers might come after Salem next.

So no other choice had been left to Salem. Better his boys have a father here in Birmingham than a father who was dead.

Blood revenge, honor crimes, and virgin blood made him think of his sister, Maryam, who had died when he was a boy. Her killers had accused her of being pregnant with the child of the man she loved. But after her murder, her father had requested that she be examined, and her killers had been proven wrong; Maryam had died a virgin.

He remembered her with disheveled hair and startled eyes, weary with lack of sleep. He remembered her plaintive wails and how full of sorrow he had been that he couldn't help her.

He shivered from the cold and from the memory of his sister's fate. He buttoned his thin coat as he stepped outside the airport and into a place that didn't feel like home. But that was exactly what this damp and gloomy place would have to become. The fog wrapped itself around him; he could even taste the cold as it made its way into his mouth and nostrils.

He wished he could afford to take the train to the address his father had given him on a piece of paper and shoved into his pocket as he left. The train would, after all, be so much faster than a bus. And he could stretch his limbs out and relax after the long flight, which he had spent stuffed into a space so small he could barely cross his legs. But he had to make his money last.

He got into a long queue behind a woman who was surrounded by a pile of bags. Trying his best to make himself understood, he asked her in halting English when the bus was supposed to arrive.

Wearily, she shrugged. "Who really knows?" she asked. "They say it will come at one time, and it shows up at another."

Salem didn't understand. What she said made no sense. Why did she speak of *two* times for *one* bus? And who did this woman mean when she talked about a they?"

A sense of loneliness seemed to choke him as the cold wind intensified and whipped into his face. There were people all around him, but there were so many times they used words he didn't know. And even when he knew the words, they came out strung together into sentences he couldn't understand.

How could he even hope to connect with people in this new place, once a smudged mark on a map, a place his father had pointed to with a wrinkled finger? And now here it was with its dirty smells, its hurried people, and a cold so deep it stung.

If he were home in Yemen, the air at this time of day would be filling up with the smells of lamb and rice. Friends might be calling out to him and waving, asking about his day. But his family and beloved home were lost to Salem now, all because his culture had grown obsessed with the idea of revenge—the ruinous, bloody, kind. Even men of honor were no longer safe.

The woman in the bus line gave Salem a tired smile. "What bus do you need?" she asked, trying harder now to help. His confusion and despair must be written on his face.

"What time does it say on your ticket?" She tried again, winding her scarf more tightly around her ample neck.

Ticket? Salem was even more confused than he had been before. This whole process was a puzzle. *You have to have a ticket?*

Again, she read his face. She pointed to a desk, where he joined another queue.

◆◆◆

He was tired enough to sleep on the bus despite the smells, the legs pushing hard against him from both sides, and the jerky turns and bumps. When the bus finally stopped at midnight, a cross woman

25

at the ticket desk informed him that it was now too late to board another bus to his final destination. And so on his first night in his new home, he tried to sleep on a hard bench while others at the station eyed him with suspicion. His dark skin and dark eyes, he thought, marked him as different here, marked him as one to watch. At home, he was told, he drew stares for other reasons; his broad shoulders and strong features often caught the ladies' eyes.

Early the next morning, he set off again, his stomach grumbling with hunger. He stared out at a blurry England as a constant rain drizzled against the dirty window by his seat. During a brief stop, he got off and bought a sandwich with a filling he could not identify. The bread and mystery meat tasted as old and flavorless as this dreary country seemed to be.

Then, finally, he stepped off the bus and into Birmingham, which would be his new address. He had to ask several people how to find the house where, according to his father, he'd be welcomed. Some of the people on the street waited with impatience as he tried to find the words to clarify the *lefts* and *rights* and *two blocks down* they were describing. Others just ignored him as he tried to ask for help.

After some time, he arrived at the worn and gloomy house that matched the address on his paper. The door was opened by a man whose eyes held more weariness than welcome. But he at least knew Arabic; Salem was relieved not to have to work so hard just find the words for a simple sentence.

Salem handed him the paper that his father had asked him to present.

The man looked it over and let out a deep sigh. "Not another one!" he mumbled to himself. Then he studied Salem. "Okay, you can stay, but only for one night. I'll take you tomorrow to the factory and then take you to a place where you can get a room."

After Salem had given him some bills from his father, he was shown a room with mattresses littering the floor. But Salem couldn't rest there and enjoy the quiet; he would not be welcome back until after the sun had set. His heart sank at the news. After a sleepless night, he was filled with longing for even a thin, dirty mattress that had been discarded on a stranger's floor.

And so he spent the day exploring, taking in the sights. Wearily, he sunk down on a park bench, choosing his spot carefully near a walking path. He needed people near. But most of the passersby seemed to be in too much of a hurry to spare a nod or smile.

◆◆◆

The next day, Salem's host, whose name was Samuel, drove him to the tall brick structure that was the home of the HP Sauce factory. *What is this sauce?* Salem wondered. After the proper introductions, Salem had a job, and he started right away. Some of the men he worked with spoke his language, and Salem found a little comfort in drinking in the sounds of home.

At the end of the first day, Samuel returned and drove him to a sad and small building on Frazer Road in Small Heath. He told Salem that this was to be his home. After brief instructions on how much to pay and to whom and when, he went on his hurried way. "Good luck to you," he called out as he disappeared around a corner. But his tone indicated that he didn't care at all what fortune (or lack thereof) Salem met with in this place.

◆◆◆

On weekends and sometimes after work, Salem would sit by himself in the park, or he'd walk downtown and gaze at the strange goods advertised in windows. Most of all, he'd watch the people. They laughed so easily! They smiled at one another in a way that was only possible for those who haven't known the misery and sadness his people had endured.

And the women! Oh, the women, with their tiny skirts and low-cut tops that made Salem blush. *Come with me,* their eyes seemed to say as they watched him carefully. Something stirred in Salem when they looked at him that way, but he dared not meet their eyes. For him, modesty was the way of honor, and every lady that he met was to be treated with respect. But something in his body cried out *yes,* even as his conscience and his better self-held those desires at bay. With his thick dark hair and handsome profile, he was used to being noticed, but females here were different in ways that he found shocking.

Visions of these women filled his thoughts at night, because the nights here were the worse. On more nights than not, he'd wake up with his arms and legs so chilled that he could barely feel them. It was all that he could do to throw off the thin blanket and make his way across the room to feed more coins into the heater. Finally, when the old thing had eaten up its greedy fill of coins, a tiny bit of heat would come out with a whir and a hiss. Salem would huddle as close to it as he could, desperate for the smallest trace of warmth. Then, with his body warmed a little, he'd head back to bed. After all of that, maybe he could sleep.

On nights he couldn't sleep, his thoughts sometimes turned to his young wife. They both had been too young for the marriage forced on them by their parents. One minute they'd been playing games of chase, concentrating hard as they threw a ball, or hiding from their friends amid bursts of giggles. The next minute they were wed, with expectations that neither one of them fully understood.

Then everything went wrong, and Salem had been

banished to this city, where he felt so out of place. Each day brought new bewilderments, and he would sometimes have to point to things or come up with hand gestures just to ask a question. But he made it work. His duties at the factory were easy enough to carry out, and the people there were pleasant—if uninterested in forming connections that went deeper than How are you today?

Then, finally, in his rooming house, Salem made a friend—an older man who, in many ways, was the opposite of Salem. Still, Marouf brought to the friendship much-needed company and a listening ear. Well, *sometimes* a listening ear; mostly, Marouf loved to talk. Salem was always cheered to open up his door to find the short, round man with the bulging belly, who usually had a smile already plastered on his face, as if in anticipation of the stories he soon would be spilling out to Salem.

Yes, Marouf loved to talk, but what he didn't like was work. The man, Salem learned, was frequently unemployed, and while he was always full of ideas for a bit of fun, his pockets were often empty when it came time to pay. If Salem could spare just a little a bit . . . new job coming soon, excellent opportunity . . . the lousy heater ate the last coins, such an awful winter.

At the center of all of Marouf's plans was one shining goal: Marouf loved the girls. "Such gorgeous girls at this place. Girls like you've never seen!" he would exclaim, proposing a night out. He'd look at Salem hopefully, knowing that his new friend kept a respectful distance from the ladies while Marouf greedily ran his eyes up and down their bodies as they passed.

Salem would agree, anxious to ease his loneliness with the one man in Birmingham who'd reached out to be his friend. Besides, Marouf's stories always made him laugh — although Salem doubted that even half of them were true.

As he walked along the streets with Marouf, Salem would glance around him at the city, hoping that this place would be good to him. The last words he'd heard his mother speak had been a prayer for him. May God protect you from the jinn and from the worst of mankind. There had been fear in that prayer, but Salem was trying hard to hold on to hope as well.

One night, Salem was nursing a beer across from

Marouf at another dirty table in another pub. As on many other nights, the promised "girls from paradise" had failed to show. The weather must have kept them in, said Marouf with a dismissive wave of his right hand, as if the next time, surely they'd be greeted by a roomful of beauties.

Salem nodded to his friend. "It's okay," he said. All he'd expected from the night was a little conversation over beer, a chance to be with others and not in his tiny room alone.

Sometimes they went to dingy pubs, where old men stared into their pints and mumbled about the weather, the economy, and "bloody politicians." Or they went to nicer places, where young girls arrived in groups, gazing nervously around them and dissolving into giggles—which turned into shrieks of laughter after several drinks. Sometimes there were bands, but Salem was never glad to see the musicians warming up, as they were always loud and mostly out of tune. He missed the music of his country, music you could dance to.

On this particular night, he startled when Marouf nudged him in the ribs.

"Check out that one over there." His companion spoke in a low voice, staring off into a corner.

"Where? Who do you mean?" asked Salem, who'd been lost in his own thoughts.

Marouf let loose with his loud laugh, his hand on his big belly. "You're useless, boy. I'm not sure there's any hope for you. How can you miss *that one?* She's spectacular. A beauty! Right there—by the bar." He indicated her location with his eyes.

Salem looked that way, and his heart skipped a beat. This time, his friend was right. She had long blonde hair that caught the light and looked soft to the touch. Her red dress hugged her curves in a way that, while not immodest, gave tantalizing hints of what lay beneath.

A warmth rushed through Salem as he stared at her, entranced. Something told him that this moment would stay in his mind forever: a blonde beauty in a red dress and a room infused with magic. She was leaning on the bar, and her full lips, painted a soft pink, were turned down in a frown. She held her hand up to the man behind the bar, who walked past her thoughtlessly as if he didn't see her standing there.

"Go on." Marouf grinned. "You know that you want to."

Salem hesitated.

"I'll have another drink and sit back and enjoy. You go and try your luck."

Salem headed toward the bar before he could change his mind. Something drew him toward her. Something big was about to happen. Somehow he was certain his life was about to change.

She turned to him and smiled. Her eyes were a deep bluish green, and in them, he could sense enduring sorrows but also victories won. He saw kindness and a sense of fun as well.

Then he caught himself and stood up straight. He was staring like a fool! "Oh, hi! Hello!" He stumbled on his words. "Can I get you a drink?"

She nodded, shy and pleased. "I would love that. Thanks." She held his eyes in her gaze.

They were quiet for a moment, each studying the other. Then she glanced at the bar. "That guy behind the bar has been ignoring me for ages, and I'd love to have a Guinness."

Salem tapped his fingers on the bar, holding up his money. The bartender came right over, and Salem bought their drinks.

She laughed. "Well, my goodness, that was fast. Perhaps I was invisible, waving at him for a drink." Then she swayed a little, and Salem caught her shoulder, reveling in the touch. She might be a little drunk, he thought as he watched her.

"You rescued me!" She smiled, and Salem took note of the way her eyes crinkled at the corners when she laughed. He was mesmerized by the smooth and shimmery pink gloss on her lips. He imagined she would taste of flowers or sweet berries. Her hair curled a little in the heat of the bar, and he longed to sweep it from her eyes.

"Would you like to sit?" he asked, and then it hit him. "Or are you here with someone?" What a fool he'd been. He should have known a girl like her would not be by herself.

She shook her head, looking around for a table. "I was supposed to be with someone, but, as you can see, that someone isn't here. Since he hasn't turned up yet, I don't suppose he will." She tilted her head to the side and studied Salem, blushing. "Which might not be a bad thing. Because here you are." Then her teasing smile turned quickly into embarrassment. "Unless . . . you might not be alone. Oh, can you please forgive me? You see, I didn't think."

She followed Salem's eyes as he found Marouf, who grinned at them and waved. A middle-aged man had joined Salem's friend at the table. Both of them were prattling away with enthusiastic gestures to go with their stories.

Two to talk, no one to listen, Salem thought. But never mind about Marouf. Salem turned to the girl and grinned. "Some friends you need a break from. Perhaps it's you who rescued me! I think I see a table—over to the left."

At the table, they nursed their drinks in silence, sneaking glances at each other. At last, she broke the silence. "You don't even know my name. I'm

Mary, Mary Norman."

But he knew *her*, he thought. He'd waited for her all his life. He'd always sensed that something special was in store for him, although he couldn't name it. "Salem Al-Qahatani from South Arabia. And it is my great pleasure to be here with you."

"Tell me more about you. Have you been in the city long?"

"Only a few months," he replied, happy that he had gotten better with the language. "My home and my family are in Yemen, and now I have found good work here in Birmingham. Through some contacts of my father. The sauce factory. Do you know it?"

She nodded, smiling up at Salem as if she were fascinated by the ordinary details of his life. Could she feel it too, a kind of force that seemed to pull at them, like something in the universe wanted them to be together?

"I come from Northern Ireland. I work for the council here." She rolled her eyes and smiled.

"Most days it's pretty blah, but it could be worse, you know?"

The council? Salem wondered what she meant by that.

When the initial shyness left them, they told story after story about their lives, their fears, and the random things they loved to do to pass the days. As a child, she said, she had hoped to be a barrister. "Don't we all dream big?" she asked Salem, smiling. "Before we grow up, that is."

Salem shook his head. "I wanted only simple things," he told her. But—dreams? That must be the way of children in the West. Children who grow up here must anticipate some shining kind of future, their hopes extending far beyond enough food on the table, a family that is safe, and a soft place to lie down when the working day is done.

"If I had grown up here, I might have wanted more," he said. Strains of music filled the room from a speaker system. "What would I have dreamed of?" he wondered out loud. "Perhaps to be a doctor?" Could a doctor have helped his sister as the life drained from her body?

"I also played around with the idea of drawing for a living," Mary said.

"Yes, it would be quite nice to be paid for that." Salem picked up his mug. Both he and Mary laughed, and that felt good. It had been a long time since Salem had felt playful.

"Drawing little pictures is still my go-to thing." She reached for her Guinness. "When the boss is acting crazy, when I'm stressed about the rent, I draw ballerinas, stars, or moons — or I draw whatever — on old envelopes or menus. And it kind of makes life better, as crazy as that seems." She looked down at her mug. "It's better than my chums' way. They all go out and drink, and they say they wake up feeling like their heads might just explode."

He told her about the things he missed most about his country, like the music and dancing that his family once enjoyed. "So different from the music here." He took a swallow of his beer. "There's such nice music back in Yemen. You would like it."

"I'd love to hear it sometime," she said to Salem softly. "Which is more than I can say for the band that's here most weekends. I'm glad they're off tonight."

"Yes, there are bands here in this country that make you long for . . . silence," Salem said.

He loved the way that Mary laughed, and somehow he just knew that if he only heard the laugh—the musical rise and fall of it—and not the joke itself, his joy would be the same.

He told her how he missed the laughter of his family when they'd gather over coffee after a big meal—cousins, aunts, and uncles, the whole lot of them. He didn't tell her how those gatherings had come to a sudden end, with some members of the clan demanding blood from one who was once their own. There were so many things about his life that she could never fathom. So many things about his life that would never happen here; they'd seem like the things of stories to a girl like her.

Then, before he knew it, he'd told her about the loneliness that had come to engulf him since he'd arrived in Birmingham. It was a loneliness that sometimes kept him up at night—much more than the cold air did or his aching muscles.

As soon as that confession had come out of his mouth, Salem sat back, shocked. He was not a man who talked about his feelings to his friends, much less to a girl who had been a stranger when he walked into the bar.

She reached out and took his hand. "I know," she told him softly. "I've felt that too," she said.

It was like a drug almost, saying things out loud and having someone listen, wanting you to tell them more rather than rushing off.

Then, to his surprise, the bartender yelled, "Last call!"

It seemed they'd just sat down. Salem looked around, surprised to find that the bar had almost emptied. At some point, Marouf had gone. As for him and Mary, their mugs were still half full; the Guinness almost forgotten with all they had to say.

Now, Mary was pulling on her jacket.

"How are you getting home?" he asked.
"Somehow, it's gotten late. Please, let me make

sure that you get there safely."

"If you'd walk me to the bus, that would be really nice," she said as she grabbed her purse.

In the quiet night, Salem walked beside her, not close enough to touch, but close enough the heat coming from her body warmed him against the wind.

As the bus approached, the shyness once again took hold of them both; he could see she felt it too, that this meeting was important.

"So, what happens next?" she whispered.

"Same place tomorrow night?" Then right away, he wondered if he was taking things too fast, if he appeared too eager. Should he have said "next week?"

She reached into her purse, pulled out a sheet of paper, and wrote down an address. "This place is much better. Meet me there at eight." She smiled. "They have a band that's brilliant. It's not the kind of band that makes you long for silence."

He smiled at the remark as he glanced down at the paper. Then he looked back up at her to nod, but she was already gone, rushing toward the bus.

◆◆◆

That night he barely slept with his mind so full of visions: soft blonde hair, pink lips, the way her eyes lit up when he made a joke. For the first time since he'd started working at the factory, he was almost late reporting for his shift. He hurried past the tall clock on the street, barely registering the distinctive, white *HP* in the factory's name as his destination at last came into sight. It was a tall brick building with an array of windows that looked out at the city like so many eyes.

Once he began his shift, the hours seemed to drag, separating Salem from the girl that he would see again that night. He kept feeling in his pocket for the paper, fingering it like a charm. She had touched the paper. Even the smell of sauce that filled the air, with its vinegary notes of dates, tamarind, and spices, seemed infused with magic on that day.

After a quick lunch break, he returned to the line of

workers, glancing always at the clock. She'd said there was a band, and if they played a slow song, he could hold her close and sway with her to the music. He reached into his pocket for the paper, which had begun to feel so familiar to his fingers, like an extension of his hand.

In that moment, Salem's heart stopped. There was nothing in his pocket except a few loose coins. Wildly, he looked around him on the floor, underneath the big equipment that was scattered all around him, beneath the ever-moving feet of the busy workers.

He rushed back and forth, drawing stares from his fellow workers. "Small piece of paper!" he called out. "Did anybody see it? A folded bit of paper! With an address! It's important. It was in my pocket when I went to lunch."

Lunch. A hard knot formed in his gut. Could he have dropped it at the table when he took his break to eat?

Ben beside him laughed. "Man, Salem really wants that paper. This girl must be *hot.*" To some men in the factory, everything in life was about a girl.

Another worker, James, slapped Salem on the back. "If we help you find the paper, you'll have to give us all the details—every little thing—about what happens with this girl. It sounds like you have *plans.*" He winked, and Salem cringed. How dare these men disrespect his Mary? But for now, he had to find the paper.

Bill, who was a quiet, thoughtful type like Salem, gave the men a look. "Hey! Leave the guy alone. Can't you see that he's upset?" He stopped what he was doing to look around him on the floor.

Visions of Mary waiting, confused and alone, for a man who never showed twisted the knot in Salem's stomach even tighter. He ran to the lunchroom, knowing all too well that it could mean a reprimand and a dock in his pay. But Salem didn't care.

The room was almost empty except for a maid in a black shirt and black pants taking out the trash. Salem eyed the bulging bag of rubbish in her hand. Could his little piece of paper—Salem's very future—be wadded up in there among other people's dirty napkins, chicken bones, and already-browning apple slices?

Then he caught sight of something in the corner: a folded piece of paper whose shape he knew by now. And he could finally breathe.

Tonight, he'd dance with Mary after all.

◆◆◆

After drinks and a shared snack of pub chips, which they hardly touched, they stayed on the dance floor for almost every song.

This pub was a step up from those favored by Marouf. The seats in the booths were plush, and nearly every surface gleamed, from the counters to the gold-framed pictures on the wall.

When the band began a slow song, Mary had grabbed his hand as if to say, *Let's go,* and Salem had led her onto the crowded floor. She wore a tight black top that hugged her upper body and a skirt with blacks and pinks that twirled around her when she moved.

Now, he could feel her tremble as he held her

gently and they moved to the music. She moved in a little closer as the singer's voice grew more insistent as he hit the melody.

It was a song that Salem loved: A Beatles song about a man and his need for a woman here, there, and everywhere. The Beatles had it right.

She pressed her face gently into his chest, and he buried his face in her hair, breathing in the flowery, slightly spicy perfume that she wore. He kissed her soft hair lightly and pulled her even closer. As the song came to an end, they were barely even moving to the music. He didn't care about the song now. All that Salem cared about was the feel of her against him.

Then the song was over, and the band announced a break. Dimly, Salem was aware of the other dancers exiting the dance floor toward the tables and the booths. But there was Mary in his arms, and he didn't want to move.

She took his face in hers and gave him a long kiss. "Come home with me," she whispered.

He should not do that, he thought, even though he

longed to. And thus began a battle, as his body cried out for a kind of closeness he knew would not be proper.

He went home with her that evening, and in his first sweet nights with Mary, his mind warred with his need.

Most nights after work, he went straight to her apartment. It was a simple place that was decorated with a Mary kind of flair: black and white artwork all around and fresh flowers on the mantle. After a small dinner that she'd made or takeout brought by Salem, they would sit and talk. Or they might move to the couch, already wrapped up tightly in each other's arms before they reached their destination. When Mary reached to undo the buttons of her blouse or move Salem's hands to places that they hadn't been, Salem would resist.

"Tell me, please! What's wrong?" She grabbed his hand one night as a knot of worry creased her forehead. Then she brought his hand gently to her lips. "No need to be shy with me."

"In my country, there are things that we are taught to save until the day we're married," he explained.

"Or at least *some* men—men who show respect—will court a girl that way."

She smiled, and then very slowly she took off her top and moved in to kiss him. "Welcome to the West," she whispered in his ear.

At night, he slept in her arms, no longer depending on a stack of coins and a faulty little heater for a bit of warmth. At the factory, the others watched with interest as Salem went through the motions of the job with a new air of content. He performed his duties well—as he was a man of honor—but his mind was far away.

"I'll bet you anything that your mind's on a lady." Ben loved teasing Salem as they went about their work. "Hey, man, good for you."

One night soon after that, Salem stopped back by the rooming house to grab some things on his way to Mary's. As he walked down the hall, he saw Marouf lingering not far from his door, as if he had been watching for Salem to appear.

Marouf broke out into a grin. His eyes seemed to reach into Salem to search for private things that were not for him to know. "I leave you with the blonde and then you disappear," he teased. "Let's go and grab a pint so you can tell me more. Every. Little. Detail. I want to know it all." He winked.

Then something odd occurred to Salem. His friend had the same name as the man who'd watched his sister fall in love at the well. How had he not remembered that? A coincidence, of course, but a chill ran through him.

"How about that pint?" Marouf raised an eyebrow.

Salem hesitated. Marouf had been a friend when no one else had seemed to care about spending time with Salem. But Salem had come to see a darkness in the man, and now he felt a need to be very careful when Marouf was around. Plus, Mary was waiting for him at her place, making a lentil stew that a friend from work had promised was divine. And Salem had told Mary he'd pick up some chardonnay while he was out.

Marouf threw back his head and laughed. "I can see you're anxious. Go!" He grabbed Salem's arm and grinned. "Did I not promise you? Girls like you've never seen! And now you have such a girl, and all because of your chum Marouf! And speaking of that pint, I was wondering if maybe. . "

Salem reached into his pocket. The bills needed for a pint were a small price to pay to stop the flow of words coming from Marouf.

◆◆◆

One night soon after that, Mary asked him if he would meet her at the pub where they'd danced to the Beatles the first week that they met. As he ducked in from the rain, pushing the heavy door open with his shoulder, he was filled with a sense of anticipation.

But she was running late, which was not like her at all. He kept glancing at his watch. Fifteen minutes passed, then twenty. He grabbed a stool and got a beer, keeping a close eye on the door as the pub grew crowded, as pubs did in the rain. Passersby rushed in, having seemingly decided that Neddie's Public House was the perfect place to wait out the rain, which was coming down in sheets. Soon, the crowd had grown so huge that he couldn't see the door and watch for Mary.

The band began to play, and the crowd moved onto the dance floor. Couples pressed close against each other. They twirled. They laughed, and they stole kisses, whispering in each other's ears. Everyone but Salem seemed to be holding on to someone as the music soared. Salem watched the women, not one of them as pretty as his Mary. Had she come in already and been pulled away by someone who'd been struck with her beauty?

"Just one dance," they might have said, "then you can find your date."

Salem sighed and took a long swig of his beer. This was not the first time that he'd worried about whether this could last. Was it possible that he could hold on to a woman each man in the place must surely long to have? But every time he worried, she covered him with kisses that sweetly reassured him that what they had was real.

Then he heard her familiar laugh, and he turned toward the sound. She was talking to a group of women—and holding on to the arm of a tall, handsome man. Salem closed his eyes, trying to calm the rush of disappointment that made it hard to breathe. When he opened them again, Mary's face was pressed against his in a kiss.

"There you are!" she said. "Come and meet someone." She pulled him through the crowd, and Salem followed, stunned, until they reached the man that Mary had been touching.

"Salem!" The man put out his hand. "Paul. From Mary's office. All day, she talks of Salem. Ever since she met you, our Mary's in a daze. So finally, one workmate says, 'That's it!' He says that one of us should come along with Mary after work and see you with our own two eyes!"

Mary held on to Salem's waist, resting her head on his chest. "Paul cannot be trusted to ever tell the truth. I stepped out into this weather, and my cheap umbrella broke. I'd have gotten soaked! Can you imagine? So Paul said he'd walk me here so I wouldn't have to swim."

Paul gave her a little bow. "And now that you are safely delivered to your love, I'm off to see some mates. You two have a brilliant time. I hear the band's amazing."

She pulled Salem to the dance floor and sang into

his ear as they moved to the music. He softly kissed her shoulder and whispered that she looked amazing. The band started on a new song, this one about wedding rings exchanged beneath a tree. Mary glanced at Salem shyly, then she ran her hand through his hair and kissed him.

Salem felt two things at once: dizzy from the kiss and paralyzed with fear. Did she have weddings on her mind? And how could he tell Mary that he already had a wife? In Yemen, it was normal for a husband to court another wife, but that was not the way here. Would Mary understand?

Chapter Two

He began to stay the nights with Mary. It just felt wrong to leave when he could drift to sleep with Mary in his arms. For the first time, this new country had begun to feel like home.

At the factory, as he played his part to move the bottles down the line, he barely registered his movements, which by now were second nature. He no longer even noticed the smell of vinegar, which had once been so overwhelming. It was as if the flowery, slightly spicy scent of the perfume Mary wore followed him around; she was that present in his mind.

One night as he prepared for bed, he turned around to catch her staring, as if she couldn't get her fill of drinking in the sight of him. "I just like to look at you," she said. "Those gorgeous eyes. So handsome."

As he smiled and went to her, he wondered: Who did Mary see? Could he really be *that man*, one that a girl like Mary would cover with her kisses before wrapping him up tightly in a hug?

"Handsome—no one has called me that but you," he said, burying his face in her hair.

"Well, don't suppose they didn't think it. I saw it right away."

He moved his lips to her shoulder and thought how right this felt, his skin against her skin. At the same time, he wondered how he could feel so connected to her when the expectations and traditions that had shaped them were not at all alike. The heartbreaking stories and the happy ones that lived in Salem were so very different than the ones that lived in her. He thought now of the miles and the vast blue waters that lay between his homeland and her Northern Ireland. It was a place so foreign to him, and yet it was the place that had produced this gift of a woman whose soft hair was now tickling his chest.

She ran her hand down his bare back, and his lips

moved to her neck as his heart cried out for more. Yet another part of Salem knew that this was wrong. He was a man of faith, and he should either marry Mary or walk away from this. He was not her husband, and she was not his wife, and this intoxicating closeness wasn't his to have.

He'd known that all along. But things had moved so quickly.

She was pulling at the buttons of her shirt now. "Let's go to bed," she whispered.

But Salem pulled away. "I'll be back tomorrow — as quickly as I can. But it's only right I sleep at my own place. I must!"

"This *is* your place — with me." With her lips on his, she pulled him to the bed, and Salem followed. The heart was fierce that night in its insistence of a *yes*. And he could barely hear the small voice of his better self that told him, *Salem, no.*

Sometimes at night they'd talk for hours. But there was still so much each didn't know about the person intertwined with them on the bed.

At times, he thought he knew her well, but then she would surprise him. One night when she couldn't sleep, Salem found her in front of a late-night movie he would have never dreamed she'd like. On the screen, a disembodied hand floated in the air while some kind of monstrous figure moved about the woods with a gleaming knife. Mary was scrunched up on the couch underneath a blanket and staring at the screen, transfixed.

"This is the kind of film that you choose to watch?" asked Salem, who had been woken up by a scream coming from the TV—although Mary had been careful to keep the volume low.

"Oh, scary movies are the best. I absolutely love them."

Salem would have guessed she'd have chosen some news show. She always seemed to have some cause on her mind that she was intent on seeing righted. New rules should be enforced to see that animals were treated more humanely; Mary would tell him often. British rule in her Northern Ireland must come to an end! She was livid that a woman who did the same job as a man was often paid much less. "Our work is every bit as valuable.

Robbery is what it is!" she told him one night over drinks.

But, for now at least, her causes would have to wait while she indulged in her love for horror films.

And Salem also learned that she had some secret talents. One Saturday, after she'd been on the phone with a friend, he happened to catch sight of the elaborate doodles that she'd drawn on an envelope while she carried on the conversation. There was a ballerina, a long-eared dog sitting on a moon, geometric shapes, and more. She'd said she loved to draw, but he'd had no idea how talented she was; Salem was impressed.

Yes, there were surprises. But there were also things he knew. He knew she loved to keep fresh flowers all around the bedroom and the den. He knew pink roses were her favorite and that it thrilled her no end when they went on sale. He knew that she grew more talkative and happy with a second glass of wine but woke up feeling dreadful if she had a third.

Of one thing he was sure: he loved everything thing about her. And there was much more to discover during those sweet early days of peeling back her layers to find new and wondrous things.

At the same time, he could tell that she was eager to know more about him too. She asked a lot of questions: Do you have regrets that wake you in the night? Things you wish that you could change? If you could have one wish—no restrictions—tell me what it would be.

He told her things that scared him that he'd never said out loud. A man's job, after all, is to be strong and carry on. But it felt good to talk to Mary. She loved him in a way that made him stronger. He was a better man with her than he was before.

And yet could it work when she was not a Muslim? She was, after all, a stranger to the sacred way of being, passed down for generations and now ingrained so firmly in Salem's daily life. It was something that sustained him, some vital part of him she could never understand.

"Sometimes I worry we're too different, you and me," he said to her one night. "Because of our religions."

She reached for his hand. "But we're more alike than different. And I think it's rare to find the kind of love we have. Because of that, we'll make it work. We'll *more* than make it work; we'll have the best life, Salem."

But Mary didn't know just how different his culture was from hers. A tight knot of worry formed in Salem's chest when he thought about the one important fact he had not yet found a way to share with Mary. It would be permissible in Yemen, part of the normal flow of life, for him to take a second wife. But here in England, what he was doing would be thought of as betrayal against the woman that he loved—as well as a lack of faithfulness to his wife back home.

Mary noticed right away that there was something on his mind. And, as she often did, she seemed to read his mood. "Talk to me," she said.

"I belong with you," he said. "I *need* to be with you. But my country's ways are different, and there are things about me that might hurt you—although I would never mean you harm." He was surprised to feel the sting of tears forming in his eyes. "Because to hurt you, Mary, is the last thing I'd want to do."

She pressed her lips to his. "Don't you think I know that?" she asked. "And while I don't know your country's ways, Salem, I know *you.* Remember what we both thought that first night that we met?" She held his eyes in hers. "My sweet love, I know you. From the first day that I saw you, I knew you were mine. And, whatever it might be that you have to tell me, it will be okay."

He felt warmed by her words yet chilled by what he had to say. *Would* she understand? Should he have told her sooner?

He took a deep breath to try to calm the beating of his heart. "In Yemen, things are different. A man can marry more than once—and it means no disrespect if he cares for all his wives. If he treats each of them with the honor that is due a woman."

A pained look moved across her eyes, and the room was filled with silence.

Finally, she spoke. "So you have a wife—or wives?"

"One wife, who was my parents' choice for me.

That is another difference. Here, when you are ready, it you who picks a mate.

Her voice was small. "Were you happy with her there in Yamens?"

"We've made a life together, and we make it work. But what I've found with you is different." He ran his hand along her cheek. "What I've found with you is not a thing two sets of parents can arrange."

"But I don't understand. If you have a wife . . ."

He could tell that it was hard for her to say the word.

"If you have a wife in Yemen, then why did you come here?"

"I had to do it, Mary. I wasn't safe at home. You see, Mary, in my country, there are clans that go to war with other families." The old anger bubbled up inside him. "There's a thing called *blood revenge.* And what it means is that people die—fathers, brothers, sons. My father came to me one day and said it was time for me to go—that I might be the next one to be murdered. All because of things that were going on before I was even born."

Her face was white. "Oh, Salem."

"You can't know how hard it was to leave my family and everything I ever knew. But when I saw you at the pub that night? This rainy, foggy place— all at once, it felt like home."

Her smile was bashful as she took his hand.

"I should have told you sooner, but I couldn't."

"I can understand," she said. "It's a lot to tell."

"And what I have with you feels . . ." He paused to think of the word. "Like some bit of magic that I didn't want to break." He watched her, frightened now about what she might say next. "Can we still be okay now that you know . . . my story?"

She was quiet then, and her silence scared him.

"I had wanted the whole wedding thing—the white veil and the music, one husband and one wife. And those vows that I always thought sounded so romantic. Forsaking all others, keep the only unto her." She paused and looked him in the eye. "But Salem, I don't need those things. What I need is you."

A long-held tension drained out of his body, and at last, he could breathe.

With tears in her eyes, she gave him the kind of kiss that was filled with desperation. It was as if she, like Salem, was scared of losing something precious.

But when she moved away, Mary still looked troubled. "What is her name, your . . . wife?"

Salem took her hand. "My wife's name is Yasmine."

"You say she was your parents' choice, but did you *come* to love her? And do you love her still?" Tears streamed down her face, and Salem almost couldn't bear the look of pain he saw on her face.

He brushed away her tears with his finger, then he stroked her cheek. "Mary, never in my life have I ever felt the way that I feel with you. What I have for Yasmine is respect. On my wedding day—and even now—I thought of her fondly as a cousin—and as a childhood playmate, because that is what she was. On the day that we were married, she was twelve."

Mary's eyes grew wide. "A child!"

"And I was just fourteen. Hardly old enough for that."

She snuggled closer to him. "It's a lot to take in, Salem. It's a lot, but it's okay."

What Mary didn't know was that it wasn't over yet. "And Mary, one more thing . . ."

She looked up at him, fearful, a question in her eyes.

"I have two sons with Yasmine. They are Ahmed and Omar."

"Salem." Compassion filled her eyes. "How hard it must have been to leave them. How old are your boys?"

"They are five and three, and I think about them all

the time, how hurt they both must be. And how confused they must have been to find me gone. But what could I do but go? And this blood revenge might one day put their lives in danger just like it has mine. And then it might be *me* who sends word to *them* to run as my father did for me. Or since I'm not there to watch, I hope someone will warn them . . . before it is too late." The knot of worry began to tighten in his stomach. "And now you know the reason why my mood is sometimes dark and why the nightmares sometimes come." He gave her a small smile. "Although those have eased off since I've been sleeping in your bed." He took her hand and kissed it. "I feel safe with you, Mary. You have given me that gift."

Her answer was to hold him. It was good to say the hurt out loud and have her bear it with him.

"So there is no need for marriage," she said after a while. "Let's just go on like this. I promise that's enough — to be with the man I love."

"No, it's not enough. Because we must have more."

She looked at him, confused.

"I want you to have a wedding. As a way for me to honor you in the way that you deserve."

"But . . ."

He stopped the question with a kiss. "I'm told that in England, things start off with a proposal. So Mary Eileen Norman, will you marry me?"

"But can we really . . ."

He kissed her once again. "No more words," he whispered. "Except for one word — yes.

He would find a way.

Chapter Three

Family Pictures

Soon they had a date. They'd go into the ceremony as simply Mary, simply Salem, and leave as man and wife. He'd informed Yasmine of his plans, and she had agreed to a divorce so that his and Mary's union would be legal. Yasmine would remain a valued part of his father's household, where she would continue raising the two boys.

"There's no rush with the wedding," Salem said to Mary one day as they walked in a nearby park. "Don't you want to plan a party? Or wait till we have the time off to take a trip and celebrate?" He could not afford a big trip, but they could go somewhere special for a few days. His mates at work could surely give him some ideas. The whole thing seemed to lack the festive feel it needed. For one thing, there was no ring, which he knew was the English custom. He still needed time—just a bit— to save up for that.

For his part, of course, there was no need for frills. He only wanted Mary. But from the way she talked, he assumed that she had always dreamed of a special wedding. In the West, he understood, it could be a grand occasion with parties, fancy clothes, and months and months of planning. She deserved no less.

"Soon we must arrange for me to meet your mother and speak with her about my plans," he said. Her father was no longer living, and he understood that she and her mother had become somewhat estranged. But, still, Salem felt it was important for him to take that step.

"Oh." Mary looked surprised. Then she shook her head. "Salem, there's no need to involve my mother. This should be a time for joy. And my memories of my mother? Well, there's a lot of hurt."

"But I must go to her. I must assure her, Mary, that I can care for you in the way that you deserve, show her that her daughter has chosen a good man. Hopefully, the meeting will put her mind at ease.

They slowed down a little, and she looked down at her hand, which was intertwined with his. "I love that about you, Salem—that you'd think to go to her. But I'm sad to have to tell you that my mother wouldn't   care."

"Surely she'd care, Mary." He could not imagine that a parent would not want to meet the man her daughter planned to marry. In Yemen, it was a parent's solemn duty to see that their son or daughter found a match that would ensure a happy future (and the continuation of the family line).

"Plus, good luck even finding her at this point. I have no idea where you'd even start to look." A hardness filled her eyes. "So I guess that's your proof of how much my mother cares."

Salem paused along the path and looked at Mary, stunned. "How long has it been since you've spoken to your mother?" he asked her.

Mary watched the ground and kicked softly at a bramble. I don't like to talk about it, but, Salem, it's been years. And even then, it was just a real phone call—very brief. There was not a lot to say between me and my mum—if you could even call her that. She left when I was ten. She left me with my sister, who did the best she could, but we weren't old enough—not really—to be left on our own."

He stood there quietly as he took that in. "Shall I talk to your sister then?" he asked her gently, pulling her closer to him.

Mary shook her head "We're not in touch that much. I guess we each remind the other of all those awful years, of feeling desperate—and unwanted."

All he could do was hold her.

She leaned in for a kiss. "You'll be my family, Salem, and if we are very lucky, maybe more will come along. Little ones, I mean."

Some of Salem's friends at work had told him that they also had little contact with their parents because of disagreements or just a lack of effort. This was one more thing about the West that Salem found confusing. In the Arab world, the family was the center of everything important.

They continued their walk in silence, Salem's arm around his future bride. "We don't have to do this in a hurry," he assured her. "Don't you want more time to plan?" Then there'd be time to do a little more to mark the commitment they were making.

"I used to think I'd want that. I had all these fantasies—like a lot of girls, I guess. Flowers and the lacey dress. And dancing! Lots of dancing." She gave Salem a shy smile. "But now that I understand what a dreamy groom I'm getting, I just want to be your wife."

He stopped walking and put both arms around her waist. "If I could marry you tomorrow, you know that I would." A fog had moved in to make her hair curl at the ends, and the coolness brought a color to her cheeks that only added to her beauty. "Are you sure there are no aunts or cousins, other friends or family, you'd like to stand beside you?" he asked, kissing her.

"You *are* my family, Salem. Let's just keep it small, okay?"

♦♦♦

She was quiet that night as they ate their simple dinner. Salem had the idea that their talk at the park was still heavy on her mind.

Later, with the dishes cleaned and put away, she reached up to the top shelf to pull out a photo album. "Want to see pictures of my mother? And me as a girl? I feel like I should show you that part of my life."

That sat together on the couch, and Mary pointed to a photo of a mother and a daughter sitting on a stoop with a wreathed door behind them. "Here we are at the house where I was born in County Antrim. I think I was maybe four. We left Northern Ireland a few years after that, after my father died."

First, Salem's eyes went to the girl, gorgeous even then, laughing at whoever was behind the camera. He marveled that her capacity for joy somehow had survived in the grown-up Mary — despite the abandonment and neglect this young girl would endure. A fury overcame him, anger at the woman who could leave this child when it was her job, her solemn duty really, to give her the best life that she could.

Moved, he looked again at the small girl in the photo. It's okay. I'm here now, he told her silently. Taking care of you will be the thing I wake each day to do.

He looked then at the mother, who had Mary's eyes and smile and held on protectively to the child in her arms. Salem wondered what had happened and if he'd learn more in time.

"And here she is with my first stepfather. They both look happy here, so this picture must have been from the early days. Later, they just fought. I don't remember happy."

The couple was pictured clasping hands with a fountain in the background. They gazed at each other, giddy with delight at their life together, which must have been just starting. Salem recognized that feeling, and suddenly this newfound joy with Mary seemed like a fragile thing. He recognized the passion in the couple's eyes as the same thing he felt now. Could that kind of wanting and devotion simply disappear?

He turned another page. "Do you have pictures of your dad?"

From the back of the book, she took out a picture of a handsome dark-haired man. "He used to read to me. I remember that—a little—and the smell of his pipe. But he died when I was three."

"The stepfather from the picture—was he kind to you?"

"He was not a fan of children. I used to listen to their fighting. Of course, I couldn't understand. I just knew that it was loud. But my sister told me later what she heard. And I think that she and I were the reason that he left."

He pulled her close and kissed her. "You will always be," he whispered, "the reason that I stay."

Salem was filled with thankfulness for the family he'd grown up in. His father was a busy man with work and so many sons and daughters. But for him, contentment meant the knowledge that his children were safe and doing well. Of course, his father hadn't seen that wish fulfilled; blood revenge had taken one and sent another here to England. But Salem knew his dad would do anything he could to keep his children safe, as would Salem for his boys.

In another picture, Mary's mother and another man smiled broadly at the camera. But by now, Salem was suspicious of any smiles that he might see in this book of photos.

"Stepfather number two," said Mary. "For a few years, at least. By this point, we were here in Birmingham."

Mary and her sister stood between them. Mary looked to be five or six, about the age of Salem's oldest boy. In the photo, Mary frowned, irritated, at the camera, as if she were ready to get the picture-taking done with and rush off from the grip the man had on her shoulder.

"You don't look like you're a fan," said Salem. "You didn't like the guy?"

She shrugged. "He never really did father kinds of things. And there were so many times he made my mother cry. That breaks your heart, you know? To see your mother weep. And then he was gone—which *I* thought was a good thing." She touched her mother's picture. "But she had a real hard time."

Then she turned to a large, professional-looking shot. "And here we have their wedding." The newlyweds were pictured with a gigantic cake topped by enormous flowers. "This one lasted three years," said Mary with a sigh. "I guess maybe there's a reason I'm not up for the whole cake-and-flowers kind of wedding. In my mind, all of that is tied up with love that isn't love. And you and me, we're different."

Salem wasn't sure if that was a statement or a question.

But nonetheless, he answered. He kissed her on the cheek. "I promise you we're different. You're stuck with me for life."

She smiled a little, grateful for his tired attempt at humor, but mostly for the reassuring hand placed protectively on her leg.

"I'm not going anywhere," he said. He'd honor his commitment to her, as he'd been taught to do, but it was more than duty that would keep him at her side. "You are part of me now. I *need* you with me,

Mary. Without you, I'd be lost."

He studied the picture of the groom, a tall, imposing man with a mustache and salt-and-pepper hair.

"He was an awful man," said Mary. "The way he used to watch me always creeped me out. Back then I didn't get it. I just knew that it was wrong. And what a relief—oh, happy day—when that man was gone." She pulled the photo album from his hands. "Okay, enough of that. I just wanted you to see. Of course, that's a part of me that I wish I could forget. But you can't forget, not really." She looked down at the floor. "I know all that stuff was *their* fault; I was just a kid," she said in a small voice. "But some days I'm still that girl, you know? The girl nobody wanted—until you."

He brushed a stray hair from her forehead. "I'm sure everywhere you go, people want to be with Mary." Because how could they not? She was always full of fun and was quick to listen when others had a problem. Compassion seemed to spill out from her blue-green eyes. But now that he thought about it, she seemed to keep a distance from the people that she knew, revealing very little of herself. She didn't have a lot of close friends. She knew a lot of people, who'd flock to her at the pubs or call to her on the streets, always thrilled to see her. But all of them seemed to be acquaintances more than they were friends.

"Okay! Your turn." She smiled. "Tell me every single thing about growing up as you. What was it like, Salem, to have a mom and dad, to be a normal, happy kid?" Her expression turned a little wistful.

A sense of melancholy swept through Salem. How would he begin his story? Yes, he'd had the comfort of knowing that his parents held him always in a protective watchfulness. But *happy?* Well, that was not the way he would describe his home. A huge sense of loss had touched every facet of their lives since the day his sister died. It seemed his mom was always weeping or on the verge of tears. And even as a young boy, Salem understood that while the world can give, it could also take away the people you held dear.

But he didn't start with that. "As I've said, my mother was not the only wife. For my father, there were four."

"*Four.* And how was that? Four wives. I can't imagine."

Salem smiled, leaning back against the cushions of the couch. "It was not without its drama, but most of the time we got on well." He had warm memories of his household, so full of wives and children. It seemed the opposite of Mary's home, where everyone had left.

"And he was a tribal leader?"

"Yes, my father was a sheikh."

"And were there brothers? Were there sisters? Jean was so much older that we never had a lot in common. Then when my mother left, my sister was distracted, which now I can understand. She was way too young to have had me in her care. But I was so lonely, Salem! In fact, when I was I was six, I made a sister up. I'd talk to her every night. It was my dream to have a sister who had time for secrets and all of my little games."

I had such a sister, Salem thought. *And it was my dream to have my sister back.* Maryam had been the one to teach him little songs and tell him fairy tales each night before bed. She would use hand motions to illustrate his favorite stories, which were Cinderella and Aladdin and the Magic Lamp. And she had an expressive voice that made the stories more exciting.

"We were mostly boys at my house, and the youngest one was me. Fifteen boys and two girls, seventeen in all."

"Oh, Salem, that's amazing. Was it perfect? It sounds perfect."

"Sometimes we thought it was." He smiled. "Well, that is, until . . ." A shadow crossed his face. "Well, you have to understand that *perfect* doesn't last. I've come to understand that more and more. It might seem to you that you see a family that is happy—walking in the street or running in the park. But they might be hurting on the inside and trying to forget. Or maybe they *are* happy. It's their golden time! And if that's the case, oh Mary, you hope they love it while it lasts. Because their time together might be shorter than they think."

She took his face in her hand. "Hey, what's wrong?

What happened?"

"My sister Maryam. She died. She died when I was seven."

"Salem, no! I had no idea!" She put her arms around his waist and leaned her head against his chest. "Was it an accident?" she asked. Her voice was soft and careful.

"No, Mary. It was murder."

She looked up and him and gasped.

Salem took a deep breath. "There is great beauty in my country. Part of my heart is still there in my village. But for a long time, Mary, we have lived with terror. Not terror from the outside—but terror from ourselves. It's family against family." His heart began to pound. The anger, it seemed to him, would never go away. "Do you know why she was killed? Because she met a man she loved." He closed his eyes against the searing pain. "Love!" he said to Mary. "Love should never be a reason for a bullet through a heart."

Mary's eyes were wide. "Who killed your sister,

Salem?"

"There were rumors of an affair with her lover, Mohsen. And someone in my family killed my sister—as a way to clean the shame that they thought she brought upon us."

 A silence fell between them before Mary finally spoke. "I don't understand."

"If a woman in my country is suspected of a sin or brings shame upon her family, then her death is what some refer to as an honor crime."

"And so that is allowed?" Mary's face was white. "For someone to be shot because . . . of a pregnancy?"

"My sister wasn't pregnant. That's just what someone thought. But, yes, it is allowed. And when she was taken from us, many of my neighbors slept the better for it." The hard knot tightened in his chest. "To them, the world was better—because my gentle, joyful sister was no more."

She absorbed that information in a state of silent shock. "So no one's tried for murder? They are just allowed to . . . get away with a thing like that?"

"They more than get away with it. They are considered by their clan to have done their solemn duty for the family."

"Salem, I'm so sorry. I don't know what to say." A silence overtook them as Mary held his hand. "There's just so much that we don't know," she said, "about how other people live. Most of us spend our lives in this tiny little fraction of the world. And we live our lives just *blind* to the bigger picture." They sat lost in thought before she kissed his hand. "Tell me more, but this time, make it happy. Tell me a happy story."

"Well, as the youngest of the seventeen, there were a lot of eyes on me. More eyes than I wanted." He smiled. "You can imagine that a young boy liked to have his secrets! I was sent to school at three, and I worked hard. By the time that I was twelve, I'd memorized the whole Quran."

"That's impressive, Salem." She smiled. "Well, just look at me, marrying a man whose ability to memorize is close to genius. Seriously, Salem, that makes me so proud." She leaned in for a kiss. "Not that I didn't know that first night at the pub that you were absolutely brilliant. So many great ideas you had! Ideas on everything."

Salem blushed. "And then that led to other things. Memorizing the Quran helped me when I wanted to learn other languages. When I memorized the last part, that was quite a day for me. I won't forget it—ever. My father threw a party to boast to the other sheikhs. It's a good day for a son when he makes his father proud."

"And what happened after that? When you got out of school?"

"Although my father was a sheikh, he taught us all responsibility. We should depend on ourselves, not him, he said. We should find our own ways to contribute. After school, my job was to help my father cultivate our land. Oh, you should see our palm trees. I'd love to show you, Mary." The thought of the majestic trees reaching toward the sky brought a sudden ache for home. To Salem and his family, the palm was everything. His people ate its dates, and from its branches, families formed the homes and tools that were central to their lives.

"I'd love to go there, Salem."

"That will be the best day." When he could introduce his precious Mary to his revered Aunt Palm, whom he also loved, something deep in Salem would finally feel complete. He was eager for the day it was safe for him to return. But how long would that be?

She kissed his hand again. "We'll see it together."

He closed his eyes. "If Allah wills."

Before the ceremony, Mary waited next to her friend Ann. She wore a simple white lace dress that she'd found on sale. Her eyes sparkled when she grabbed Salem's hand and gave him a shy smile. "Look at my handsome husband. Well, my *almost-*husband. Soon now. Very soon!"

He handed her pink roses, which had not been on sale. But a bride should not be married without the flowers she loved best. The small group was completed by Marouf, who was grinning broadly, his suit-coat buttons straining hard against his bulging belly. "Do not forget me, Salem!" He clapped Salem on the back. "This is because of me. Did I not say that you would thank me for dragging you out to the bars? And you found a good one quick. You moved right in and took the most magnificent of all the fine girls in the place."

Salem didn't like the way he talked of women—and especially his bride—as some kind of prize to be claimed and hunted. But his mood could not be spoiled. He shook Marouf's hand. "It's good to see you, friend," he said. "Thank you for being here."

Ann snapped some pictures before the ceremony started, and what followed that was brief. Salem held on to just two memories: hearing the word *wife* and the look of thankfulness and love that shone in Mary's eyes. Later, they toasted the occasion over a pint at the pub where the bride and groom had first laid eyes on each other.

When they started out for home, he tugged at her arm, pulling her west instead of east.

"Where are we going, love?" she asked.

"Just trust me, wife. You'll see."

Although the preparations had been minimal and rushed, something that she'd said had weighed on his mind. I had a lot of fantasies, she'd said about her wedding. And dancing! Lots of dancing.

He'd scoured all the papers until he found a band that would be playing at a small park that very afternoon. He'd asked around at work to see if they were any good, and now he had a way to make the day more festive, if only just a bit.

She smiled and understood once she heard the music.

"I wanted you to have the roses and the dancing." He held his face close to hers. "I want you to have everything." Because everything was what she deserved. "And I promise, Mary, here and now, that I'll do my very best." Although he knew what he could give would not come even close to what he wanted for her.

She pressed her lips tenderly into his and let them linger there as if to say her life with Salem was everything and more.

With their faces still held close together, they moved slowly to the music.

"This is okay?" he whispered. "That there was no big wedding?"

"I dreamed of all that stuff," she said, "before I knew there was a you." She put her hand gently on his cheek. "If I had seen this face, I would have spent my whole life dreaming of my groom instead of dreaming of a wedding. I would have dreamed of doing this." She put her lips once more to his.

A cool breeze brought the scent of lilacs to help them celebrate as they enjoyed the songs, their closeness to each other, and the music. When a light rain began to fall, even that seemed like the perfect touch with Mary as his new bride pressed up warm against him.

She looked up at him and smiled. "Do you know what it means for it to rain on the day that you get married? It's like a signal from skies; the rain means that we'll be blessed."

"It is mercy from Allah," Salem said.

And blessed is what we'll be, he thought. And so it begins.

◆◆◆

The joys of their first few weeks as a married couple were mixed with small aggravations. Crusty dots of gravy were left on dinner plates lying in the sink. Mary's dainty flats, kicked off in the middle of the floor, made Salem stumble on more than one occasion. One day she put his socks away in a different drawer. "See how much sense it makes?" she'd cried out happily. "They're closer to the shoes!" But he was almost late for work as he searched frantically for his socks as well as for his razor, which was in the wrong place as well—a place that, of course, "made so much sense" to Mary.

Not that this was new since he had often stayed the night with Mary before the two of them were wed. But now that it was his place too, the order and the cleanliness mattered more to Salem.

"I'm organizing the apartment for our life together," she said to Salem proudly. And Salem couldn't bring himself to say that he couldn't stand the changes and the small bits of disorder in the home they shared. Salem liked things kept in order; he liked things kept neat, each thing in its place. With all the violence that he'd seen—so much uncertainty— neatness helped him cope. He could not control the monstrous urges of the men who wished to take his life in retaliation for a thing that Salem had no part in. But he could keep his books, his shirts, his mail, and his other things in their proper places—right where he could find them. Of them, he could be certain.

"One soul in two bodies," she had once said of their union, and Salem knew that it was true. More and more each evening, he felt a sense of rightness when he took her into his arms after a long day. But more and more, he found, the one soul had two opinions. Going out or staying in? The Beatles or the Rolling Stones on the record player? Staying up a little later just to talk some more or heading off to bed? Mary thought one thing, and Salem often thought the other. The days at the factory were hard, and most nights Salem liked to relax at home and go to bed before eleven. Pub life on the weekdays had less and less appeal.

The man over him at work had decided that the

team should increase production and move faster. *Too slow,* he was always saying. *Men, pick up the pace.* Most nights, Salem's energy was spent when he pushed open the apartment door to the welcome smell of Mary's stew or roasted chicken. If she pushed too hard for dancing and the pubs, he occasionally gave in to the eagerness in her eyes or the way she'd press her lips into a pout that begged him Pretty please! as she grabbed his hand.

But more and more, he'd simply kiss her forehead after dinner and hold her close for just a moment. "You be safe," he'd say. "And don't stay out too late." But of course, he couldn't sleep until he heard the turning of the doorknob when she came back to the apartment. Stretched out on his bed, he'd listen for the sound of her shoes being kicked off onto the floor (most likely in a spot that would later trip him up). Salem couldn't sleep until he knew that she was home and safe.

Salem understood the reason that his wife had more energy than he did for dancing and the pubs. Her workdays were much shorter. And, from what Salem understood, her superior at work was more of a chum to Mary than a demanding boss. There were no long days on her feet for her; there was none of the constant stress of being pushed to be better, to be more.

Salem's boss was a good man, who set expectations for his workers in a way that was kind but firm. Mainly, Salem pushed himself, hoping for a raise or a promotion, now that it was his job to provide for Mary as well as for himself.

From the outside looking in, his life might have appeared to be about the same as his previous existence as a single man. Since he'd practically moved into her apartment as soon as they had met, the day-to-day business of their lives just went on as before. But now that they were married, each little bit of trouble felt permanent in a way that sometimes seemed alarming. In Salem's mind, each argument that they had stretched into similar refrains that would likely fill their home again—for years and years and years.

The thought made him even more exhausted one cold day in November as he pushed the door open to their place. No smells welcomed him; he'd been hoping for a nice soup to take off the chill.

Mary ran to him with a smile and took his face in

her hands for a deep, long kiss, which he eagerly returned.

"I've thought of you all day," she said, her lips pressed against his neck.

With his arms still around her, he pulled her toward the couch. "Let me just sit awhile and hold you and let this day drain away."

Stretched out with her on the couch, he let himself be soothed by the soft warmth of her skin and the perfume of her hair. He closed his eyes, half asleep.

She took his hand and kissed it. "Rest your eyes, my precious. And then I thought the two of us could run out to the pub for a bite to eat. What do you think, Salem?" She snuggled even closer. "And then if I'm very sweet, perhaps you'll dance with me? Just one dance, maybe two?"

"Mary, I can't do it. You don't understand the way they push us all day long. But we'll go on the weekend. How does that sound? I promise."

"Oh, Salem. It's so boring at the council. I was hoping we'd go out." She moved to get up. "Well, let me warm some dinner, and then maybe I'll still go. One drink, a nice laugh or two if some of my chums are there, and then I'll be back early. I'll make it an early night."

Salem watched her sleepily as she headed to the kitchen. He took in her shapely hips and dainty shoulders, the hair that shone like silken sunshine, the very Mary-ness of this precious creature who, amazingly, was his, as he was hers. Other men would see it too. Perhaps they'd see it at the counter, where she might struggle once again to flag down a busy worker to pour her a drink. Of course, another man would grasp eagerly at the chance to come to her assistance as Salem once had done. And then a little talk would follow and perhaps a dance . . .

Salem had no doubt that Mary would be faithful; that was not his worry for a second. But Mary couldn't help it that her movements would be followed by the eyes of other men. She couldn't help it that the sight of her would stir desires within them. She wouldn't let them touch her, but a pub was still the wrong place for a married woman out on the town alone.

"I'd rather that you not," he said. And that settles that, he thought. He didn't want to spoil her fun. But there were certain issues that had to be considered — for safety and decorum.

"Oh, nonsense. You won't miss me. You'll be sound asleep." Mary smiled as she pulled some bowls out of the fridge.

Salem was surprised and a little hurt. But this was, after all, the West, where a man's request was not given the same honor it would have been met with back in Yemen. There, family and home were central to a woman's life — not this idea of running out for fun and conversation. Although enjoyment had its place. And so on the weekend, they'd go out to the pub of Mary's choosing.

Mary's mind, however, still seemed stuck on *yes*. Dancing to some music in her head, she twirled from one side of the kitchen to the next, turning on the oven, then moving to the fridge. She swayed her hips and sang as she spooned leftover meat pie into a baking dish. "But Salem, I want to dance! My whole day has been so . . . dull!" She looked him in the eye. "I won't beg you to go. I can see that you're exhausted. But if I want to have some fun, what can it really hurt for me to go out for some laughs?"

He was almost too tired to argue, but he couldn't stand the thought of her alone at some pub in a sea of men. "Our ways back home are different. To you, it might seem foolish for me to ask you to stay home, but it's important to me, Mary." He let his voice grow soft. "Because you're important. Because I want to keep you safe."

She sighed. "I will stay tonight if it means that much to you. Because it's important to my husband, and I love him more than life." She looked him in the eye. "But you have to understand that I'm me and you are you. And sometimes you just have let me go and do my thing — whatever that might be."

"Thank you." He went to her and held her. "I *want* you to be you. Because who you are is amazing. But the ways of my country work. I saw it for myself with my father and his wives. They were happy, all of them, although it wasn't easy. And that kind of happiness is what I want for us." It was his fervent wish to protect both her heart and his — and their life together — through the way he ran his home.

"Well, what do *I* know, really, about happy homes?" she asked. "I grew up in a house where everybody left." She took out some lettuce and began to slice it. "Stay home or go out? We will make it work. Marriage, after all, is made up of compromise." But she was quiet as they ate their dinner. And later, she sat apart from Salem on the couch, not touching him at all, as they watched some movie on TV that Salem was way too tired to follow.

The next day, unsettled thoughts made his hours at work even harder to get through. That night, he walked through the door, hoping to find Mary in a better mood; he longed to have a quiet night, taking comfort in her presence with no further conflict, only peace.

He walked in to find her taking tissue from around an item she had just pulled out from a Rackhams bag. She looked up and smiled. "I splurged—but just a bit." She held up a silver frame, which she placed next to the bamboo plant that she kept by the window. "What do you think?" she asked.

"It's very nice," he said, confused. "But I believe that it is meant to have a picture stuck inside it?"

"Oh, it will," she said. "I was just thinking of the way that our whole lives are stretched so far into the future. So many reasons that we'll have, you and I, to take a picture and put it in a frame."

"So this is for a picture that we might take on some future date?" He still wasn't sure that he understood.

"It is! And that one too, and that one." She nodded toward a blank frame she'd set up on the mantle, then she pointed to another, placed behind the couch. "Oh, I know it's kind of silly to put them out like that—with all those big blank squares where the pictures ought to be. But I couldn't wait to buy them." She walked over to him and put her arms around his waist. "As I guess you could tell, we didn't take a lot of photos when I was growing up. And then after I was grown, I was not the type to take a lot of pictures. But now that I have you, I want to photograph every minute of our lives." She snuggled into his chest, gazing at the silver squares bought to showcase pictures of the adventures they would share. "So that's our future, Salem, right there waiting for us. I splurged on the nicer frames. Because we're worth the splurge."

The last of the day's sunlight glimmered on the frame closest to the window. A sense of peace filled Salem. He felt celebrated; he thought things would be okay.

◆◆◆

A few weeks later, he decided that the time was right to ask her what she thought about a possible conversion to his faith. "Not that it is something that you'd decide today," he told her gently. "It would take much thought and a lot of deep discussions of the ways of Muslim life." He reached for her hand. "When I pray in the morning, I'd love to pray with you." To come together before Allah with the one he loved would be the very thing to make his life complete.

"Oh, Salem, that's so sweet." She reached up to touch his cheek. "But I've never really been too keen on religion. I don't think that's for me."

"But there is much about my faith that I feel you could embrace if you'd take the time to learn. We could sit together and discuss some of the teachings. And then you could decide if you feel called to make a change." He smoothed back her hair. "I want for you more peace, and I think that this could help."

"But are we really meant to have peace in this world—that can be kind of awful? Because if your God—or your Allah—is really in control, I'd think he might step in to stop some of this madness that's always in the news."

"Allah can bring peace in the midst of *all* of that. And if more people turned to Allah—"

Mary squeezed his hand as she interrupted. "Salem, I adore the fact that it works for you. And I know there's something *more* . . . something that's much higher than the minds of me and you. I think there is a God—and I can glimpse him, just a little, in the way you live your life. I can see that when you pray, you become a better man, the best man that I know. And, Salem, how I wish that I could make that work for me. But I just don't think it will."

"We could find a church for you," he tried. Perhaps

that would be the place where Mary could find comfort. He thought of Islam's teachings about the baby Jesus, who spoke in his mother's arms. I am Jesus Christ. I am God's servant. He has given me the scripture and made me to be a prophet. The blessings of God are with me withers ever I will go.

Mary looked him in the eye. "Salem, you were lucky. You grew up with two parents who loved their child enough to teach you the ways of Allah. My mother never once took me a church. All religion ever did for me was make me feel set apart. Because here I was in school with all these Protestants while I had a different label, although what does it even mean to be a Catholic? I had no idea. I still don't, I suppose. And my father, he was Jewish. So what were we, really, as a family? Religion was a jumble, not a source of peace."

"But it *could* be, if you let it." He would pray for that for her.

Chapter Four

Clashes

Two weeks later on a Friday, they went to a Christmas party thrown by one of Mary's friends. They pushed their way through the crowded room to find some drinks. Someone had put on a Beatles record, so they had to edge around the dance space. Some guy almost fell into Salem as the man drunkenly gyrated to "Yellow Submarine." Irritated, Salem put a protective arm on Mary's shoulder. It wasn't even half past seven, and this guy was already wasted.

People Mary knew would grab her hand or shout into her ear things that made her laugh. She'd pull Salem closer to include him in the conversation. Or at least she tried. But he could barely hear the talk over the music, which seemed to be turned up at full volume.

He looked around the room and spotted the

English version of a Christmas tree. But Salem knew that Christ was born beneath a palm, its fruit offering nutrition for both Mary and the child. So why this lighted pine? It was if the people in this country didn't understand the importance of the palm, which Salem's people had the knowledge to revere.

"Christmas trees," he knew, had a varied history here. In early times, the Europeans had used hawthorn or cherry plants that they would bring inside and hope would bloom at Christmas. If they could not afford a real plant, pyramids of wood were sometimes decorated with candles and with apples. But Salem had never heard of a family here who gave the palm an honored place in their Christmas celebration.

They grabbed some whiskey and munched on some cheese and crackers when they could get to the crowded table with the food. Then they found a spot on the dance floor, where by that time a second Beatles album had begun to play. Several times, he'd watch as Mary smiled across the room at someone that she knew. *That smile.* He hated everything about this party, but that smile filled his very being with a rush of warmth. He'd get through the party, then he'd be the lucky one to go home with her.

Friends of Mary would squeeze in to press drinks into their hands. "No thanks," he would mouth. But out of politeness, and perhaps out of boredom too, he drank more than he'd intended. As did Mary; he could tell from the way her dance moves got a little looser and her voice grew louder when she'd yell into his ear: something about the music or about another person that he *had* to meet.

When he felt enough time had gone by, he suggested that they leave, and she said okay. But on their way to the door, they kept getting pulled into more conversations that Salem couldn't hear. At one point, they found themselves in a small knot of people. Standing across from Mary was a well-built man who did not take his eyes off Salem's wife the whole time that they talked.

Salem squeezed her hand three times, a signal they had worked out to say *Time to go.* And soon they were on their way. The last thing he remembered was heading to the door with Mary's hand in his.

But somehow he ended up slumped over on the

host's couch, fast asleep. At some point, he sat up groggily and looked around for Mary. The music had stopped playing. People were huddled in small groups or talking quietly in corners, but Mary wasn't there. One couple in a chair across from Salem was wrapped up in each other, whispering and kissing.

Salem stood up slowly and wandered down the darkened hallway, wondering exactly how late it had gotten. Then he came upon two shadows, and his heart stopped. It was Mary—with the man who'd watched her so intently when they tried to leave. They were sitting with their backs against the wall, so close that their arms were touching. They seemed deep in conversation. And Mary was looking at the man with the smile that Salem thought was reserved for him, a smile that seemed to be keeping secrets—and making promises.

Then she noticed Salem and gave him a drunken smile. "There you are! You fell asleep."

"As I told you—hours ago—it's time for us to go." He tried to hold in the fury that was threatening to explode within him.

The man glanced at the floor. Salem couldn't tell if he was ashamed—or perhaps furious at Salem for the interruption.

What gave this man the right to sit so close to Mary and look at her that way? Salem watched them closely. Had the top button on Mary's blouse always been undone? Was her face flushed from alcohol—or from something else?

"Mary, let's go. Now!" He grabbed her arm with a force that he regretted right away.

In the car, they didn't speak except for when she asked him to pull over for a minute so that she could throw up by the roadway. At home, she fell into a deep sleep as soon as she hit the bed. Salem, on the other hand, could barely sleep at all, and when he did, he was haunted by dreams of Mary in a darkened hallway with a stranger.

The next morning was spent in the house together—but apart. They said little to each other beyond mumbled, glum good mornings. For a while, Salem sat in his chair with *The Guardian* but couldn't concentrate enough to read. Had he overreacted the night before to a simple conversation? Or had the man come on to Mary and, in her drunken state, had she let things go too far?

At one point, he heard her in the bathroom. She was sick again. He went in to check and found her doubled over by the toilet, wincing, her face grown white with the wave of nausea that had overtaken her.

After she'd thrown up for a second time, he gently rubbed her back. "I propose we both take it easy with the drinks when we go out from now on."

She smiled gratefully at him. "Yeah, you're right," she said. "But there's something else, I think, that's making me this way." She gave him a tired smile. "I think it might be a baby. I might be pregnant, Salem."

Salem took a deep breath; not sure he'd heard her right. "I thought we said we'd wait." He wanted very much to raise a family with her, but he'd hoped to find a better-paying job before a baby came. He sent money when he could to help his boys in Yemen.

Plus, there was something almost magical about this time in his life, when it was just him and her. He wanted Mary for himself for just a little longer.

Now she was laughing at him. "Yes, we said we'd wait. But it's not always up to us. Sometimes a baby comes when a baby wants to come. I'll go to the doctor soon. And then we'll know for sure."

The silence that had shadowed them all morning fell over them again. "And about last night," she said. "I'm really sorry, Salem."

Sorry for what? He wondered. For staying out too late or for something more?

Noticing the question in his eyes, she made herself more clear. "I'm sorry I was drunk. I should have woken you, and we should have left much sooner."

So that was all that happened, he reassured himself, although a hint of doubt still lingered.

He ran warm water onto a washcloth and handed it to her. "I think it would be best if you didn't drink at all in this new condition. That's what I prefer. And I should cut back too." With drinks, you lost control. And even sober, Salem knew, there was so much of life that that took you by surprise.

"Not drink at all? But Salem, you know how much I love to go out and be with people. Last night I overdid it, but one drink out with friends won't do any harm at all."

"But one drink can lead to two and then . . . well, I prefer you not. Especially if there is indeed a new little life in there." The news still seemed unreal. He gazed at Mary's belly. "Whiskey, beer, and all of that can't be healthy for the baby." *A baby. He and Mary.* He began to get excited. A new family of three.

She closed her eyes and held her stomach, bracing for another round of nausea. "Right now, I have to tell you, I am not a fan of drinks. So we'll talk about it, Salem."

The next week, Mary's doctor confirmed the pregnancy, and Salem seemed to go through the next weeks in a daze,

On one Saturday shortly after Christmas, he

decided that a film might distract her from her sickness, which had continued off and on. They caught an early showing of the movie that everybody seemed to be discussing all over Birmingham. All of Mary's friends had loved *Doctor Zhivago*, and some of the men at work had also raved about the film. So far, Salem had resisted because of the movie's length. But he and Mary both were mesmerized, caught up in the romance and the wartime setting.

Through much of the film, Mary's hand was near her mouth, holding in her gasps of delight or fear or sorrow. The combination of the plot and her pregnancy left her in a sea of tears.

The next night after dinner, she was still debating which scenes might have been her favorites as she lazily flipped through a movie magazine. "Salem, did you know that Omar Sharif was born in Egypt? Wasn't he just perfect in the film?"

"One of the all-time greats." Salem was, in fact, familiar with the background of the star. Sharif, he thought, was proof that art could be a unifying force for people whose cultures might be different.

"His life was fascinating in so many ways," Salem said to Mary. "Does that story that you're reading say that he is Muslim? He wasn't born into the faith, but it was something that he chose upon his marriage to his actress wife. And there's something, Mary, about your handsome movie star that you and he have in common. His father was a Jew."

The subject of religion still came up from time to time, and it seemed more important now with a baby on the way, a child who would come into the world with roots in Islam, Christianity, and Judaism. Three sets of beliefs indeed, but all of them built upon the ancient teachings of the prophet Abraham.

But Mary didn't seem to have her mind on religion. "Interesting," she said. "I wonder if he has another film already that he's working on." Slowly, she turned the page of her magazine. "Officially, I declare that Omar Sharif is the second most handsome man ever on the planet. And the first most handsome man? Well, he belongs to me."

Chapter Five

Two months later, Salem touched Mary's still-flat belly with both hands, feeling a deep reverence for the new life just beginning.

"There's nothing to feel yet," she told him gently, covering his hands with her own. "I can't wait to feel him kicking. But the doctor says not yet."

"Or it might be a *her*." Had she even thought of that? When he thought of this baby, he saw a tiny Mary. He could even hear the way she'd giggle when she got old enough for Salem to twirl her in the air.

He stood very still, reluctant to move his hands from her warm belly. Even though the pregnancy was too new for him to feel the baby move, he imagined that his little girl could sense that he was near.

Again, his life was changing, and Salem's mind was filled with visions of small hands reaching out for his. At night, he dreamed of a face that held a mixture of Mary's features and his own. What a pure expression of his love for her; parts of her and parts of him would soon be mingled into a whole new soul. Some days, Salem thought he might explode from joy.

And some days this new and overwhelming love was mixed with a kind of terror. Because he had to face it: the more fiercely that you cared for another person, the more violently your heart could one day be ripped in two if they were taken from you. Amidst the violence of his homeland, he'd seen so many taken. Birmingham, of course, was safer. But no place in the world was immune to tragedy. He'd have to be vigilant, even more so than before, he thought as he pulled Mary to him in a hug.

Suddenly, she pulled away to cover up her mouth. "Here I go again," she said, running for the toilet. Some of the foods she used to love—crispy potatoes, for example, like the ones she'd fixed tonight—would often come back up.

"No fair," she playfully complained when he went in to check. "Will I be stuck for nine months with tasteless, mushy yuck? It seems that mushy yuck is the only food I can keep down."

When she wasn't working (or bent over the toilet), she was often curled up on the couch asleep, which the doctor said was normal.

Now, she moved toward the kitchen to grab a pot to scrub. The dirty dishes from their dinner still sat by the sink, waiting to be done.

Salem followed behind her quickly and pulled the pot out of her hand. "You sit down and rest," he said. "And go to bed early if you'd like." The sleep her body craved must be what the baby needed. They had to work together for a healthy pregnancy, he thought. Their job as parents had begun.

So there was more to do at home, even as the pressures at the factory continued. His anxiety moved through him like a knife with each cry of *Too slow! You need to step it up!* Salem had to stand out from the others so he might be chosen for any extra jobs that could earn him extra pay. Plus, he'd heard that someone from his team might get promoted soon.

He wanted that promotion! Because soon somebody new would depend on Salem to provide for her (or him.) And he was hoping that Mary would agree to give up working at the council to be home with their child. They'd have to be more careful with their money, but it could work, he thought.

In the kitchen, she turned to gratefully touch his shoulder as he took the dirty pot. "Thank you for doing that, my love." She gave him a kiss. "I'm really feeling better. So much so that I was thinking I might check out the scene at Tinker's. It's been a little while since I've been out for some fun."

Salem frowned as he began to scrub some sauce off of the pot. Tinker's was her favorite pub, although Salem preferred the ones that were quieter and not so full of people jostling up against you. Tinker's wasn't far, but it was on the border between their neighborhood and the rougher part of town.

"Some of my friends from work told me they were going, and I guess I should go now before my belly gets so big that I can't squeeze myself into those tiny booths." She gave him a rueful smile.

"You know I wish you wouldn't drink. It's not good for the child."

"Only one. I promise!"

The doctor had told her that drinking alcohol while pregnant was not a good idea. But Mary said she was craving a Lambrusco, her favorite sweet red wine.

Now, she looked Salem in the eye. "I've cut back on my nights out. You asked me to. I did! And most nights I do without my one nice glass of red at the end of the day—because of what the doctor said. Almost every single night, I sit here alone while you doze off on the couch." She reached down to touch her belly. "And, well, who really knows how my life might be about change. So if you'll please excuse me, I'll just freshen up and grab my coat."

"But, Mary . . . "

"No buts. I've decided."

In a silent fury, he picked up a pan and scrubbed at it hard. It wasn't safe for Mary to set out by herself like this to the pub, where men might try to take advantage. Or where it might be too crowded for her to even find a seat if she suddenly grew tired — and she grew tired a lot. That's because her body was adjusting to the change — and working hard to grow a baby. That's why she always seemed so tired, the nurse had explained to them at her last appointment.

"So get lots of rest," the nurse had said to Mary.

And what does Mary do? She goes out to a pub! How could Salem keep her — and the baby — safe and healthy when she was so intent on this foolishness?

He thought about the way Marouf used to watch the women in the pubs. Tinker's would be full of men like him. And like that other man, who'd watched her at the party and then found a way for them to be alone, arms touching as they bent their heads together in a darkened hall.

Salem knew that kind of fellow, adept at using

"accidental" touches and soft words to get the things he wanted from a woman. There were special dangers for a girl as pretty as his Mary. Without Salem at her side, she might be lured into a conversation that turned ugly when she said no to a dance or perhaps to a kiss.

And he had another worry, one so dark that Salem dared not say its name. That night at the party, he'd abhorred the way the stranger had gazed at Mary in the hall. But that was not the thing that stabbed Salem in the heart. It was the look on Mary's face: happy and expectant as she looked into the eyes of another man.

She called to him from the closet, where she was looking for her coat. "I don't tell *you* what to do," she said. "When you ask your work chums to come over with their wives, I cook them a nice dinner and I don't complain. The same friends every weekend! Although you never think to ask, 'Hey, Mary what would you prefer to do?' Because maybe I would rather have a nice walk in the park. Or see a film. Did you ever think of that?"

As she left for the bedroom, Salem closed his eyes and tried to control his anger. He'd planned the dinners with his friends because he thought that it would please her to meet Bill and Khalid's wives. More than once, she'd said she longed to have "real girlfriends. Not just girls to chum around with but ones who tell you all their secrets and always have your back."

Soon, she breezed back into the kitchen bundled in her red scarf and coat that matched her newly applied red lipstick. Her perfume filled the air as she moved in to kiss his cheek. "Come out with me? One dance? They've got a band tonight."

She was trying now to make things right between them, but he just shook his head.

With one hand on his back and one hand on his waist, she playfully pulled him into a slow dance in front of the stove. When her lips found his, the sweet taste of her cherry lipstick made some of his anger start to fade. It was a kiss that seemed to beg, Come out with me and play!

"We'll have a good time. Promise!" she whispered in his ear.

The feel of her in his arms almost pulled a yes from

Salem—until he saw the rest of the crusty dishes waiting by the sink. And that's what won out in the end: the realities of scrubbing and putting up and catching the early bus tomorrow for the factory, where he never really felt fast enough or good enough for the ambitions that he harbored.

♦♦♦

The next night, as they talked after dinner, she was full of stories about the laughs she'd had at Tinker's with her chums.

"Paul was there," she said. "Do you remember him? Oh Salem, you would love the way that Paul can tell a story. We laughed until we cried." She put her stockinged foot in Salem's lap so he could rub her sole. "And you'll be glad to know he walked me home. Because I told him you were worried that I might not be safe."

"That was kind of him." Salem felt a mix of thankfulness and irritation at the thought of Mary walking home with this co-worker by her side. What a place this England was, where women felt so free to talk and laugh with men who were not their husbands.

Mary closed her eyes in pleasure as Salem picked up her other foot and began to rub. After that had gone on a while, she stood up and stretched. "I'm so glad I'm feeling better. The doctor said the nausea sometimes doesn't last for long—for women who are lucky."

She disappeared into the kitchen and quickly reappeared with a glass of wine. "I'd offer you a glass, but you're such a fuddy-duddy." She kissed him on the nose as she sank back down on the couch.

"No, what I am is a father. And I want what's best for her." He glanced down at her belly.

"Her . . . or him." She reached for his hand. "You know what? I'm jealous—just a little bit." She put down her glass to rest her hand on her stomach. "Because he . . . or she . . . will have the kind of father that I've wanted all my life." She looked him in the eye, and her voice turned soft. "Thank you so much, Salem, for giving that to her."

He leaned in to kiss her forehead. "It is my great honor, Mary."

A period of peace followed for the next few weeks. Mary still turned to the occasional glass of wine after a bad day at work. One of her workmates had just gone on extended sick leave, making more work for the others. But her after-dinner glasses were more often filled with water than with wine. The doctor had said to try for six glasses of water every day, and she found that it gave her energy to get through the day. The pub visits were infrequent, and Salem tried to keep his silence on the nights she did go out. Once, he even went along, to her surprised delight.

Mary's focus now seemed to be on the baby. Their spare bed was filled with paint swatches for the nursery along with sheets and blankets for a crib. The linens were folded neatly beside the smallest little outfits in shades of green and beige and yellow.

While Mary eagerly prepared the nursery, Salem also had a newfound source of joy. One day after dinner, as he was dozing to the TV news, Mary shoved a book into his hand. "Wake up, sleepyhead," she said. "It's time you had a proper introduction to one of England's treasures. Much more fascinating than the TV news! Goblins, trolls, and battles!" Salem carefully examined the book in his hand: *The Hobbit* by J.R.R. Tolkien. "I've heard of this," he mused, turning the first page.

Now there was something to look forward to each night after dinner. Sometimes he could hardly wait, having left the characters at the very height of danger when he had to go to bed. "Wonderful!" he said to Mary. "How did I not know to read this book before?"

"And the good news is," she said, "there's more of Tolkien after that. "Did you know that Tolkien grew up close up to here?"

"I did not," he said, intrigued.

They were peaceful and content as Salem read, enthralled, by the glowing fire and Mary folded baby clothes or picked up a book of her own.

But the old resentments stirred again when Salem came home on a Friday to announce that Khalid and Sabina would be coming by the next night for dessert. "Sabina's very anxious to see the baby's things." He winked. "I think she's after Khalid to have one of their own. He says that it's our fault; we've given her ideas."

He thought that Mary would be thrilled. These days, she loved nothing more than showing off the small stuffed lambs and toys and little outfits that she'd begun collecting.

But to his surprise, she frowned as she stirred the soup and sprinkled some oregano into the pot. "Oh, Salem." She got the glasses from the cabinet and set them down hard on the table.

"*What?*" he asked, confused. Life with Mary could be breathtakingly sublime — or it could be a puzzle.

She moved to the stove to check the soup, then she turned to face him. "I love Khalid and Sabina. But I thought we had decided that we would plan our weekends as a couple from now on — that we'd decide together how we spend our time. Which is really so much nicer than just you deciding and announcing it to me."

Well, yes, he supposed they had, but it had slipped his mind. And he'd planned the night for Mary more than for himself. He'd just as soon be home alone with her and his book than to have people over. Most of his plans, in fact, were designed for pleasing her. But as a woman of the West, she found his ways to be "controlling." He understood that now, and he understood that it was important for her to have more say about how they lived their lives. But it was just dessert. Was it that big of a deal?

"Mary, I forgot. And I'm really sorry. But don't you think we'll have a good time with them while they're here?"

"Oh, I'm sure we will, but Salem, don't you see? That is not the point!" She began to set out their dinner; there was soup and bread and fruit. She paused to look at him. "Salem, let me ask you: How exactly do you see me? As a capable, smart woman? Or as some foolish girl who has to have a man to look after me so I don't lose my head?"

What an odd thing to ask, he thought. Then he saw her face, and the sadness brimming in her eyes hurt him to the core. "Oh, Mary," he said softly, "you know I think you're brilliant."

"How would I know that, Salem? Because, I have to say, it doesn't seem to me that you think that at all."

Oh, but Salem did think exactly that. He marveled at the way his wife had a plan for everything—from saving money at the grocers to finding small cafes or walking trails that were like hidden treasures. When they watched the TV news, she would shout opinions at the people on the screen. And she sounded much more sensible than any of the fancily dressed "experts" who always seemed so smug, so sure that they were right.

When she wasn't watching with him, Salem let the news drone on, unheard. Because what did Salem know about the problems of the world? Weren't the problems of one household enough for any man? But when he watched with Mary, Salem paid attention to the things he heard. His wife explained things in a way that showed him how important the topics really were. To Salem, air pollution, for example, was just an ugliness that hovered in the air and in his nose, not something that could kill. Until Mary set him straight.

Now, she looked distressed as she set the knives

and forks neatly by their plates. "When you don't even ask me before you make your plans, it doesn't seem to me like you value my opinion—or my mind."

He kissed her on the forehead. "I love your mind—and you. In fact—do you know what? —you might just be the smartest person that I know."

She rubbed his arm. "Thank you for that, Salem. I know it's different in the home that you were raised in, but remember we're a team. Equal partners. Right?"

He nodded, and they ate their soup, but Mary became quieter as the next few weeks went by. Salem could sense a distance begin to creep in between them.

Arriving home one Friday, he did not feel the normal sense of thankfulness for the weekend break. Most likely, Salem figured, they'd stay around the house, glum, not talking to each other. That had become their pattern.

"What would you like to do?" he asked her the next morning over eggs and fruit. He was feeling hopeful. Glancing out the window, he saw that the fog had cleared to reveal a sun-kissed day, a rarity for Birmingham at that time of year.

"Oh, I don't know," she said. "We can just stay in; that's fine."

"Would you like a walk?" he asked. "Looks like a pretty day."

"I don't think so, Salem."

"What is that I see outside my window? Could that be the sun?" he teased.

She smiled at him weakly, barely acknowledging his weak attempt at humor as she reached for her juice. He knew the pregnancy had put a strain on her body. But something else was up as well. He saw it in the way her smile never seemed to meet her eyes, the way she touched him less now when they passed in the halls.

"The sun might do us both some good," he tried again as he reached for more eggs. Although he couldn't wait to meet his son or daughter, he'd miss their time alone. "And tonight I thought that maybe I could take you out to Tinker's for some dinner. Or we could go wherever else you might prefer," he was quick to add.

"I'm a little tired," she said. "I think that I'd prefer to just head back to the bedroom now and try to get some rest."

They mostly spent their time in separate corners of the house, Salem finishing *The Hobbit* and Mary working in the nursery or resting in their room. The old loneliness he'd felt in his first days as an expat crept back into his being. Yemen and his family felt so far away. And some nights it seemed to him that the distance between him and Mary was even further still.

After the disagreement about the dinner invitation to his friends, they seemed to have reached a kind of understanding. But then he'd brought the subject up of her quitting work once the baby came. She'd seemed to bristle at the thought. "I've got things going on," she said. "I've got some long-term projects that I'd really like to see through to the end."

Salem had kissed her forehead and touched her growing belly. "But there's a joyous project here, a precious project in our home," he told her gently. He knew that many women longed to stay home with their babies, although some had to work. Salem was determined to give that gift to Mary, even if it meant he had to work some extra hours or even take a second job.

"But what would *you* know about my projects?" Mary sighed. "You don't ask about my day enough to have the slightest idea what goes on at my office." He could see the anger, long suppressed, burning in her eyes. "The fact is, it might be hard for the others at the council if I chose to leave. *Some* people—at least people in my office—think that what I do's important."

"I didn't say it wasn't," he replied, frustrated. "I was only trying to do something nice—for us."

Then he'd spoken up one night when she'd left for the pub in a lacey top that was way too sheer and low-cut to be proper.

She'd wheeled around and stared. "Do I tell *you* what shirt to wear? Or is that another thing that only *men* get an opinion on?"

But that is not the point, he thought. "Do you not see how much that top reveals? Have you looked in the mirror, Mary? What will people think?"

"They'll think I'm dressed the same way as every other woman in the place. This is England, Salem. This is the way that women dress. And since the clothes go on my body, I'm the one who gets to choose."

Salem was astounded. "Mary, I'm your husband." It's not like Salem was some stranger commenting on her clothes. "Does a man not have the right to say such things to his wife?" he asked.

Her answer was to simply shut the door on her way out to meet her chums.

Now, as they began their Saturday, she stood up from the table. Most of her breakfast, Salem noticed, was still left on her plate.

In the days that followed, the mood in the house grew darker. Some spark between them, some connection that was everything to Salem, seemed to just be gone. Some days, he was angry. Other days, he was bereft. How had his father ever managed to have a somewhat peaceful household with four wives when Salem couldn't even seem to make it work with one? (And he'd also failed at finding happiness with Yasmine; he had not forgotten that.)

The next Saturday, he slept in. Equipment failures and other issues at the factory had made the week especially stressful, and stress exhausted Salem. Plus, why not stay in bed? He and Mary had no plans for the weekend, and this time, he hadn't bothered to suggest a film or walk.

Bill had asked if he and Mary would like to meet him and his wife to listen to a new band at a club downtown. But Salem had made excuses and not mentioned it to Mary. Doing so, he feared, might make matters even worse. Although it really shouldn't. After all, it was a pub! And music! Two things she adored. He knew now to ask her before committing to a plan. But he was never sure what might set her off. Would the mere *suggestion* of a plan bring a barrage of accusations that he was controlling, chauvinistic, and didn't care what Mary thought?

But that Saturday brought a nice surprise. He awoke to Mary's kiss upon his forehead, her gentle hand resting on his back. "Aren't you a sleepyhead?" she teased him. "Did you know it's half past nine? Get up! We have some plans."

Salem looked up groggily at her. The softness of the sheets against his aching legs seemed like an invitation to sleep a little more. In addition to the problems that had occurred at work, the tension in the household only added to his sense of fatigue. Now, he felt like he could close his eyes and sleep for hours.

"Plans? What plans?" he asked. "Let's wait till after lunch. It's been such an awful week."

But how nice that Mary wanted to go out and spend some time together. This might just be a nice weekend after all.

"Come on." She sat down next to him. "We have to hurry, Salem, or we'll miss the bus."

"The bus? The bus to where? Let's leave a little later so we don't have to rush. That's better for the baby." He closed his eyes again to rest.

Just a hint of anger seemed to flash across her eyes, but it quickly disappeared, and she took a deep breath. "Up, up, up," she told him. "You won't be disappointed. And as for the *where,* you'll find out when you get there. Don't you like surprises?"

Well, no. No, he didn't. If he had no idea where it was that he was going, how would he know what to wear? Or what he should take along? Or even if he'd like the place he was going to.

He took her hand, trying to appease her. "Mary, tell me where it is that you want to go. And then we can discuss if we can leave a little later. Perhaps there's a later bus that would work out better for us. That way, I at least could have some breakfast and a little coffee before I start my day." Why had she not brought this up last night over dinner?

"Salem, there no time. I've packed a picnic, and you'll love it." She threw back the covers. "Get up, get up, get up," she sang out with an eager smile.

Salem felt a flash of anger at the rush of cool air that met his bare legs, but then he caught sight of

Mary's face. There it was—that spark. Here she was again, the Mary who'd gone missing.

He stood up and kissed her. "Give me fifteen minutes."

◆◆◆

Ninety minutes later, he found himself looking across a pond at an old brick building. "What is this?" he asked.

"This very spot, my love, is my favorite place in all of Birmingham to come for a picnic." She began to set out deviled eggs and apples. His stomach grumbling, Salem looked on eagerly as she took out ham, homemade bread, and thick slices of pie from the bakery down the street.

He looked again at the building, which offered him no hints about the reason that his wife so adored this place. The surroundings, though, were lovely. He felt an instant peace as he gazed at a ring of tall trees reflected in the pond. "What place is this?" he asked again.

"It's called Sarehole Mill," she said. "And now for

the surprise. Salem, can you guess who used to live across the street from here and take in this very view?"

Salem thought about it. "Did you grow up near here?" he guessed.

"No, not me." She laughed. "Once upon a time, very close to here, there lived a young boy who dreamed of writing books. He dreamed up all kinds of creatures, who he liked to pretend lived right here in these woods."

Salem didn't have to think for very long. "Tolkien," he said, excited.

When Mary nodded to confirm, he looked around, amazed. He had often wondered if he might be walking in some of the places the great man had stood.

"So you see, my love?" She gave him a kiss. "Surprises can be nice. We've arrived in Middle-earth! The last place in the world you'd expect to go today."

After their picnic feast, they walked hand in hand across the property. His mind on the baby, Salem constantly asked Mary how she felt and if she was getting tired.

"I feel great," she said as they got closer to the mill. Then she stopped and pulled him to her. "Salem, I'm so sorry for how things have been between us," she said into his chest. "This should be a happy time. A baby! We should be excited—and I am." Then her voice grew quiet. "When I was growing up, I never had a family. So this will be a first for me—a family, a real family."

"I can't wait," he said, kissing her forehead and then her nose, her cheek. "And thank you for today. You could not have found a place that I'd love more than this."

"Oh, I knew you would! Tolkien and his brother used to come here to play, and they'd get chased away when they were little boys. Then later, in the book, he wrote that Bilbo Baggins was right here in this place— 'running as fast as his furry feet could carry him down the lane, past the great Mill, across The Water and then on for a mile or more.' Bilbo Baggins! He was here!" She smiled. "I memorized that part when I first found this place."

They continued with their walk. "When you fussed at me this morning," Mary said, "I almost just gave up on my little plan. But I have special places that I want to show you, Salem. I understand you need your rest—and that your job makes you exhausted. And I *love* the way you work so hard for me . . . and especially for her." She glanced down at her belly. "But you have to make the time for some of the things that *I* plan—and leave room for surprises." She squeezed his hand. "And if you want to do more things with your mates from work, we can do that too."

A gentle breeze brought the woodsy scent that must have inspired the author of the magic that enthralled Salem every night. A sense of peace swept over him. "I have a feeling, Mary, that you will show me things that I never dreamed existed." He pressed his lips to hers. In fact, you already have."

"Oh, and one more thing." She reached into the purse and pulled out a camera. "Remember those silver frames I bought? All of them still need pictures." She nodded toward a couple just ahead. "I bet they'll take our photo." She grabbed Salem's hand. "Let's go."

◆◆◆

As the months went by, the nursery came together with a crib and rocking chair set up against freshly painted yellow walls. Mary's stomach grew rounder with new life, and an excitement filled the home as her time grew close.

But the tension in the household hadn't disappeared. Mary's growing belly made her tired and cross; some nights she couldn't even stay up much past dinner. On rare occasions, she still smoked, much to the alarm of Salem.

One night Salem watched as she lit a cigarette in front of the TV news. Salem often wondered why she even watched the news; almost every time she did, some story made her angry.

She caught him looking. "Salem, don't. Please don't even say it. It's my business if I smoke."

Untrue! Salem thought. As the father of the child who might be being harmed, it was Salem's business too. But he didn't say a word. He was tired of fighting. And embarrassed at his failure to control the goings-on in his own home. What kind of man was he?

In frustration, he asked Mary if she had another and if she had a light. She passed him a cigarette and lit it for him. Then Salem closed his eyes and put it to his lips, hoping to find some comfort in a habit that he'd broken long ago.

Some nights he turned to alcohol as well when the trouble between him and Mary wouldn't let him sleep. But that backfired every time and made him sleep more fitfully when he finally did manage to doze off. On mornings after drinking, Salem moved more slowly at the factory. That, in turn, led to even more stress about what the bosses might be thinking of his poor performance. And *that* stress made him want to go home to drink or have a cigarette. It was a vicious cycle that he had to break.

◆◆◆

Then—for a time, at least—their stress turned into joy when Mary, three days before her due date, woke him up. "I think it's time," she said.

It was just after 2 a.m. when they arrived at Queen Elizabeth Hospital after navigating the darkened route that Salem had carefully practiced earlier. In the back was Mary's small blue suitcase, which she had packed a week before. Be prepared, the doctor had cautioned her at her last appointment: babies had a way of coming early.

In the waiting room, Salem was too anxious to sit still, so he paced the hall for hours. The sun was coming up in the hallway windows when he heard footsteps behind him, and a nurse called his name. Anxious, he turned around and searched her face for a sign. Was everything okay?

She gave him a big smile. "Someone would like to meet you! It's a lovely little girl."

A girl. It was a girl!

He hurried behind the nurse into Mary's room.

With a small bundle in her arms, Mary looked up at him, exhausted, but there were happy tears shining in her eyes. "She's gorgeous, Salem. Look!"

Very carefully, he pulled back the soft pink blanket from around the baby's face, marveling at the softness of her skin. The baby's eyes stayed tightly shut, but she moved her head a little in response to Salem's touch.

"She knows you're her daddy," Mary whispered; her voice was full of awe.

The little girl had a tiny fuzz of dark hair, and already there was something of Mary in her face—and of Salem too. She belonged to many. His beloved family that stretched back for generations far across the sea would continue with this child.

"Would you like to hold her?" Mary asked, and Salem was already reaching out. He'd forgotten how very light a newborn was.

"Her name is Maryam," he said. He hadn't even thought about a name until those words came out.

Mary shook her head. "You know, you're a lucky man. I'm too happy in this moment to be mad at my baby's daddy." She leaned back against the pillow with an amused smile on her face. "Did you think to ask me first? After all, I was the one who pushed this baby out, and I've got to tell you, Salem: the pain of childbirth is intense," she teased. Then she looked lovingly at the child in Salem's arms. "Not that she isn't worth it."

"It was my sister's name. Mary in Arabic is Maryam, so she will have your name and my sister's too."

Mary hesitated. "Was she the sister who . . .?"

"She is the one we lost. But today someone is found." Salem's voice was hushed.

"Baby Maryam. I love it. I think it's the perfect name."

Then the baby opened up her eyes, and in the baby's face, Salem saw his sister. This tiny newcomer to the world had his sister's wide-set eyes, his sister's heart-shaped face. *I know you,* he thought. *Although we've only met.*

His daughter looked like Maryam, whose body had borne bruises from the chains that kept her from escaping in search of a lost love. Now that Salem understood how intense a love could be, he understood her desperation—and sometimes wept at the thought. What would the future hold for this little one?

By now wide awake, the baby stared at him, curious and expectant about this brand-new world. Would it treat her well? *Please, treat her well,* he thought. For those who were unlucky, the world could be so cruel.

Feeling his knees go weak, he handed the baby back to Mary. And then Salem wept: tears of sorrow, tears of joy. For life lost and life continued.

Their first days at home passed in a kind of haze with

very little sleep. Maryam always seemed to cry as soon as they finally managed to drift off to sleep.

"How can I go back to work when Maryam won't sleep?" Mary asked one morning as she fumbled into her robe. "As soon as she is napping, I just collapse across the bed. Salem, I'm exhausted. Who knew it would be so hard?"

They heard the baby stirring, and Salem went to pick her up. She felt so fragile in his arms as he met Mary in the den. "Your place isn't at the council," he told her. "Your place is here with her. No one else but you and I can keep her safe. Don't you see?" A surge of fear swept through him as he thought of the child-minders and day-care centres they'd managed to check out; none of them would do.

"Oh, but Salem, I miss people. I miss talking to adults. And besides, we need the money, don't we?"

Baby Maryam nestled against his chest. A helpless, tiny baby, trusting them to keep her safe.

"You must stay home," he said. If not, he couldn't stand it.

A tiny fire seemed to flash across Mary's tired eyes. "What did you say? I *must?* Like you're giving me an order?"

He sighed. "It's not an order, Mary." That was the last thing he would do. He was slowly getting used to the ways of marriage here, with the decision-making shared between a husband and a wife. Not that *giving orders* would have ever been the way Salem would describe his role with Mary or with Yasmine. His role was to lead and to protect.

"It's not an order; it's a plea. A plea from father's heart. Please protect her, Mary. Please be here with her."

She opened up her mouth to speak, but then something stopped her. Salem wondered if she had caught a glimpse of the terror in his eyes that he tried hard to hide. Had she seen the tears that, embarrassingly enough, had just begun to form?

"Will we be okay—without the money from my work?"

"We will be okay. I promise. I will make sure that it is so."

She gently touched his arm then took the baby from

him. "Then I will call today and let them know at the council. Being mom to Maryam, that will be my job." She touched her nose to the baby's nose and began to coo. "Will it be you and me at home now? What do you think of that?"

♦♦♦

Maryam's first visitor was Marouf, who came bearing gifts a week after they got home from Queen Elizabeth. "Beautiful!" he said when Mary came out with the child and held her close for him to see. "And now you are a family." Playfully, he punched Salem in the arm. "Aren't you the lucky man? First, one gorgeous girl, and now you have another."

They sat in the den and talked till Maryam began to cry.

Mary stood up from her chair. "Time for a diaper change and bed." She gently held the baby to her chest and rocked her. "Isn't that right, little princess?"

After she was gone, Marouf looked Salem in the eye. "Pay attention to me, friend. With this baby in the house, you keep away from other women. That just wouldn't do now that you have a family."

What? Salem stared at the man in disbelief. "How dare you say a thing like that to me? I would never even dream of doing such a thing." He glanced toward the hall, wondering if Mary had overheard the conversation. That wouldn't do at all. The stress of late nights with the baby and the new routine had left her fretful and exhausted. The simplest of things—like running out of milk—could reduce his wife to tears. And now this crazy talk might give her something new for her long list of worries.

Quietly Salem said, "It might be a game to you, chasing after women, but I've never been that way. There's nowhere I'd rather be than here at home with them."

Marouf shook his head. "You might say that now, but the lure of a shapely figure has felled many a weak man." The sound of Marouf's laughter brought an ugliness into the house that Salem wished he could wash off.

"This kind of talk is disrespectful to my family. And it will not go on in this house. Do you understand me, Marouf?"

Marouf smiled in a way that seemed more mocking than apologetic. "Please make me some tea, mate, and tell me how your job is going. Then I can tell you all the gossip from your old rooming house. So many foolish goings-on! You will not believe it, Salem."

Again, Salem recalled the man of the same name who had lurked in the shadows when his sister met her Mohsen at the well. He had spread the rumors she was pregnant, false rumors that had caused her death. Salem had come to understand that the man had been connected to the Sultan, the Ruler of the Sultanate, who is in turn has strong connection with the British Authority in Aden. This Marouf, as well, seemed intent on seeking and spreading information. Could this Marouf perhaps have connections with the CID in England?

◆◆◆

While at work, Salem envied Mary, home with Maryam. But when he got home, exhausted, she seemed jealous, amazingly, of *him.* She always met him at the door, anxious for any news that he might bring from the outside world.

"Did you walk by the new café? Tell me how it looked," she said to him one day. There were dark lines below her eyes, and it looked like she had not had time to even brush her hair. "Oh, I used to be so anxious to have a new place on the street with sweets and homemade bread. And now that we finally have one, I sometimes think it might be *ages* before I can even leave the house."

The sound of Maryam waking up interrupted her complaints.

"Daddy's turn to take her," Mary called out as she headed for their room. "I *must* lay down for just a minute. And I'm not even sure I ate a thing today."

Salem went to pick up Maryam, whose cries were louder now. He reached down to take her in his arms. "For such a tiny little thing, you're wearing out your mommy," he whispered in her ear. He loved the warmth of her against his chest. And he especially loved the way his touch could calm her in an instant.

As he sat in the rocking chair with Maryam and began to gently rock her, Mary walked into the room.

"Get some rest," he said. "I've got her."

"Salem." She studied him and frowned. "Why were you

so late?"

Wearily, he smiled. "They gave me more overtime. Isn't that good news? We could really use the money." He took the extra hours when he could, but that money was hard-earned. It was all that he could do sometimes to simply stay awake at work. Maryam woke them up at least two times every night, and it was getting harder to fall back to sleep.

Mary stared at Salem. He'd seen that look before. It was a kind of warning of trouble on the way.

"It would have been nice of you to tell me that you'd be working late. And not just left me wondering where my husband had decided to run off to after work."

"Decided *to run off to?* What were you thinking, Mary? That I'd gone off to some pub? You know I wouldn't do that. I know you need me here." Maryam began to whimper, and he rubbed her back. "I didn't know until this morning that I could get the overtime," he said. "Or else I would have told you."

"Oh, I'm sorry, Salem. I do appreciate you staying late, and I know you're exhausted too. It's just that, well, sometimes I get . . . well, I get a little scared. I get afraid that I'm no good at being someone's mother." Her voice cracked a little.

"Don't say that," he told her firmly. "The only reason I have peace is that I know she is with you."

"And can you imagine, Salem? Here I am all day with not a soul to talk to." She managed a weary smile. "Maryam is precious, and no doubt she will grow up to be fascinating to converse with. But for now, she doesn't really have a lot to say."

The next night after work, Salem made a stop at the new café that she'd mentioned to him. If she could not go out to see it for herself, he'd bring her home a treat. But he was dismayed to see a long line out the door despite the freezing rain that had begun to fall. The neighbors here, he guessed, were starved for something new. He pulled his coat more tightly around his shoulders, thankful when he finally made it to the counter to order a fresh blueberry loaf and two Chelsea buns, which were Mary's favorite.

Ten minutes later, he walked into the den to find her curled up on the couch. Her reddened eyes were Salem's first hint that his wife was distraught.

Frantic, he set down his bag. "Mary, are you crying?

Maryam—is she okay?"

"Why are you late again?" There was desperation in her voice. "Salem, this can't happen every single night. I really need you here."

"But I'm barely late at all. And wait! I've brought you a surprise. I stopped by the new café, and I . . ."

She sat up on the couch. *"Stopped by the café?* Stopped by the café with who? Tell me who you were with! Here I am, stuck at home all day with an unhappy baby—who will not stop crying—and you *stop by a café?"* In her eyes, he saw a mix of fear and anger.

He was angry too. "If you have to know, Mary, I was in the company of a crowd of strangers in the pouring rain." What reason had he ever given her not to trust him? "And the reason that I stood there in the freezing cold was to get my wife a treat." He retrieved the bag from the kitchen counter and shoved it into her hands.

Sheepishly, she looked into the bag. "Chelsea buns," she said softly, recognizing that he'd picked her favourites. Then she burst into tears. "Oh, Salem, I'm so sorry. It's the lack of sleep. And I miss my life so much. I miss all the laughs, and I miss having chums around for conversation. And with no one to talk to, I guess my thoughts run wild and I think some crazy things. I don't have any doubts that I can trust you, Salem. But other women have to notice that you're such a handsome man, and with me stuck at home, I . . . "

 He sat down beside her and took her in his arms. "You're the only woman that I'll ever want. You must believe that, Mary."

She wiped away a tear and smiled. "What a lovely wife you're stuck with. I think I've worn this same shirt for three days—at least. And I probably smell like spit-up. Yes, she spits up. Again."

What Mary didn't understand was that Salem was more in awe of her than he had ever been. He'd thought she was beautiful that first night at the pub. But even that could not compare with the beauty that was Mary with his daughter in her arms. That vision stopped his heart.

"I love you so much," he whispered.

"Those words—they scare me sometimes, Salem. Although I know that's weird."

"Mary. Tell me why."

"Because *he* said that. To *her*. Stepfather number two. He said that, and then he left. I heard her tell her friends about it."

"But, Mary, I'm not him." He glanced at a photo of their baby, taken on the day they brought her home. It was now framed nicely in a silver frame. "And we have Maryam," he whispered, stroking Mary's matted hair.

"And my mum had me. But still she left."

All he could do was hold her. If he couldn't ease her hurt, he could keep his arms wrapped around her tightly while she sobbed.

She reached for a tissue. "I just look at Maryam sometimes and think: how you could leave a child? As soon as I knew that she was coming, I loved her—just like that." Her voice grew small and teary. "And whatever happens, she always will have us."

◆◆◆

Perhaps soon, he thought, Maryam would sleep the night. And with both of them more rested, they could ease into a nice routine.

But that didn't happen. Just as Salem seemed to be on the edges of a dream, settling more deeply into sleep, Maryam would wail. Sometimes they'd wake up to find the baby nestled between them in the bed, both of them too exhausted to remember who had gotten up to get her last.

Pleased with Salem's work, the boss gave him more hours. That brought some relief to Salem, since sometimes there was just enough in his bank account to pay the rent and bills. Especially with a baby, it was Salem's duty to his family to have extra funds on hand. Emergencies could happen, and they could be expensive. That fear and that need kept him going despite the lack of sleep.

Mary had her own way to keep going in the haze of feedings and diaper changes and the endless rocking of a baby who sometimes wouldn't settle down. Salem feared that, more and more, his wife was finding comfort in her wine.

One day, after working extra hours, he stumbled through the door to find no dinner ready, despite the dirty dishes that were strewn about the kitchen

"Oh, hey! Thank goodness you are here." Mary handed

him a bottle of Maryam's formula. Then she poured herself a drink. "One for her and one for me." Salem watched as she closed her eyes, savouring her first sip of Lambrusco, the red wine that she liked.

Salem fed the baby, checked her diaper, then put her in her crib and made himself a sandwich. A sandwich often passed for dinner now, or he'd check the fridge and heat up whatever leftovers he might find inside. He saw a half-filled wine glass by the sink and glanced at Mary. Was she drinking now in the afternoon as well?

"Don't give me that look," she said. "It's just a little bit to get me through the day." She frowned. "These are the kinds of days a girl needs a cigarette. But I don't want Maryam around the smoke. So if I drink a little wine in the afternoon, it's no big deal, okay?"

Salem moved into the nursery to check on Maryam. She smiled when she saw him, and his mood changed all at once.

"Hey, Mary! Her first smile."

It was Mary's smile mixed in with the smiles that he remembered from the days when his grandparents sat beneath the palms as the cousins played. This child was a part of something grand and ancient—and also something new. With this child, he thought, something hopeful had begun.

Salem smiled back at his daughter.

Perhaps, he told himself, things would be okay.

Chapter Six

Rose and Palm

A few months later, Maryam's first smile was followed by her first words.

"Are they really words? I don't even know." Mary laughed one day as she picked up the baby. In truth, they could only guess at what their daughter might be trying to express with the constant stream of chatter.

Buh ah, the baby might pronounce. *Da!* She'd wave her fist and babble with such intensity that Salem longed to understand what she meant to say.

As their first year with their daughter neared an end, changes were occurring in Mary and Salem too. Mary seemed to have somewhat settled into her role as mother with fewer tearful outbursts. That was no doubt due in part to the fact that Maryam was allowing them to get a good night's rest—on most nights at least. Salem also noticed fewer half-empty glasses of Lambrusco on the counters and the table. But he also couldn't help but see that some spark was gone from Mary. Gone was what he thought of as a kind of inner light, a thing so essential to the very Mary-ness of the woman that he loved.

The change in Salem took the form of an increased, fiercer ambition. A factory job was fine for an expat on the run, but now he was something more. Now he was the father of another miracle, and he needed money for his boys as well; his arms often felt so empty with them so far away. His three gifts from Allah! They all deserved the world. But Salem didn't have the means to provide so much as the top brand of diaper for his daughter, let alone the world. Small treats to send his sons were hard for him to afford as well.

He was pondering his options for new work. He looked to his friends for their ideas as they also strove to find their places in the world. Bill had set out on his own to try to make a go of it in insurance. Salem watched with interest, feeling brave enough for a transformation of his own. Just what kind, he wasn't sure. Opportunities were plentiful in the south of Birmingham. Factories were booming, and new businesses were thriving, giving birth to even more gleaming stores and restaurants and places of employment. As he mulled his future, Salem continued to take on as many extra hours as he could—grateful for the work but exhausted nonetheless.

Then more months went by. Before Maryam turned one, she took one stumbling step and then another from her mommy to her dad's open arms, laughing all the way. Despite the tension that continued in the household, she was a happy child. She always smiled, delighted, when Salem walked into the room. And Salem's heart was warmed by the baby's adoration; it had been a long time since he'd felt the same from Mary. Perhaps they were simply both too tired to say those kinds of things out loud.

The small apartment was now strewn with harshly spoken words along with toys and dirty dishes that no one seemed to have the energy to pick up and put away.

The bills continued to get paid—but barely. Without Mary's job, Salem was frankly terrified about the minuscule amount that separated what was owed from what he was bringing in. The HP Sauce factory people paid their workers a good wage. But unlike his co-workers, Salem had two families to support.

Plus, he was trying hard to put some of his funds away to start a business one day to provide his family with a better style of living. But what kind of business? Salem's friends were moving in various directions. Some had decided to stick around at the factory and look for advancement there. Others, such as Bill, were starting out in new careers. Bill seemed optimistic when he checked in with Salem periodically by phone. But the money wasn't flowing yet into his bank account. "It takes time," he explained to Salem one night on the phone.

Time: it was a luxury that Salem didn't have. At the factory, at least, they'd give him extra hours, which he needed if the light bill was more than normal or Mary splurged a little at the grocer's. He'd told her to only get the things they needed and to look for sales. But he found it hard to protest on the rare occasions that she'd pop a bit of caramel into his mouth and smile. His job, after all, was to provide for her—and should the mother of his Maryam not be allowed to indulge in a tiny something sweet?

One thing that he always did was make time for Maryam. Here in England, fathers helped more with their children's daily care. At home, the roles were clearly marked; the mother was the nurturer, the father the provider. In this case, at least, England had it right, he thought. He lived for the moment he could walk through the door at night and feel the warmth of Maryam against his chest. He'd make up little songs to sing into her ear. *Is this Maryam, the princess? Or Maryam, the dancing horse? Or is it Maryam, the little girl, the best one in the land?* Or he'd make funny faces that would make her laugh so hard she squealed.

But the baby's laughter could also leave him wistful; Salem missed his boys. In addition to sending money back to Yemen whenever possible, he kept in touch with Yasmine to the extent that he was able.

From what he understood from Yasmine, the boys were doing well but were full of questions about where their father was. And how could Yasmine answer? How to explain such hatred to young children when it was a thing that Salem as a grown-up could barely comprehend?

Ahmed, he was told, had shot up to such a height that he now stood taller than his older cousins. Omar also seemed to be a different boy than the one that Salem left behind. He had finally lost his shyness, from what Salem understood, and had a million questions for everyone he met.

Thoughts of his two boys drove Salem to stay up late on some nights just to hold his baby while she slept.

"Salem, put her down. You need to come to bed," Mary would admonish, poking her head sleepily into the room.

"I'll be there soon," he'd tell her. "Just a little longer."

◆◆◆

One day he arrived home to find his wife in tears. "Oh, Salem, I know how much you want me to stay home with her, but it's just not working. Don't you see? There is just no way! We have to have my check! Now we really *have* to."

His heart froze at the *now*. What did Mary mean?

He put his arm around her and led her to the couch. "We'll be just fine," he told her calmly — although he only wished that he could be that sure. "I'm looking into new work, and until I find the job that's right, we'll have everything we need."

"Everything we need?" she asked as more tears streamed down her face. "Do we not need *food?* I try so hard to budget when I go to the grocer's. Honestly, I do. But now a whole week's worth food is spoiled. Just gone! You won't believe the things I dumped into the trash."

A sense of foreboding engulfed Salem. "What are you saying, Mary?" He glanced at the fridge, which he had noticed just last weekend didn't seem to be keeping their food as cold as it had before.

"The fridge! It isn't working. It's gone all hot inside. And if *a night out at the movies* is a splurge, how in the world, I ask you, will we afford a fridge?"

Salem thought about the numbers in the bank account. He'd been hoping for a party—just a small one—for Maryam's upcoming birthday. Plus something nice for Mary to honor her first year as a mom, which he knew had been difficult for her. Still, he had been amazed by the gentle way that Mary loved their child. The sight of her singing softly to their daughter was something that he treasured, and he'd love to find a way to show how much more he'd grown to love her since Maryam had come into their lives.

Now, the money for the party and the surprise for Mary would have to be diverted. "We have money for the fridge," he said. "We have it in the bank. Why don't I run out right now and get us a nice dinner? And tomorrow you can write a check at Ellington's and ask them to deliver as quickly as they can. They are honest in their dealings, and they'll give you a fair price." He was happy to see Mary close her eyes in relief. But he hated that a thing like money had such a grip on their emotions, such a power over them.

He sighed and watched the floor as he continued.

"Of course, you understand that we will have to take the least expensive model that they sell." Then he pulled her close and gently kissed her forehead. "I'll find a better job. I will! But until then, I promise that you and I will be just fine." He smiled. "And Maryam will live like the princess that she is." Her daddy was determined that he would make it so.

He had wondered for a moment if they should try to see if the old refrigerator could be fixed. But he knew that it was ancient; she'd had the thing forever. And he didn't want to have to pay some guy to come out to the apartment just to say the old machine was now beyond repair.

His chum Alvin at the factory listened sympathetically the next day when Salem told his story. Alvin was a supervisor with a good job and good pay, but he remembered his own days as a young father starting out with a job like Salem's. "The day the heating went out in our house was the same day that we noticed this big leak in the roof. Can you believe the luck? And I thought to myself, the same way that you did, 'How will I ever handle all of this?' But that's not all. Just wait. This thing gets worse—way worse. If you can believe it, Salem, the date on the calendar that day was December 28, 1956."

Salem's eyes grew wide. "The spill. The same day as the spill." The date was infamous in Birmingham. It was the day a vat exploded at the HP factory, sending vinegar—fifteen thousand gallons of the stuff—flooding into city streets. Residents still told their stories of the day. Some had watched as heavy furniture bobbed along through town in the pungent-smelling streams. Startled lookers-on, some of them waist-high in vinegar, raced to seal their door gaps while children, rallying to help, filled jugs and bottles in a vain attempt to ease the sudden flood.

Alvin shook his head. "Surprises happen, Salem, and they mess with your head. But the thing about it is that we get through them. That day—when the bills started mounting—was my impetus to go to the bosses here and ask them for a raise." He laughed. "Of course, I had to wait a bit to do that. As you can well imagine, they were just a little busy at the time. But I got the raise and, in fact, a big promotion. Fixed the roof and fixed the heater. And now life is pretty good for the wife and me." He looked around the busy room. "HP survived as well. More than survived, I'd say. People everywhere still love their HP sauce; people pour this stuff over anything and everything they put in their mouths."

HP Sauce and food—that gave Salem an idea. All of his favorite restaurants were packed with customers almost every time he tried to get a table. Birmingham was booming, and owners of pubs and restaurants were among the smart crowd cashing in on the success. A restaurant, he thought, might provide a steady income—and eventually a large one if he worked very hard. The gourmet crowd in Birmingham was not afraid to pull their wallets out and meet the sky-high prices on some of the menus around town. Or so Salem understood. Of course, he could not afford to see that for himself.

He was not naïve. He knew that being your own boss also meant that the responsibilities and decisions were a hundred percent on you.

But he liked the idea. Food had always held an interest for him. On the rare occasions when he went out to eat with Mary, he'd often ask to keep the menu to peruse while he waited for his food.

He'd find himself intrigued by the artful mixes of ingredients in some of the entrees and appetizers he saw listed.

Alvin put a hand on Salem's shoulder. "Salem, you'll get through this. Just take the good with the bad. Your day, my friend, will come. Of course, I didn't think so back on that dark day in 1956 — with my roof leaking and my house so cold and streams and streams of vinegar rushing down the streets." He shook his head and sighed. "Can you imagine how that smelled?" Then he smiled at Salem. "I made it through the vinegar, then I got the sweet."

Salem was feeling hopeful; he'd wait for the sweet. All day long he thought about the idea of opening a restaurant of his own. He'd talk it out with Mary and see what she thought.

Arriving home that evening, he was eager to share his thoughts with his wife. But he was also frightened about the somewhat risky undertaking that might lie in his future. Working at the stove, Mary listened carefully as he told her his idea. For the first time in a long time, he saw a spark of interest flash across her eyes.

She smiled as she stirred some meat and potatoes into a casserole. "I've always really hoped that you'd find a job that stirred your passions. Like when you helped your father with the palms! I used to love the way your eyes would light up when you talked about that job. You know I think you're brilliant, and you should have a job that makes good use of that."

"It's just a lot to take on, and I worry," he told her. What he felt was a strange mix: apprehension and excitement. One of his mates at HP worked after hours at a sandwich shop that had been in his family for years. The restaurant business, he'd told Salem, was one of the hardest to succeed in. Restaurant people, he complained, always had to work when their mates were on holiday. And the hours could be grueling. Salem was aware that his buddy Albert's family had struggled many years before their shop had finally turned a profit.

But Salem would be opening during an economic boom. Plus, he also sensed that any kind of business had an element of risk, and his mind was already turning with ideas about what he'd like to serve. He would love to put some Yemeni dishes on the menu among the usual British fare. He wondered if he could source the ingredients locally to make some of the old favorites his wife and mother used to serve. And it that went well, he could add more ethnic foods. People were settling in Birmingham from so many different countries. A plate of familiar food, he thought, might make them feel less lost.

"I'm a little scared," he said to Mary, having finally embraced the way of men in England who were not afraid to say such a thing out loud. When Mary held him tightly, a sense of warm relief rushed through him. And in that moment, he fully understood how very right it was to let Mary share the burden. Sometimes for a man to be the strongest he can be, he must borrow extra strength from those he's closest to.

He explained more of his worries. "At HP, the check might not be big, but I can count on it at least. If I open up my own place, there are no guarantees."

"We'll make it work," she said. She looked excited and not fearful, as Salem had expected. "I've gotten good at using coupons. And if it comes to that, there might be things that I can do and still stay home with Maryam. Like watch other people's children. Maryam would love it. She quite sociable, you know." She turned back to the counter and began to chop an onion. "Did you know your daughter charms every single person in line at the grocer's? And she babbles on and on when we go to post the mail, although I suppose most of her words aren't really words at all. People love it even so."

Salem smiled. The last thing that he wanted was for Mary to take on a job other than the raising of their daughter. But he was touched to the very core by her eagerness to support his dream.

"I want this for you," she said. "You deserve to have a life that makes you excited every day to get out of bed."

He kissed her in a way that he hadn't for a while. "I have you—and I have her. I'll always love my life."

"And I love the way that you work so hard for all of us—Maryam, your boys, and me. You're a good man, Salem. I think you should do it."

That night he decided he'd look into it further. He'd look into a bank loan and check out some locations that were up for sale or rent. He'd see what it might take to hire a chef who had some talent but wasn't too expensive. And perhaps Albert would make some introductions so Salem could sit down with someone at the family restaurant, someone who knew about the daily operations and the finances it would take to make it work. If Salem was really going to do this, he'd make sure that he knew exactly how much risk was involved.

But a part of him was already saying yes.

That night after Maryam was sleeping, Mary poured them each a drink. This time it was in celebration and not a way to escape. Something new had started. *His own place,* thought Salem. His father would be proud.

Chapter Seven

Bombs Too Close to Home

It was happening.

Salem managed to find a decently-sized space in an up-and-coming part of town. The building had formerly housed a fish and chip shop whose owner had retired.

Some of Salem's friends from work helped him fix it up in exchange for jobs for family members or for part-time work for themselves on weekends. Together, they cleaned and painted until Salem was proud of the gleaming floors and windows. Next, he'd put up a sign welcoming his customers to The Rose and Palm. The name interwove the symbols of the places Salem considered to be his two homes.

He'd managed to get a small loan, enough to

update some of the equipment and to hire a chef and a small staff, including a waitress from the business that had formerly occupied the space. Salem was excited to have found Sadeq, another Yemeni expat who had cooked for a well-loved restaurant back in his native country. Sadeq had been working in another factory and was excited to have found work in which he could use his skills.

The week before the restaurant opened, the chef had Salem and Mary over to his home to celebrate over Mandi and Malawah, the traditional crusty, butter-filled bread that Salem missed so much. The occasion marked one of the few times they'd gone out as a couple since Maryam had been born. Mary's friend Ann, who'd stood next to Mary at the wedding, had agreed to babysit.

After Mary had nervously bombarded her with a detailed list of dos and don'ts, Ann had waved away their thanks. "Oh, Mary knows that I am dying to have one of my own," she said as she gazed down at the baby in the crib. "I've been looking forward to some time with this precious little angel."

Later, after a satisfying meal, Salem raised his glass

of wine to his host. "To Sadeq, who will soon be a hero to the hungry and to me as well." He hadn't realized how much he'd missed the flavors of his country. He missed it in the same way that he missed the wise counsel of his father and his mother's smile that always made him understand two things: that he was treasured beyond measure and that he would be okay.

He managed to scrape one more half spoonful of the stew from the bottom of the bowl. As the flavors melted in his mouth, he could almost feel his father's hand resting firmly on his shoulder; he could almost smell the subtle floral scent of his mom's shampoo.

"And to you!" Sadeq replied. He drank and then ran a finger through his thick black curls. "For such a long time, Salem, I have dreamed of this. I've missed working in a kitchen."

Salem had decided: they would serve typical British fare alongside traditional Yemeni food. That way, if a group of diners disagreed about the kinds of food they wanted, they could choose The Rose and Palm and have a variety of choices to satisfy all cravings.

Salem was pleased to hear Mary shyly ask for a second piece of the bint al sahn. As was the tradition, Sadeq had brought the dessert to the table and then liberally poured honey over it as his excited guests looked on.

"Please. Just a tiny little bit," Mary had replied when Sadeq had asked if they'd like more. "This is wonderful, Sadeq."

Although he knew that Mary wouldn't understand, Salem had caught on to the symbolism behind the choice of dessert. Honey for Yemenis was a sign of wealth and status. By choosing to serve the bint al sahn, Sadeq was saying Salem's restaurant would put them on that path.

As Salem savored the buttery layers and the sweet taste of home, he tried to tamp down the feelings of excitement that were rushing through him. He had a solid business plan, a good location, and he had a chef who could create menu items that people would come back to taste again. But Salem had done his research. He knew that many a restaurateur had failed with those same pluses in his column. He'd stay positive and give it all he had, but he wasn't used to happy endings, and it wouldn't do to count on the one thing he couldn't plan ahead for. That one thing was luck.

The only place where happy endings could be certain was in his sister's fairy tales. He remembered the excitement that would fill her voice as she reached the high point in a story. Aladdin rubbed the lamp. And that's when the magic happened.

Maryam would smile like she was sure there was magic in the world. So Salem as a boy had believed in magic too. Until the magic failed his sister. He'd been only seven when he learned the truth. If magical beings really could appear to save those who were most deserving, they surely would have come to help his sister. On the day she died, Salem grew too old to believe in magic—or in happy endings.

Mary must have sensed his melancholy because she reached beneath the table and took Salem's hand.

He gazed over at his wife, who gently intertwined her fingers with his own and placed them in her lap. Well, perhaps, he thought, there are *some* happy endings in the real world. And a bit of magic too. In the haze of attending to their child and keeping up with the apartment and the bills, he sometimes forgot—that with Mary, there was magic; there was magic still.

♦♦♦

The next week he hovered anxiously near the door, the staff standing at attention while they waited for the first customers to come.

Beside him, Mary moved the baby to her other hip. "They're going to love it, Salem. I just know they will." She couldn't stay for long. The baby would get fussy, but she wanted to be there for Salem for the exciting start of his new venture.

For the first hour, nothing happened. Salem's heart was racing as he tallied up the money he'd already spent on this shiny place with its enticing smells— and its twenty-two tables sitting empty.

Sadeq strolled out from the kitchen. "Hey, it's all good," he said. "This is how it goes when you're just starting out. People haven't learned you're here. These things, they just take time."

Watching him carefully, Mary gave him a reassuring smile along with a thumbs-up. She'd moved to the window, trying to appease a fussy Maryam with the sight of people rushing by.

Then a young man stepped through the door. He glanced around the room. "Hey there. You guys open?"

"We are indeed. And welcome!" Salem nodded to the closest waiter to indicate that he himself would see the young man to his table. He would take great pleasure in making sure this customer, his very first, was well taken care of.

He led him to a table by the window and handed him a menu. "On the left side, you'll find fish and chips, meat pies, all the favorites from the place that was here before us. On the right is something new: dishes that the chef and I both loved in Yemen, where we're from." He pointed to the middle section of the right-hand side. "My personal favorite is this chicken, roasted to perfection and topped with a mix of nuts and onions. And all of our entrees come with bread and soup."

The man nodded, looking somewhat confused. "Shepherd's Pie? Do you have that?"

"We do indeed," said Salem. He heard movement near the door and watched a waiter greet an older couple. Customers. It's working! Here we go, he thought.

The first two weeks went well. While they were never full, the restaurant always had a busy buzz of conversation. Salem had hoped more of the customers would try the offerings from Yemen. But Sadeq had cautioned him that would take time as well.

"When it comes to food, people tend to stick with what they're used to," he told Salem. "But once the word gets out, I think we'll see success on both sides of the menu."

Salem especially loved the nights when mates from the factory would come in to say hello and try out the food. One night he looked up from serving a customer and saw two of his former co-workers who also were Yemeni. They had come in with some friends. Salem had missed Samir and Hamed and their talk of home. He personally brought out their orders of lamb stew, Mandi, and Saltah, which was meat served in a flavorful salsa of chilies, tomatoes, and herbs.

Next to their table, two women were looking over menus. "Excuse me, please," a middle-aged woman called to Salem. She pointed to the Mandi. "Could you tell me what that is? It smells just divine."

As the weeks went by, the Yemeni offerings gradually became more popular as customers took note of the enticing appearance and aromas. Of course, there was the lure as well of trying something new. In addition, more Yemeni expats had learned that The Rose and Palm was now open with the foods that they missed from home.

Some of Salem's nervousness began to dissipate. This might really work, he thought.

Then a review appeared in The Guardian. One of the waiters saw it first. He came rushing in one morning with a stack of papers in his hand, holding one of them out to Salem. "The Guardian was here! They were at the restaurant! They were really here! You won't believe it, Salem."

Salem's heart was pounding, despite the fact the boy's smile should have clued him in that the news was good. He quickly found the headline: "New Eatery Delights, Welcome Addition to the Scene." The article below used phrases like "artful flavor combinations," "exciting menu options," and best all, "potential to be a superstar on the local dining scene."

Luckily, the restaurant had yet to open for the day, so they could whoop and high five each other, bringing Sadeq out to see what on earth was going on.

The result was that the restaurant was now full most nights as well as during most lunch hours. Often, there was a small crowd waiting to be seated, and Salem had to add chairs to the lobby so they could comfortably wait until tables opened up. Sometimes he offered appetizer samples to make the wait more pleasant. By the time the first year was over, he had hired more staff and added an extra hour onto the dinner-service schedule to accommodate more guests.

For the first time in years, the knot of anxiety that lived deep in his stomach began to loosen up and he could breathe. He'd forgotten what that felt like: not to worry. There was now no need to debate whether the last bit of his pay should go for groceries or the phone bill or be sent to Yemen. Now there was enough to go around. Plus, there was money left to save for his family's future. For a house perhaps? Or if Maryam had her mother's drive and heart for big causes, she'd want to go to college. So might her sister and her brother. Because, yes, Salem longed to feel once again a small head against his shoulder as he dozed through the evening news. He missed the feel of a little body nestled against his.

As for Maryam, she was past her baby days. And she was never still. Quite often, Salem found, she was too busy for a cuddle. She would rush, delighted, from one room to the next to show Salem a new drawing or ask him another question. So many, many questions all day long! What did he eat for lunch? Did he like the color purple? Did the moon feel hot or cold, and who put it in the sky?

This should have been the sweet time in their lives, mused Salem, the time they'd worked so hard for. But Salem came home most nights to discover Mary staring, morose and often tearful, at the TV screen. While the family's dinner simmered on the stove, she'd be sipping wine as if the liquid in the glass were a kind of shield against the world around her.

Salem didn't understand. They had a steady income, a precious little girl, and a loving marriage. What exactly was it she was drinking to forget?

One night he came home with news of more success. The Rose and Palm was set to be included in the next edition of *Best of Birmingham,* a well-read magazine. Some of the reporters had been in and especially loved the bint al sahn and the minced lamb with onions and tomatoes.

"They're coming tomorrow for an interview about my life in Yemen," Salem said to Mary, kicking off his shoes. His legs were aching, as was usual after a long day on his feet, but his excitement energized him.

With a bowl in her hand, Mary frowned as she gazed across the kitchen, more intent on Maryam than on Salem's news. "Don't you put that in your mouth!" She sighed. "Salem, will you please take that away from her?"

Salem rushed to get a used tea bag out of the child's hand.

Mary sighed. "I swear, the child exhausts me." She turned off the stove and poured some pasta into a colander as she stood over the sink.

Salem picked up Maryam and bounced her on his hip. "Did you hear me, Mary? About the magazine?"

"Oh, yeah. I forgot. Which magazine did you say it was again?" She pulled a tomato from the fridge and frowned. "How on earth has this gone bad so quickly? These greedy business people. They don't think a thing about selling you bad food if they can make a dollar."

"Best of Birmingham." He did not elaborate. How he would have loved to come home to a wife who cared—a tiny bit at least—about his day.

He could not decide if he should be angry or if he should be worried. Somehow, the joy in her had disappeared once more. In the weeks that followed, he tried to talk to her about it, but she just waved him away or gave him an evasive answer.

"You ask me what the problem is," she said to him one night. "The problem is the world we live in! It's the whole awful world."

But what did that even mean? He felt the way he'd felt when he was new in England and the language was confusing.

More and more, he found himself reaching for his drink of choice as well, which was a glass of gin (and on bad days, two). It was a special kind of sadness, he decided: a life full of things to celebrate and no one there beside you to share in your enjoyment.

In addition to the gin, he tried to lose himself in the day-to-day operations of The Rose and Palm. In December, he could feel excitement building up as the holidays grew near. Customers seemed cheerier and often lingered longer over meals. Work was seemingly not as urgent as thoughts of gifts and parties filled their minds instead.

With no family around, he and Mary usually had a no-fuss kind of Christmas with some friends, who'd join them for dinner with everybody bringing food. And this year, of course, Maryam talked incessantly of Santa. Salem had already bought a dollhouse and a big blue rubber ball, which he'd hidden in a closet. And he had promised his little girl they'd leave some mince pies out for Father Christmas before bed on Christmas Eve.

He had sent a note to Ahmed and Omer about this grand tradition.

There's a fairy tale in England about a bearded man who rides through the sky at night—on a sleigh that's pulled by reindeer! The children leave him treats, and he leaves them toys. In just twelve days, he comes. I am sure this "Father Christmas" will leave some gifts for you—which I will get to you when I can.

At The Rose and Palm, he strung up twinkling

lights, but he needed something more. All up and down the block he saw businesses bedecked with wreaths and lighted trees. What he needed was a palm. With lights and Christmas balls, it would make his business stand out since Europeans had an odd insistence on decorating firs and pines for the holiday. But instead it was the palm that had given nurture to the Christ child's mother. So what better tree could there be to celebrate that sacred birth? The palm should wear lights for Christmas!

In a sea of "Christmas trees," it took a lot of searching, but Salem managed to find two small palms suitable for the restaurant and, most importantly, his living room at home. He'd already begun to tell Maryam about his family's business and the place the palm held in both Christianity and Islam.

He'd told her about the time that the mother of the baby Jesus spent beneath the palm tree long ago. "And the baby Jesus told the palm tree, 'Please, my mommy's hungry,' and that is when the palm tree reached down with its dates," he said to her one night as he tucked her into bed.

She'd given him a sleepy smile as she closed her eyes. "Wasn't that so nice?"

When patrons asked about the palm, Salem would reply that palms, not firs or pines, were found in Beit Lahem at the time of Jesus's birth. "I think the palm might be feeling sad not to have its rightful place of honor on the holiday."

Christmas passed and New Year's. Then came the day that Mary had some news. He came home to find her weeping on the couch. He could hear the sound of music from Maryam's room across the hall, which meant the child was in there playing.

"Mary!" He rushed to sit down beside her, pushing her hair from her eyes. "Honey, what's the matter?"

"Oh, Salem, I've been throwing up, and that just confirms it. I've been thinking that it might be true but hoping that it wasn't." She put a hand on her stomach and closed her eyes against the tears.

A rush of emotion swept through Salem. "What are you saying, Mary?"
She gave him a small smile. "You know, you really

are the best daddy in the world—although I really stink in the role of mum."

"Mary, do you mean . . .?"

"I'm afraid another one is coming." She nestled against his side. "And soon we will be four."

He kissed her forehead and then her cheek. "Mary, that's the best news!" He put both arms around her and pulled her close to him. "Do you know how much I love you?" he whispered in her ear, kissing her again. "Nothing is more precious to me, Mary, than you and our little girl." He rested his hand on her stomach. "And there's nothing I want more than this news that you've just shared."

She sobbed into his chest as a mixture of elation and confusion bubbled up within him.

"Why aren't you happy, Mary?" Salem asked her gently. "You've been so sad for a long time. Aren't you happy with our life?" Dare he ask the question? "You still love me. Right?"

"How could you ask that, Salem? You and Maryam are the *only* good things in my life." She paused.

"But sometimes I watch our daughter, and I feel certain that she needs so much more from me than I could ever give. Oh, Salem! All day long I just feel . . . I just feel so depressed. And I don't have the energy to get down on the floor and play, to be a fun mum like some others, which just makes me feel worse." The tears came harder than before. "Because she is like her daddy. She is such a special child. She deserves a mother who's more present in her life."

He gently wiped her tears away with his thumb. "But I don't understand what's wrong. Of course you're a great mum. What's making you depressed?"

"Oh Salem, I don't know. I sit around all day with only Maryam and the TV to keep me company. And so what do I hear in the background all day long? All this talk of bombs and crooked politicians, the whole world going nuts." She rested her hand along with Salem's on her stomach. "And *this* is the world I bring another child into?"

He leaned in to kiss her. "It's a world that has you in it. And that's good enough for me."

She buried her face in his chest. "I love you so much, Salem," she said in a muffled voice. "And you deserve a better wife than the one you've got."

"What are you saying, Mary? I would never want to be with anyone but you." He ran his fingers through her hair. He would love her through this. What else could he do?

After he'd held her for a while in silence, he noticed that Maryam had come into the room, her eyes grown big with fear. It was the first time in a long time he'd seen the child stand still.

"Is Mummy feeling bad?" she asked.

Salem held out his arm to invite his daughter into the embrace. "I think what Mummy needs is a hug from you and me."

As the pregnancy progressed, Mary had a few more tearful episodes, but she also took a turn for the better. Soon, she grew excited about the new addition. She and Maryam threw themselves into a project of making a nursery out of the small sitting room off the master bedroom. Maryam took great delight in choosing yellow paint and giraffe decals for the wall. As instructed by her mother, the child carefully folded the small outfits that she had outgrown to put in the baby's drawers.

Then that August, Salem, Mary, and Maryam welcomed baby Jamal. Life fell into a routine of work and childcare and falling into bed exhausted. Salem couldn't wait to get home from work and just take in the innocence of his new son as he slept. (Sadly, Jamal was usually sleeping when Salem finally dragged in from The Rose and Palm.) Maryam, who was still full of words, would give her dad reports about their day while Mary would smile peacefully and get Salem's dinner ready as she listened to her daughter talk.

If there was a certain joy missing in the interactions between him and Mary, neither one of them had the energy to comment—or to even notice, really, that there was something wrong. Again, there was the familiar tiredness that came with a new baby who woke up at all hours.

Salem was exhausted now when he woke up for his morning prayers. Mary would complain that he always woke her up. "First it's Jamal, then you," she'd tell him sleepily. But the first prayers of the day must come before the sunrise. In them, Salem found his peace.

Life came at them quickly in the time that followed. They moved into a house, which was much more suited for a family of four. And soon, that number became five. Almost a year exactly after the birth of Jamal, daughter Sara joined the family.

As the children grew, Salem could clearly see that raising three young children was taking a toll on Mary, who sometimes got teary eyed as they watched the evening news. Other nights, she seemed to just zone out when he spoke to her, as if she didn't even understand that he was talking.

"Let's get a babysitter and go out this weekend," he said to her one day.

"I'm surprised you thought of that." She looked up from the dishes she was washing. "Sometimes I imagine you've forgotten that you even have a wife—or that you, in fact, have children who'd need looking after if the two of us went out." Then she froze and stood very still with a dish in one hand and a rag in the other. "Oh, Salem, I'm so sorry. That was mean. You can't imagine how long and exhausting these days at home can be."

"I think we're both exhausted. I'm on my feet all day, dealing with reservations, checking orders." He wished she'd understand: his wife and his children were the very reason that he worked so hard. Hopefully, in a few years, he could hire a manager and spend more time at home. But for now, he had to be there, or things might fall through the cracks. And he didn't want to lose what he'd worked so hard to build.

He took a deep breath and tried to choose compassion over anger. "I'm sure we could find a sitter. And we could go to dinner or go out and get a drink. Maybe dancing later? What do you think of that?"

She grew quiet and then smiled at Salem sadly. "I remember dancing. That was so long ago."

He took her in his arms and began to slow dance with her in the kitchen, holding his cheek close to hers. "I miss this. I miss you."

She moved in a little closer. "Okay, I'll find a sitter. I think I'd like that, Salem. Mona might be willing to come and stay one night."

Mona was a grandmotherly woman Salem had encouraged his wife to hire to give her some relief in the afternoons. Once a week or so, she would stay for a few hours so that Mary could have some lunch with chums or go out to see a film.

"I'm glad that you found Mona to come in and help," he told her as they danced.

She broke away from him and frowned. "I'm really not so sure that it does me any good. Once a week. That's all! Once a week I get to go out and be a grown-up for two hours, maybe three. Oh, lucky, lucky me. While look at you. You get to be a grown-up all week long."

◆◆◆

The next week, they had their date night.

To try to bring back the thing that had been lost between them, he took her to the pub where they had met. But unlike that first time when the words flowed like a flood they couldn't stop, they spent a lot of time in silence. How could it be, thought Salem, that she seemed like a stranger?

Two nights later, he got home late to see fire in her eyes as she moved to the stove to heat up his dinner.

What now? Salem thought. He was already spent. The night had been horrific with two local pubs blown up by bombs. News was still pouring in, but the injuries and deaths appeared to be catastrophic.

"Well, I suppose you heard," she said. "We could have died, you know. And where would that have left our children?" She took out a plate and slammed the door of the cabinet with a bang.

"*What?* I don't know what you mean. You're not making any sense." He took off his coat and shoes and massaged his sore left foot.

"Don't you listen to the news? I'm talking, Salem, about bombs. There were two of them — in two of the pubs downtown. *Let's go for dinner or a drink,* you said. We should have just stayed home."

He sighed and sank down in a chair. "I think I'm still in shock. But, Mary, we're okay." He stared at her flushed face. "None of our friends were . . .?"

She shook her head. "Not that I know of, Salem." She sighed. "It just scared me is all. It's just so . . . close to home."

He closed his eyes, exhausted at reports of the kind of violence that he thought he'd escaped when he came from Yemen. Now this was happening near his children? It made him want to hold them against him tightly and never let them go.

Mary set the table. "Going to the pub on Tuesday, that was a bad idea."

"You're blaming me? For taking my wife out to dinner? Blame the IRA!" That was who his customers said was responsible.

"Yeah, right." Her tone turned sarcastic. "Everybody here always blames the IRA. Because they dare to be offended that their country is under British rule. You don't know a thing about the IRA. Do you even listen for one second, Salem, to the news? Do you for one second think of anything at all besides sauces and desserts and the special of the day?"

Salem sat up straight. "Well, excuse me, Mary, for thinking of the things that allow a man to make good money to take care of his family. And I will *not* apologize for not paying any mind to the dreary news when, finally, I get a break. And yes, I'll put the blame on anyone and everyone who dares to plant a bomb that could take the life of innocent bystanders. Because you're exactly right. It could have been you or me."

Why was this an argument? Salem didn't know.

"Of course, it isn't right. I think about a young mom who might have been out dancing. 'Oh!' she might have thought. 'Here comes a Beatles song.' But instead, all hell breaks loose. And all she wanted for the night was to have a laugh and talk to people her own age for the first time in a week. She shouldn't have to suffer. None of them should suffer. So many people suffer—and for so many different reasons. It's not as simple as you think. That's all I'm saying, Salem."

Of course, it wasn't simple, he thought wearily. And it wasn't fair. But why would she glare *at him?* As if he somehow were to blame for the troubles in the world?

Quietly, she shut the bedroom door and went to bed, leaving him to eat his soup alone in front of the TV.

After washing up and before he got too tired, he tried to clear his mind for the Salat al-'isha, the last prayer of the day. As he closed his eyes and prayed, a sense of peace began to warm him, slowly easing out the anger brought on by Mary's words and the thought of bombs so close to the home where his children slept. Allah was still with him, in control.

After he was finished, he noticed Mary watching from the open door of their room.

"Does that really help?" she asked him quietly.
"It does."

"I wish I had that, Salem—something that would help."

He nodded. "Perhaps we could find a mosque and go

together. I would like that very much." With more Muslims moving into England, some had begun to gather in living rooms and buildings that had extra space. But, although he had asked around, no one knew of any gatherings close to where he lived. He missed that community, the call to prayer in Yemen that meant that others also were taking time to pray.

"Or perhaps you could find a church?" he asked. He so wanted Mary to find a sense of peace.

"I don't know," she said. "I went once or twice with friends when I was young. But it was only songs and music. Nothing that connected to . . . to the part of me that hurt."

He put his arm around her and led her back to bed. "Perhaps another church might suit you better, Mary. I hate to see you hurt."

"I wish I could be like you. That I could just concentrate on my children and my life and turn off the world. But Salem, I can't do that."

He gently kissed his wife. "I know that you can't. I'm so sorry, Mary." If she saw someone hurting—on the news or on the streets—her mind would go into overdrive, searching for solutions. As if she could fix the world.

He settled her into bed and rubbed her shoulder. "I'll check on the babies. You try to get some sleep."

Chapter Eight

Battles

Over the next year, Maryam started school, and The Rose and Palm continued to draw crowds. To a stranger, Salem's life might seem to be progressing well. But, more and more, Salem found himself longing to be home. More and more, that word—*home*—made him think of Yemen and of his family there. In this house he shared with Mary and the children, there was only stress.

Hard to believe that once she could make him feel like the smartest, most handsome man around. Now, from the minute he walked in after work, he was hit with a shouted list of all the ways he'd failed her.

Did you stop to get some fruit like I asked you yesterday?

Did you forget the bread again?

I was so hoping, Salem, that one time in your life you'd

be home when you promised. I need some help here with the kids.

He was making a real effort to help more with things at home. The success of The Rose and Palm had enabled him to hire a manager so that he could be home more. Now, he got home earlier in the evenings to help Mary with the children, who seemed to have grown more active. One of them always seemed to be in tears or asking questions or needing one thing or the other.

Many nights he was home for dinner with the family, and he was always there to tell the children stories as he tucked them into bed. But her complaints just seemed to grow. Instead of an eager kiss hello—how long had it been since he'd had that? —he might be told that Sara had a splinter in her thumb. *You should check that right away.* Or she'd nod her head toward a corner where Jamal might be wailing because some toy had failed to work. *Salem, help him please. Go see to your son.* A tone of accusation would creep into her voice as if Salem were at fault for all of the cheap and broken toys that someone had failed to manufacture like they should, for the pitiful cries of Sara as she stared down at her thumb, for every single problem in the whole damn world.

And what about *his* problems?

If the dishwasher had broken, if a waiter had failed to show during the evening rush, Salem had no one waiting at the house to hear about his day. He longed to come home to a sympathetic smile and a warm hand on his shoulder to rub away the tenseness. He still found comfort from Maryam's eager greetings and perhaps a smile from Jamal, who seemed to always have a list of new accomplishments to show off to his daddy—perhaps a crayoned drawing or a tall tower of blocks. But in a place deep inside him, the loneliness in Salem could be chilling. He longed to talk things over with his father, to take a long walk through the palm groves with Ahmed and Omer, who must have changed so much by now.

But one day at The Rose and Palm, as he was working on some orders at the counter, some hopeful news drifted over to him from a table in the back. With just a few tables filled with those finishing late lunches, a group of men was lingering over coffee. From their thobes and headscarves, Salem knew that they were Muslim. And snatches of their conversation let him know that they attended mosque together—hopefully close by.

Salem made his way to them to top off their coffee. "I hope that you fine gentlemen have enjoyed your dinner."

"This is our favorite place," said one. "Your Mandi is the best."

"And the coffee!" said the other.

"Oh, how I used to miss the coffee from my country! Until I found The Rose and Palm." A third man picked up his mug and sipped.

The first man smiled and nodded. "I am a different man after my first sweet sips of this fine Yemeni Mokha."

Salem smiled. "I do have to say that my British customers are no less than amazed when they first try our coffee. Now all of Birmingham will understand what we Yeminis have kept as our little secret for all these centuries." At one point, in fact, most of Europe's coffee came from Yemen, where it was thought to have been first cultivated by monks in the 1400s, perhaps to keep the holy men awake during lengthy nightly prayers.

"How long have you been in the country?" the first man asked his host, and soon Salem found himself seated at their table. They talked of things they missed from their beloved homeland and the challenges they'd overcome in their lives as expats.

Then Salem broached the subject that was really on his mind. "You say that your heart longed for the exquisite coffee of our country, but my heart longs for something deeper, even more essential. Did I overhear you speaking of a mosque? And could you tell me—is it close?"

And that is how he found a mosque and a community just fifteen minutes from his home. Amid the busyness and clamor of the restaurant and his family life, he finally had a place where he could find some peace.

The Rose and Palm continued to grow in popularity even as the boom in Birmingham began to slow as a result of oil shortages and economic woes that had followed the Arab-Israeli War of 1973.

In many ways, things were good for Salem. He took great pride in his work, and the ability to worship with others at the mosque soothed an ache that had become lodged deep within him. The mosque was a busy place with festivals and classes, which he eagerly attended when he could find the time.

But as he found his people, Mary longed for hers as the children became older and grew more independent. "It's time," she told him one day, "that I return to work. I miss talking to adults. You know, there was a time—when I worked for the council—that I really mattered, Salem. A time when I could work the phones and schedules like a pro; I could make things happen. Things that did not involve chauffeuring ball players all over town and back. And moderating fights over whose turn it is to clean up or who did what to who or ate the last bit of the pudding."

This request of Mary's disappointed Salem. His hard work at the restaurant had resulted in an income that gave her the privilege to stay home with the children. Now that they were older, there was a whole new set of problems that required the vigilance of a mom at home. Could Mary not see that? This seemed to be a thing in England: mothers returning to the workforce (out of choice, not need) with children still at home. It made no sense to Salem.

But more often than he worried for the children, Salem

worried about his wife. More than anything, he longed to fix the sadness that lived in Mary's eyes.

Now, he took her in his arms and gently kissed her forehead. "To me and the children, no one matters more than you. I feed people lunch and dinner; you're raising fine young people, training them to be adults. What you do here in our home—that matters so much more than my ordering and scheduling and whatever else it is that might happen in my day."

But she didn't seem to hear him. Sometimes he felt lost to help her or to explain the comfort that he found in having her at home when the kids came home from school.

They let the matter drop, and the years continued on. Maryam and Sara grew into teenage beauties, the oldest looking so much like Salem's sister that Salem sometimes had to catch his breath. His oldest daughter had his sister's long, dark hair and heart-shaped mouth, her delicate shoulders, and soft laugh. As for his younger daughter, she had Mary's blonde good looks, and when Salem looked at Sara, he could almost see her mother as she had appeared in those first blissful days when they fell in love.

Jamal now towered over Salem and always seemed to be strumming a guitar if he wasn't studying or eating.

And Mary was more restless than she had ever been, and once more she introduced the subject of going back to work. "Two of them are driving!" Mary said to Salem. "They're always off to somewhere, and its time their mother had places to be as well."

But things were happening with the children. He needed her at home.

Maryam at sixteen had her first boyfriend, Luke. Oh, she'd had movie dates before and small crushes and flirtations that had mostly gone nowhere. But this time, it was different. In his daughter's smile, Salem saw a welling of emotions that he remembered all too well. He thought back to the night he'd sat across from Mary after buying her a drink from the inattentive, can't-be-bothered staffer at the bar. He knew the kind of spell his daughter was now under.

But who was this boy exactly? Could they really trust this stranger with their girl? It was one of many reasons Mary should be home to monitor their daughter's moods and her activities.

"It's fine," Mary said to him one evening as he watched the door, waiting for his oldest daughter to get home from a date. "He's a nice boy, Salem. You are such a worrier when it comes to Maryam."

Which was true, he guessed. He loved all his children, but Maryam had always held a special place in Salem's heart. Now that she was older, she looked so much like his sister that he almost expected her at times to burst into the songs the older Maryam had sung to Salem as a child. It was almost as if his sister had returned, brought back magically to life.

Jamal, in the meantime, had developed a combative streak that caused concern for Salem. Almost anything that Salem asked of him was met with resounding opposition. The boy all but refused to finish homework or to help his mother out with the simplest of chores. Salem thought about the way he himself had longed to please his father. Was Jamal copying the way that he saw his British friends behaving toward their parents? What was going on?

Or was the tension in the home seeping into Salem's children's psyches, affecting their very ways of being? Salem felt a chill. What were he and Mary doing to their kids?

Sara, their miniature version of her gorgeous mother, had once been a happy child whose high-pitched squeals of laughter were the first thing Salem heard when he got home from work. But now at thirteen, the smallest thing—a grade, a friend's remark—meant the slamming of her bedroom door, followed by a rush of tears.

"Temperamental," Mary whispered one night after one of Sara's outbursts. "I'm afraid I was the same."

The children had reached an age when Salem longed to introduce them to the peace that came from daily prayer. To share with them the wisdom that came from the Quran on thankfulness, priorities, and goals. He himself had memorized the book by the time he was their age, he doubted if Jamal had even read a single word, although he kept one in the den, an English translation, and encouraged each of them to pick it up.

He longed for his children to connect with the teen group at the mosque—just the type of friends he wanted them to have. They were so unlike the ones that Jamal had been having over, kids who never said a word to him or Mary—not a *hello,* not a *thanks.* But some of the words he did hear coming from their mouths were unsuitable for teens. Salem was appalled.

But Mary had insisted that the kids stay home when Salem went to worship. "They've got so much on their plates without us making them go there," she explained to him. "With school. And hockey and piano. When they're older, they'll decide. Let's leave it up to them."

"But none of that will bring them joy like they will find in Allah," Salem pleaded with her. 'My success is only by Allah,' it says in the Quran. "And I see my children suffering. Don't you see it, Mary?"

But there was no use in arguing with Mary on this point. The fact was that she was jealous of his friends at the mosque. She was jealous of the time he spent away from her. And Salem picked his battles. He'd won one already when Mary had agreed to stay home with the kids. For now, they'd have their mother at home with them in the afternoons. And perhaps one day he'd win another battle and he could introduce them to the wisdom of Islam.

For now, only Maryam showed any interest in her father's homeland and the faith that had been nurtured there. Even as a tiny girl, she had loved the stories of his days in Yemen. "When can I go there?" she had asked him eagerly at age three and four. And now when she sat with her father after dinner, him with his newspaper, her with her schoolwork, she'd come up with more questions about the land by the Red Sea that she longed to one-day visit. Tell me more about the palms. How high do they grow? What kind of studies would I have if I were living there? Tell me more about my aunt. My aunt who had my name! Was she very pretty?

At Maryam's request, Salem had begun to teach his daughter the language of his country. She was good with words, and Salem was amazed at how quickly she could learn. And each Christmas, he and Maryam would locate a small palm and decorate their tree in twinkling lights, placing it near a window in their living room.

"Why are we the only ones who recognize that *this* is the tree that was present when the mother of the baby Jesus needed to be nourished?" Maryam asked one day.

Salem added more twinkling lights to the branches of the tree. "I do not know, Maryam, why they do not understand. But we will give the palm the honor it is due."

One day, when she asked about his sister, she shyly fingered the small stone on the necklace Luke had bought her when she turned sixteen. "Did your sister ever get to have a boy she loved? A boy who loved her too? I hope before she . . . well, before she . . . I hope she got to have a Luke."

"She did," Salem told her softly. "He loved her very much from what I understood." One day he'd tell her more. For now, he'd just tell her the beginning. The beginning was so nice.

Earlier that year, after many questions from his daughter about the teachings of his faith, he had presented Maryam with her own copy of the holy book. Mary, after all, had said to let them decide, and Maryam had asked: "What does the Quran say that you should do if you're feeling really scared about something that's important?"

One day, he saw her shyly watching as he washed his hands in preparation for the first prayers of the day.

"You're up early," he observed.

"Couldn't sleep," she said.

Worried, he kissed the top of his daughter's head. "Is there something on your mind?"

"Just some stuff with Luke. I feel so happy with I'm with him, Dad! But then when things go wrong, I feel like I might explode. Do you ever feel that way?" The beginnings of a good cry seemed to be just waiting in her dark, expressive eyes.

Salem closed his eyes in a silent plea to this stranger, Luke. *Don't you break her* heart? *Don't you even dare.*

Maryam watched quietly, as if she still had more to say. "So . . ." She hesitated. "I was wondering if maybe . . . could you teach me how to pray? I think that it might help."

Salem stroked her hair. "The best gift I could give you is the peace that comes from Allah. I'd love to show you, sweetheart."

Carefully, he showed her the rituals and movements. And from that day on, the two of them often prayed together at night and in the mornings. Even more so than in the mosque, Salem felt that sense of power and connection that came from the shared act of prayer. And sometimes father and daughter would go together to the mosque for Friday prayers.

Sometimes he'd catch a certain look in Mary's eyes when they left for the mosque. It was if she felt threatened by the closeness he had always felt to Maryam.

Then bad news came for Mary in a late-night phone call from her sister reporting Mary's mother's death. By that point, Mary hadn't seen her mother in twenty years at least.

Still, the phone call left her reeling. "I don't know why I'm crying," she said that night to Salem. "It's not like I even ever had a mother to begin with." She paused to blow her nose. "But I guess somewhere in my mind, I always thought there'd be a chance for her to meet you and the children. And then I guess I thought my mother might be proud of me at last. After all these years. And now that will never happen. Never in my life will I be someone's daughter—in the way that really counts."

And in that moment more than any other, Salem loathed the distance between his home and Yemen. If they could somehow make it to his homeland, he knew that his mother would gladly take in Mary as one of her very own. His own mother, with her gentle ways and her all-knowing smile, was the only one he knew who might begin to fill—maybe just a little—the gaping void in Mary's life.

In the days that followed, he'd come home more and more to find Mary gone. If she was finding comfort with her friends at the movies or in the pubs, so be it, Salem thought. But Jamal's grades were slipping, and he was now in danger of failing two of his five classes. And although he was plenty old enough to have the discipline to do his homework on his own, it often went undone without Mary standing over him to make sure it was completed.

After a few months of Mary's constant absence, his patience began to wane. Could she not see her friends or go to meetings when the children were at school?

Then he was overcome with fury when he came home one night to no dinner (once again) while Jamal lay on the couch, strumming his guitar while the TV played in the background.

"Where's your mother?" Salem asked.

Jamal shrugged, not bothering to look up from his guitar.

"Look at me when I talk to you," Salem almost shouted, stopping to remind himself to be calm, to be the adult. "Is your homework done?"

Jamal sighed and turned off the television, signaling to Salem that the answer was a no. But he could only guess since Mary apparently hadn't bothered to instill the simplest of manners in his son.

"Girls, I'm home," he called out. "Has everyone had dinner?"

Sara peeked out of her room. "I'll make you a sandwich."

He gave her a hug. "I'd love that, darling. Thanks. Where is Maryam?"

Sara nodded toward the closed door of her sister's room.

Salem gently knocked. "Maryam, you good?"

"Hi, Dad. Come on in."

He noticed her reddened eyes, and she saw him notice. She glanced down at the bed. "It was a really bad day."

"Sweetheart, what's the matter?"

She just shook her head. "You wouldn't understand. I'd rather be alone, please, if you wouldn't mind. But . . . I hope your day was good?" she asked him hopefully.

"Oh, yes. It was fine. Thank you, love, for asking." He kissed her on the cheek. "I love you very much."

He headed to the kitchen, where Sara sat with him while he ate his turkey sandwich.

"Problems with the big romance," she explained to Salem in her quietest voice.

"Really?" Salem asked her. "What's up with her and Luke?"

"I'm not sure," said Sara. "She'll talk to Mom sometimes, but, well, Mom is never really here."

"And speaking of your mother, do you know where she is?"

Sara shrugged and sipped her coke. "Saving endangered whales, I guess? Or maybe saving orphans? The politically oppressed? Saving someone somewhere. Whoever really knows?"

It was midnight before Mary finally came home, looking half-asleep.

"Where have you been?" he demanded, standing up from the couch. He was exhausted from his day but way too mad to sleep.

But she was too preoccupied to take note of his tone. "I was at the pub—commiserating mostly—because evil's winning, Salem. And there's nothing we can do. Do you have any clue what the Catholics in Northern Ireland are having to endure?"

"I have no idea," he told her, "about some Catholics who are of no relation to either me or you." He made certain to keep his voice very low. "But here is what I know: Your daughter's heart is broken, and she'll only talk to you. But because you're off again to some bloody pub or who-knows-where, she cries in her room alone. If you can't save the Catholics, perhaps you could save your child. She's your daughter, Mary. Is that too much to ask?"

"Now, Salem, that's not . . ."

"And did Jamal do his homework while you were at the pub? I'm sure you can guess the answer. What would Jamal have to do to get on your list of causes? Is there a waiting list perhaps?"

She sank down in the stuffed chair by the couch. "Don't you start acting so self-righteous. Because you have no right! You get to live your dream. You wanted to open up your restaurant. And guess what? You did! With support from me. And I've told you that my dream was to have some meaning in my life. I was asked to come back to my job, but I told them no, that I'd stay home with the children as you asked. You have your friends at work and your friends at the mosque. And you begrudge me this—a few nights out with people who care about the things that are important to me. After all I've done, you dare to complain about the little bit of time that I spend with them, doing what we can to help."

Salem's heart was pounding as he listened to her words. "The Rose and Palm is not some fun day at the park where I while away my time with no care in the world. Mary, it's a job—a back-breaking, all-day-on-my-feet, exhausting day at work." He moved closer to her. "A job I do unselfishly for you and our family! And I come home to no supper and to a filthy house and neglected children."

Fury flashed in Mary's eyes. "Perhaps you haven't noticed that the children, as you call them, are almost grown-up now. It's not as if I've run off and left toddlers home alone." She sighed and leaned back in the chair. "Don't I get a life? I have needs, you know. I'm not just someone's mother, someone's wife." She closed her eyes wearily, thinking back on Salem's words. A look of worry creased her forehead. "But Maryam . . . oh, Salem. Did you say that she was crying? Is Maryam okay?"

He shook his head. "I don't think so, Mary, and I don't know how to help." Why couldn't life in England be like it was in Yemen, where family was so central; it was everything, in fact. Every woman placed the utmost of importance on her role as a mother. Salem's mother still—even now—made a major difference in the man that Salem was. He still heard her calming voice when orders came out wrong, when new recipes failed to turn out like he'd hoped, when he fought with Mary . . .

He tried something different. "Mary, let me ask you

this: if there was one thing in your life that you could go back and fix, what would that one thing be?"

"Salem, I'm exhausted. I'm much too tired for games. I heard some things tonight that were so upsetting I could weep. Please. Let's just go to bed."

"I'm begging of you, Mary. I've seen how much it hurt you not to have a mother. Don't do that to your children. Be their mother. Please."

She stared at him in fury. "Salem! Don't you dare! You don't see the things I do while you're away at work. Of course they have a mother."

He took her hand in his, trying desperately to find some peace between them. "I'm requesting from my heart. Out of love for them. Because the children need you, Mary."

She was breathing hard. "They need me—and they have me. I can't believe you, Salem. You try to get your way by taking the most hurtful thing ever in my life and using it against me?"

He took her in his arms, but she did not return the hug. "Oh, Mary, no. I'm sorry! The last thing I would ever want to do is hurt you." He hadn't realized the hurt his words would bring. He had gone too far by bringing up her mother.

She wept against his chest. "But you don't see me, Salem! You might see a woman who sleeps in your bed at night, but you don't see me—your wife! You see that you need dinner and that Maryam needs soothing. But do you think for just one second about what it is that I might need?" She pulled away and looked up at her husband. "Because, the thing is, Salem, I have a request as well: I want you to look at me. Look at me. See me!"

She went quietly to bed, and Salem's arms felt empty. He still loved her with the same fierceness as before, but did he even know her anymore?

All he was asking her to do was to be there for the children that they treasured, who'd soon be on their own. He was asking out of love for the family they had made. And this was somehow hurtful? It made no sense to Salem, but he had seen the hurt that his request had caused. He'd seen it in her eyes, and it had cut him to the core.

I love you, Mary, but you're right. I can't see you anymore. And can you see me, your husband? He didn't think she could. Because what he felt for her was love, but what she seemed to see instead was a cold indifference to her feelings.

Love. They still had that. He'd thought it was enough. But maybe he was wrong—and perhaps the day had finally come when love had met its match.

Chapter Nine

Other Ways and Other Truths

The year that followed brought new lows for all five members of the family. Still grieving for her mother, Mary sank into a deep depression. Even more so than before, she let her housekeeping go. Dirty dishes sometimes stayed in the sink for days, and Salem had to step over piles of papers to make his way through his house. Maryam tried to help as much as she could, but she had been brought low by new conflicts in her relationship with Luke. Not that she talked that much to Salem about what was going on. But her reddened eyes were hint enough, along with the moody silences that were so unlike her.

Once he listened at the door of Maryam's room as Sara spoke in soothing tones to her weeping sister.

"I can't lose him, Sara," Maryam insisted. "If I lose him, I'll just die. But he doesn't understand! My faith—it's so important—and keeping myself pure. And if he really loves me, how can he even ask?"

"But Maryam, you have to see that his needs are met, or he'll go to someone else. And you can't let that happen! Because he loves you. And he's hot! And because you love him too; that will make it special when it happens—and that makes it okay."

It took all the self-control that Salem had not to burst right through that door. How dare Sara give her sister such advice? And how free was his Sara being with the boys? Mary really needed to have a long talk with their daughters.

But something told him Maryam would stay true to her faith. As the two of them studied and said their prayers together, he could see the ways of Islam taking hold inside her, becoming an essential part of who she was.

Most of the tears in the house that year belonged to Sara, who seemed to bring home the worst grades of the children, despite her struggles late into the night with her books and papers. Mary sat up with her some nights, using her calmest voice to quiz Sara on events for a history test or to help with algebra.

On more than one occasion, Sara had fled the table

where she and Mary had been working. She would slam her bedroom door, declaring she was "stupid."

After one tirade, Mary glanced at Salem. "She just tries so hard, and still she doesn't get it, Salem. She might need some special help. I'll talk to her teacher maybe."

Salem nodded. "That sounds good. And what is up with Jamal? I worry for him too." The boy seemed to always be incensed. Every question Salem asked him was met with a scowl.

Mary shrugged. "Things seem so much worse since we took his guitar away. Perhaps we should . . ."

"Absolutely not," said Salem. It had been a good decision. They had told him they would do it if he did not bring up his grades, and they had followed through. Perhaps now they would start to see improvements in his scores. Jamal should not be spending time in a garage band with his buddies when his grades were what they were.

Mary looked her husband in the eye. "It's just that it's the only thing that brings him any joy at all."

"There is more to life than joy. He needs to get the

grades to go to university and support a family one day. A guitar won't help with that."

"Do you think the Beatles' families said that?" She gave him a rueful smile.

"Well, the Beatles are no more. They won't be knocking on the door and begging for Jamal."

And if they did come calling, what they'd find would be a mess unfit for superstars—or for any company at all. Salem looked around at the dirty, half-filled cups and specks of dirt and paper littering the floor. No doubt the filth and odors were making everyone feel worse. But he dared not mention that to Mary lest he be invited to pick things up himself. Or he might be inundated with a list of ways she spent her time that had much more meaning than digging out the vacuum.

So here we are, he thought. Mary wanted meaning; Jamal wanted joy. And of course, so did Salem! But since he couldn't find a way to pay the bills with a search for joy, he continued to get out of bed each morning and drag himself to work. He double-checked the orders and the employee schedules. He smiled and welcomed guests, despite any inclination that he'd really rather do something else that day. It was time

Jamal—and his mother—learned to do that too.

Changes came that year as well for Salem. The reputation of the Rose and Palm began to soar even higher. The restaurant won several regional awards. The growing popularity meant extended hours and demanded more of Salem's time. As problems mounted up at home, the new success brought him little pleasure. Instead, it added in more stress.

The later hours meant less time to sit with Sara over homework. It became even harder to find time for Maryam, who at last had opened up a little about herself and Luke, although she never got specific. "He wants things that I can't give him," she said to Salem one day. "In some ways, we're the worst match that you could imagine. But if he's wrong for me, why does it feel so good to just be close to him?"

Salem's heart just ached, longing for the days when she cried for easy things that any dad could fix.

He also had less time for the mosque, and for the first time in a long time, he found himself skipping prayers. And perhaps the distance between himself and Allah was the hardest thing of all.

The busyness at work was a nice distraction, but it hurt to not have Mary to share in the excitement of the accolades that kept piling on. This should be a time of joy that both of them had earned. But she continued to be jealous of the time and attention Salem gave to The Rose and Palm.

Thank goodness there was Maryam, who was more thrilled than Salem about each new success. She now spent some weekends as a hostess at the restaurant, and she also loved to spend time in the kitchen with Sadeq, eager to learn more about the preparation of the dishes from her ancestral home. Sometimes he would hear them speaking in Arabic as they worked. That had been Sadeq's suggestion. Knowing that she had long been studying the language, he had thought the practice might help her to excel even more.

One night, Salem watched a young couple by the window while they waited for their food. The young man whispered something that made the woman blush. She reached for his hand and kissed it.

Salem saw in them a sense of excitement for the future, and he couldn't help but worry as he caught sight of the fragile hope that sparkled in their eyes. At this point, they had no idea how hard the world might treat them.

But it might be fine! He thought about his parents. They'd hardly known each other when their marriage had been planned by his family and hers, but they still held hands at every meal and shared glances full of meaning, that secret code some couples always seemed to share.

That night he stopped off at a new pub, longing for a beer and perhaps some fish and chips in the company of people who were happy. Everybody at his house always seemed so down, and he never knew if he'd find a warm meal waiting for him or be left to make a sandwich.

Soon after he had ordered, a woman nodded at the empty stool beside him at the crowded bar, a question in her eye.

Salem nodded back, indicating it was free. Right away, he noticed the tight fit of her dress, the softness of her long, dark hair, and the way it caught the light from the fixture in the ceiling. Then he felt bad for having noticed and concentrated on his chips as they were set before him.

She ordered a glass of pinot noir, then she turned to

Salem. "Thank goodness there's a seat. It's been that kind of day. I thought it would never end." Her smile was inviting. There was nothing flirty to it; she was simply being friendly. And he could use a friend.

"Same here," he replied. He picked up his Guinness. "Some days you just can't wait to lock up and go home. All day long at my place, we had customers lined up at the door, and it just never stopped. Of course, you love the business, but two staffers called in sick, and it was a lot to handle. It feels good to finally breathe."

They sat for a while in a companionable silence. Then she accepted her glass from the bartender and held it up in a toast. "To breathing," she said. "And to quitting time."

He smiled and touched his mug to her glass of wine. "I will drink to that."

She watched him with interest. "Where is it that you work?"

"I own a restaurant in the next block. Do you know The Rose and Palm?"

"Oh, I love the mandi there. And the bint al sahn."

Tilting her head to one side, the woman studied Salem. "And you really own the place? I am so impressed. Tell me how you started. What gave you the idea?"

Before he knew it, he was on his third beer and it was getting much too late. His new friend, it seemed, had question after question about his life in Yemen. She was eager to know more about the country that had given birth to her favorite dining destination.

"I take all my friends there when they come to town," she said.

Salem told her all about the way the Red Sea would look at sunrise when he used to wake up early to help his father with the palms. He told her how close big families were in Yemen, describing for her the dances that his cousins and other family members loved to do when they all got together. He knew that he should wrap it up and head home to his wife and children. But it had been so long since a woman had listened to him with such eagerness—and such fascination.

"My family's big as well," she said. "They're all still in London, everyone but me. At night I still get lonely, although I've been here for five months. Oh, and by the way, my name is Michelle."

"Hello, Michelle. I'm Salem."

Then she looked at Salem and put her hand on his. "I can't imagine how it must have felt to have moved so far away from everyone you knew," she told him earnestly. "And to just lay down every night and know how very far away they were. That's how I felt anyway, and I didn't move that far." She smiled. "Hey, but look at you. You came here, and you managed to build something just so special. You must be so proud."

He knew he should remove his hand before things went too far. But for just a moment, he'd enjoy the warmth of another hand on his. He'd give himself that gift.

The band began to play "And I Love Her" by the Beatles. They sat there in silence for a moment taking, in the words. *She gives me everything, and tenderly . . .*

"Dance with me?" she whispered.

There was still time to say the words: *I'm a married man.* But that would break a kind of spell, it seemed to Salem. Sometimes he didn't wear his ring if he had a lot to do in the restaurant's kitchen on a given day.

Now, it was well past time for him to simply leave.

"I really have to go," he said as almost every cell in his whole body begged him to say yes, to lead her to the dance floor and hold her close to him.

She looked into his eyes. "I've had too much to drink. Please forgive me, Salem, but would it be too bold of me to say you're such a handsome man?"

Sensations he'd forgotten filled his body, and he knew that if he didn't leave at that very moment, it would be too late.

She reached up to touch his hair at the temple, at the place where the gray was starting to creep in. Until then, that flash of silver in his mirror had made him feel like an old man who was past his prime.

Then she leaned into him, and her lips were suddenly on his. Her kiss was light and tender but filled with a kind of longing that seemed to match his own. Despite his best intentions, he couldn't pull away from the softness of her mouth and the sweet taste of wine that still lingered on her lips.

Then he did the thing that he had to do. He abruptly

leaped up, reaching for his wallet. "You're beautiful, Michelle. A very special woman! I've loved my time with you. But I really have to go." He called to the bartender and paid for his drinks and hers.

"Can I see you again?" Confused, she touched his arm.

"Sorry. I'm so sorry," he mumbled to her softly. Then he hurried out, as deeply ashamed of himself as he had ever been. A man should keep control of his emotions at all times. He should control his actions. Most importantly, a gentleman does not disrespect a woman. And he'd just disrespected two.

Unable to go home yet and look Mary in the eye, he ducked into another pub for another drink. Perhaps another one—his fourth—would dull his sense of shame.

A light rain was falling by the time he finally stumbled to his car, leaving the second pub. When he had trouble fitting the key into the lock of his new Ford Escort, something told him he should call a mate to pick him up; he wasn't good to drive. No way could he call Mary and give her an addition to her ever-growing list of all the ways he'd failed her. But Sadeq would come; he'd been known to have one pint too many on occasion, although Salem never did.

But home was just so close, a short two blocks away—hardly any distance. Salem decided he was fine. With the evening rush completed, there was barely any traffic on the road. He'd just take it very slowly; he would be okay.

And he would have been correct—if home had been just a little closer. But after he made his final turn, he must have dozed off behind the wheel before he was awakened by the blaring of a horn. He startled awake to find his car sailing toward another, and he slammed on the brakes just in time to avoid a crash. Both cars remained at rest in the silence of the night, the other driver surely just as stunned as Salem by the sudden miss. In the other car, a woman glared at Salem, shouting things at him that he couldn't hear.

Then he looked in the back seat of her car, and he saw a little girl strapped into the back. The child's mouth was opened in a scream, as if she still saw Salem's car flying toward her own. Perhaps she would always see that image. Perhaps this would be the nightmare that would wake up this weeping girl, even in her teens.

But what if it had been worse? What if he had woken

up two seconds later than he had? His heart seized up at the thought.

Then the woman drove away.

Afraid to drive even the short distance remaining to his house. Salem pulled his car to the side of the road. Then, with his heart in his throat, he walked back to his home and family, who were waiting for a different man—a better man—than the one stumbling home to them.

In the weeks that followed, he immersed himself in prayer and in the study of the holy book. He vowed to be the best husband he could be. If Mary told him she was tired, he would rub her shoulders to ease the tension that she felt. If she came home late from who-knew-where, he would not describe the tantrum that she'd missed from Sara, who had failed another test. He'd offer instead to make her a sandwich, and he would listen quietly as she told him about a speaker who had enlightened her on the damage being done by the male patriarchy or the latest atrocities, perhaps, in Northern Ireland.

As they made their way to bed, he'd kiss his wife and thank her for the deep compassion she had always had for the world around her. It was, after all, a thing he loved about her. When she talked about these things, it was the only time he saw the spark from their first days together.

The first time that he'd thanked her, she had looked up at him, surprised. Then she kissed him with a passion he hadn't felt from her in years. "That means a lot to me," she said. "Thank you so much, Salem, for saying that to me."

I see you now, my love, he thought. *At least, I'm trying hard to see you.*

A point of conflict between the two continued to be their handling of Jamal, who now barely spoke to Salem. The boy was furious that his guitar remained locked up in a closet.

"It's not that I'm intent on taking away this thing that is supposedly his passion," Salem said to Mary. "It's just that to get it back, he needs to show respect and take responsibility for finishing his homework and his chores. Is that so much to ask?"

"But he's not like Maryam, who's meant to take the higher math and all the honors courses." As they talked in their bedroom, Mary was being very careful to speak quietly. "Maryam's our academic. She'll go far, our girl, if the world doesn't try to stop her with its gender biases." She paused to think. "You know, Salem, when I go to these rallies, I'm not abandoning our children. When I raise money or awareness for the cause of women, that's for our daughters' futures. I do that for them."

He pulled her close and kissed her. "I understand that, Mary. We love them in different ways is all." Of course, Salem didn't want his daughters to have doors shut in their faces because of their sex. But to even hope to be successful in the working world, Sara would have to make the grades to graduate from high school. Didn't Mary understand they had to tackle first things first?

Mary snuggled against his chest and looked up at Salem. "And another thing. Although I know it's what you want, I'm not sure Jamal is meant for university. Music is the thing that he is good at. That might turn out to be how he makes his way. Or maybe there are scholarships for music programs at the college level. I know the odds aren't good for making decent good money with a band. But he could teach or something."

"Music is a hobby. A man must support a family and

contribute to the world."

"He should do the things he loves." Mary grew quiet at that point; the old sadness filled her eyes. "I didn't get to do that, and I want things to be different when it comes to Jamal. Ignoring the thing that calls to you is no way to live."

Salem sighed. He might have won the battle for her to stay home with the children, but she would not let him forget that hadn't been her wish. But had he really held her back from what she was meant to do? Weren't there rallies, meetings, protests, and the like in the middle of the day when the children were in school? Would there not be jobs waiting for her to jump into when they had the children safely launched into the world?

It was a subject, he supposed, on which they'd always disagree. But for now, there was peace.

"And another thing," she said. "I think Jamal and Sara notice the way you've always been so close to Maryam. If you could throw a little extra encouragement their way, that might mean a lot."

He started to protest, but she held up a hand. "Ask him

something about music. When Sara talks about her friends, ask her questions, Salem. They need that from their father." A shadow crossed her eye. "Take it from the girl who missed out on all of that."

Salem only nodded. She was around them more. Perhaps she had a point.

On Saturday afternoon, she packed them a picnic and told him to be ready a little after six. "It's a surprise," she said. He smiled, glad to have a break from the problems in the house along with a chance to get away with her.

Hand in hand, with Salem carrying the basket, they walked to Bay Bridge Park, where the trees seemed to be decorated with a million twinkling lights that were reflected in the lake. Long before they got there, Salem could hear strains of music. *A local band,* he thought, his spirits lifting. He could smell roasted chicken in the picnic basket along with something sweet.

After the delicious meal, which ended with slices of his favorite chocolate cake, they rested against a tree, his arms wrapped around her, as they enjoyed the songs. It was a mix of music by the Beatles, Queen, Elton John, and others Salem liked.

"The band is excellent," he said.

Mary cut off the tiniest bite of cake and held it to Salem's lips. She grinned. "A piece of cake for a dance?"

"You have a deal." He smiled.

They danced to fast songs and mellow, slow ones until most people had gone home and the band announced the final song. They swayed together, barely moving, as the band played "Tiny Dancer."

"Thank you for this, Mary," he whispered, his lips close to her ear. "I think I really needed a night like this with you."

The next morning, some of the songs were still playing in his head as he flipped through the paper after breakfast. With the kids all shut up in their rooms, he looked up at Mary. "We should do that again real soon. We should look for other places that band might be playing. We'll be groupies, you and I."

She put down the dish that she was washing and came to sit beside him. "I miss dancing with you, Salem. That used to be our thing."

He nodded and put down the paper to put his arm around her.

She rested her head against his shoulder. "You know, last night at the park, they made a difference for us: four guys with four guitars. They made us happy, Salem. Do you see what I'm saying here?"

He knew where this was going. "I suppose you mean Jamal." Had Mary really wanted a night out with her husband? Or had the whole evening been about Jamal—a way to make a point? He sighed.

"All I mean is that a man doesn't have to go to some boring office to make a contribution to the world. There are other ways." She kissed his hand. "Let's let Jamal find his."

He looked down at his wife, who still looked a little sleepy from dancing until after midnight—and who looked even prettier than on the day he met her. Wasn't she, in fact, doing the very thing that he wanted most from her? This was Mary's way of fighting for her son.

He leaned down to kiss her. "Yes, there are other ways.

Will you dance with me next weekend?”

She giggled like a girl. “I would love to, sir.”

“If I give him the guitar, will you back me up on homework? And on chores?”

She smiled at him gratefully. “I can do that, Salem.”

Salem leaned his head back against the couch. If that son of his could just wipe the scowl off of his face, he might one day play some tunes at a little park and restore a bit of romance to an exhausted couple’s life. Mary had a point. One could do worse in life.

With that decision made, Jamal was less combative, although chores were still an issue. Salem learned to love the sound of music coming from his son’s room as the holidays approached. Around them, the world sparkled with Christmas lights and was dressed up in bows.

At that point, his and Mary’s focus turned to Maryam, who had broken up with Luke and was nearly inconsolable. He was gratified to see her turn to prayer and to reading the Quran, which seemed to calm her somewhat.

Excellent, thought Salem. That would serve her well when troubles came into her life. Allah would provide.

But still, the sobs coming from his daughter's room nearly broke his heart.

And then came a letter from his daughter's school that left Salem reeling. The school was recommending that they seek psychiatric help for his Maryam, who, according to the note, was causing a great deal of "disruption" in the classroom.

"We have noted in your daughter a stubborn insistence in her efforts to spread nonsense as the truth," the note went on to say. Maryam, claimed the administrator, was being "insubordinate" and "argumentative."

Salem stared down at the paper. "She is nothing of the sort!" he said to Mary. "I don't understand."

"Let's let her explain. She must have some idea of what this is all about." Mary knocked on her daughter's door and told her to come out to the kitchen.

Maryam sunk down at the table and lay her head in her arms when she heard about the note. "It's my stupid teacher who doesn't understand. How can she call it nonsense when it's about a subject that is very sacred to me and lots of others? I 'd say that Mrs. Bulgher is the one who needs to show respect."

"What happened, Maryam?" Salem sat down next to her.

"We had to write a poem. About a Christmas tree. And she said that mine was wrong."

A chill ran through Salem. "You wrote about the palm."

"The palm that nurtured Mary before the child was born on Christmas Day! So how it is that a palm is not a Christmas Tree? Mrs. Bulgher said to change it, and when I tried to explain, she said that I was spreading 'untruths' to the class. She called me blasphemous when I tried to tell her what it says right there in the Quran. And when I refused to change it, she gave me an F."

Salem was shaking at the news. Salem couldn't speak.

Mary stood up from the table, a fire burning in her eyes. "Well, I'll have a few 'truths' to tell that teacher about religious freedom and respecting differences," she said. She put her arms around her daughter. "This won't be tolerated, Maryam. We will make this right."

"I think perhaps it's best she not go back to that school." Salem took a deep breath. "It's bad enough she has a class with that clown of a teacher. But it's even worse that the administration would decide to back the foolish teacher up. I want her home with us. I don't want my daughter to step foot again into that hateful place. Maryam's a senior. She can study here, finish with a tutor."

Ugly words ran through his head. *Untruths. Called me crazy. Spreading nonsense as the truth.*

He'd had enough of England. Perhaps the time had come to return to Yemen. Although they'd never seen it, Salem's native country ran though his children's blood. He could let its beauty shape them as they grew into young adults in the midst of his big family.

He needed to be there, with his parents and his siblings and his cousins underneath the watchful palms. He'd run from his country's violence. But somehow it was the palms who made him feel safest.

Chapter Ten

Chill of Winter, Dreams of Home

As the Christmas lights came down throughout the neighborhood and in the stores downtown, a darkness settled on the household. The surprise snow of Christmas week began to melt; the pristine whites of lawns turned into dirty sludge. As the silver lights of Christmas slowly disappeared from the rooftops and the windows, so did the fragile light that mattered most to Salem: any remaining spark of joy had long since disappeared from his oldest daughter's eyes.

She was progressing well with her studies at the house under Mary's supervision, but once the work was over, she just sat around or slept. She didn't want to pray or go with Salem to the mosque. She had no interest anymore in helping at The Rose and Palm. Her dad had tried to lure her in to sample the new dishes that Sadeq had added to the menu to welcome the new year. "You're so quick with your studies that you have time to come in and help, and you know I love it better when there's family there," he said. He had tried to tempt her with a description of the spicy beef and potato soup that they now served with a salsa of peppers, garlic, and spices. But nothing seemed to make her smile.

Finally, one day, tired of seeing her staring into space, he sat down and pulled her close to him. "Talk to me, Maryam."

She was quiet for a while, then she answered in a small voice that he could barely hear. "Why should I even bother? When the whole world seems to be telling me just to go away? 'You're no good, no good, no good. We don't want you here.' Okay! I get the message." She buried her face in her hands.

"Don't say that, Maryam. You're amazing, brilliant—my perfect, special girl." He pulled her closer, stroked her hair. "Don't you know how much I love you? You, Jamal, and Sara are everything to me."

"That's what Luke used to tell me: 'You're

everything; you're perfect.' But he changed his mind, I guess." A look that was almost haunted filled her eyes.

Salem understood that teenage love could be all-consuming. He knew it could intoxicate, and then in the end, it could cut you to the core.

"Luke said that every day." Tears spilled from her eyes. "He was so . . . important to me, Dad. And when we were together, I kind of loved *me* more. Does that even make sense?" She blushed. "Now it seems so stupid, but I felt like I was pretty. I felt, well. . . I felt *adored*." He could see the memories rushing back into her mind, and a softness filled her eyes. She put both thumbs to her eyes to stem the tide of tears. "But dad, I was so stupid! Because it was all a lie."

"It was not a lie!" he said into her ear. But all he could do was hold her. A teenage girl, he knew, would not listen to her father about a thing like that. Not when her first great love — whose opinion was all-powerful — had kicked her to the curb.

Salem was furious at this foolish boy, and he was absolutely powerless to change the way that

Maryam was feeling.

"Come back with me to the mosque," he told her gently. "Don't you think that will help?"

"I've been reading the Quran. And that does help—a little." She looked up to meet his eye. "But for just a little while, Dad, I've had enough of people. I gave myself to Luke. Not in the way he wanted. But I told him things I'd never told another soul. For the first time in my life, I let someone *see me*. Not the fake me but the real me. It felt amazing to be *seen*—really, really seen—and loved." A darkness moved across her face. "But I wasn't loved! Not really. I showed someone my *me*. And he said 'No thanks.' He looked and walked away." Tears streamed down her face.

"*I* see you," said Salem. But it didn't matter in that moment. Because Salem wasn't Luke.

"And then I was so proud, Dad, of the poem I wrote for class! I worked so hard to make it perfect. My poems are me as well. And so my teacher saw me too—the part that's really, really me. And those words she used: nonsense and disturbing. According to my school, the real me was so wrong and awful they had to write to you and Mom!"

Salem took deep breaths to keep his emotions in control. "But you and I know better. Sometimes, more than you would think, it's the grown-ups who are wrong, and that's what happened at your school. Your poem was brilliant, honey." He rubbed her arm in comfort. "You and I and all Muslims know that what you wrote is divine truth. And I loved how you wrote it." He smiled and kissed her forehead. "You have a way with words, and you made your father proud. And their pastors and their religious leaders would also tell them that their holiday—their Christmas—is not a day for hate."

"I just feel so rejected all around!"

He held onto his daughter tightly. "Maryam, you are loved." He wished he could get her out of there and whisk her away to Yemen, where she might feel a kinship with the people in his village. They would build her spirits up and love her, unlike those in Birmingham who'd been so careless with her feelings.

Mary, he'd decided, could also use a change,

although she was doing better, much to his relief. Her depression had lessened somewhat; the house was more picked up. And she interacted more these days with all three of the children. She and Sara seemed to be especially close, and he often found them giggling over stories from their day.

But more than once since Christmas, Salem had awakened to hear his wife weeping in the night. Some hurts, he guessed, were just too deep to ever go away. In addition to the wounds of growing up as an unwanted child, she seemed to carry on her shoulders all the troubles of the world, as if they were hers to fix. Perhaps that was the legacy of those who'd gone unloved as children. Perhaps they were the ones who couldn't look away from all the hurting faces on the evening news.

He'd hoped his love could bring a sense of wholeness to her life, but there was an emptiness in Mary that Salem couldn't fill. And somehow he knew that if she could walk beneath the palms, she could feel the peace of the many generations those trees had stood watch over.

Oh, those trees had witnessed bloodshed — heartrending tragedies. But through everything, the palms had persevered; they'd stood tall and strong. To him, they were a testament that there were things that lasted. Families should last, although the idea of family seemed more fragile here in England. Bill and his wife had separated just the year before, and divorce, it seemed to Salem, was getting more widespread.

His family, too, felt broken—not bonded as a unit like the family he'd grown up in. Sara and Jamal treated Salem like a stranger, despite all the efforts that he made to be part of their lives. He'd bring them little treats in foil from The Rose and Palm, and he made a point to ask about their days. But he felt an aloofness from his youngest children that left him mystified and hurt.

Reunited with his guitar, Jamal now practiced several nights a week with a group of friends who'd formed a band and got together in one family's garage. But even with his music, Jamal's anger at the world had only grown, and that anger often seemed to be aimed at Salem.

Mary smiled at Salem ruefully one day when he complained about the treatment he'd been getting from his son. He'd lingered with her in the kitchen after dinner, helping her clean up. As soon as the meal was over, Sara and Jamal had quickly disappeared into their rooms. Maryam had offered to stay and do the dishes, but Mary had insisted that her daughter go to her room and rest. Maryam had developed headaches, and that night she was feeling bad.

Salem was glad to have some time with Mary to talk over his frustrations with Jamal.

"They're teenagers, my love," she said. "What are you going to do? Teenagers argue with adults, and they've been doing that since the world was young."

"But they're family," said Salem. "Shouldn't that mean something? It doesn't feel like family with Sara and Jamal. Well, with you they're different. But they treat me like a stranger—who they wish would go away."

She kissed him on the cheek. "I do hate the way they treat you, and I'll talk to them both some more about respect—and the sacrifices that you make." She reached for another dish to dry. "From what I understand, once they hit their twenties, there aren't so many battles. I'm sure that they'll be fine. Deep down, they're good kids, Salem."

"As long as we stay here, I'm not sure it will be fine." Salem's worry for his family had hit an all-time high. His voice suddenly grew urgent. "It's time I return to Yemen, that we go there as a family. Let's plan to go this summer, once school is out for Sara and Jamal." From his brother recently, he had understood that his father wasn't well. And that brought a new worry: what if he returned too late to see his father? Plus, it had always been their plan that Salem would take his father's place one day overseeing the palm groves.

Mary sighed as she dried the last of the dishes. "We've been over this and over this, and you know how I feel. Birmingham is all that the kids have ever known. Except for Maryam, they don't even speak the language, nor do I. What you're proposing, Salem, would be traumatic for our children. Talk about a battle. You know a move like that would bring a battle on for sure."

"They're so lucky, Mary, these children that we've raised. Of course, they've had their hurts, but compared to the lives of others, they don't know a thing about *traumatic.*" As he wiped down the counter, he thought back on the losses he'd known as a boy —and his frantic flight to England in his early twenties. "The three of them have no idea how fortunate they are." Blood revenge and wailing in the night, a beloved sister gone—what did they know of that?

Even as he said that, Salem's heart still broke for Maryam. The slightest thing—a song, a scene in a romantic movie—could bring a round of sobs. And Salem wished that he could somehow take the pain on her behalf.

England had been good to him. It had brought him Mary, and it had offered him protection when his life was on the line. But he'd never meant to stay. This was not where he belonged.

As gently as he could, he told her the news. It had suddenly become very clear to him what he had to do. "I've decided, Mary. The time has come for us to go."

He understood that this was England, where such things were decided by a wife as well. In the case of most decisions, he had come to understand that the British had it right. From that first night at the pub, he had loved her for her mind as much as for her beauty. And a woman's mind was meant to be respected, and her voice should be given weight.

But there were also times when a man had to insist on doing what was best, and such a time had come. None of them were happy here, and Salem couldn't stand to see them suffer so! "We'll tell the kids next week, and this summer we will go. I'll let my father know that we have plans in place."

"Excuse me, Salem. *What?*" Mary stared at him. "Plans aren't in place at all, despite what you might think. Because it seems that you forgot a step in making this 'decision' And that would be the part where you discuss it with your wife."

He reached for her hand. "It will all be for the best. Trust me, love. You'll see!" He was sure that Yemen would work its magic on his wife. The Romans used to call it *Arabia Felix*— "Happy Arabia." The mountains and the smell of the Red Sea would soon soothe the troubled hearts of all of them, and they'd be home at last. How Salem longed for home!

She pulled her hand away. "And when exactly did *your wife* agree to this upheaval in everybody's lives? Did I okay this in my sleep? Or did you, all on your own, just decide on my behalf?" In her eyes, he saw a fury he'd never seen before. "I can't believe you, Salem. You have absolutely no right! I thought you understood by now that this is not the way it's done."

He felt numb inside, understanding how hard things would be at home until they made the move and she finally understood that his decision had been right. He'd have to steel himself against her wrath. But a man had to do the right thing to take care of his family. Even when the right thing might be very hard.

He put his arms around her. "I'll always do what's best to take care of all of us." He'd take care of her. Wasn't that the thing she'd longed for as a child and that she longed for still?

She stepped away and glared. "Salem, I am not a child, and I'll take care of myself, thank you very much. And what I will not do is uproot my children to a country where they have never been. Where they can't speak the language! What are you even thinking?"

"Mary, it is home."

"For one of us, it's home. You're thinking of yourself. You're being selfish, Salem. I can't believe you'd even dream of deciding something that's this big without consulting me."

A furor engulfed Salem. It had been decided! "I'm thinking of *my children!* Do you think they're happy here?"

"I think they'll be just fine. And is it even safe there? What about those people? Who were so intent on hurting you that you had to run? You want to take our children *there?*"

Salem clenched his fists, trying to contain his anger. Why could his wife not trust him to do what was best for them? As the man, it was his role to make decisions for his family. It was his sacred duty as decreed by Allah, and for generations, it had been a way that had stood the test of time.

But the traditions of the West sometimes made it hard for a husband and a father to see to his family's needs. A woman should be honored and respected, but a man should have control. And Salem was a *good* man. Of course, he wasn't perfect, but in every single instance, he had put his family's needs before his own. So why couldn't Mary see the light and embrace him as a leader? She could see with her own eyes that he always led with love.

And now even Salem's father was against his plan to return. Not that he'd tell Mary, but Salem's father also thought that Yemen wasn't safe for Salem's family — yet. He'd insisted that they stay. But if his father wasn't well, it was Salem's duty as a son to return and help. So many reasons to go back!

"It was always in my plans to return to Yemen." He tried to keep his voice calm, so they could discuss, not fight.

"Always in *your plans?* Did you not understand that there would be other people uprooted by these *plans* you seem to want to force on all of us?"

Force. What kind of word was that to describe a loving family man who worked hard every day for his wife and children? Such utter disrespect.

He clenched his fists again. "After all I do for you? How can you even dare to talk to me that way?"

She stared. "Is it really all that shocking—that I would dare to even dream that my opinion counts?"

His heart was pounding now. "Of course you have always counted! Of course I thought of you when I decided that . . ."

"That's the problem, Salem. *You* do not decide." Her voice exuded calmness, but Salem was incensed.

"Enough!" His voice rang out through the kitchen. He moved closer to her, almost close enough to touch, so that she would understand. Never in their marriage had he raised his voice to Mary. But he couldn't help it now. He grabbed her arm, insistent. "It's decided now. We go!" Then he took a deep breath. *A man should at all times keep control of his emotions.* He spoke in a calmer voice. "It is decided, Mary. Do you understand?"

It took a moment before he understood that she was looking past him toward the kitchen door. He turned to see Sara and Jamal at the entrance to the kitchen. Salem was devastated to see his daughter shaking. A sense of shame rushed through him as he took his hand from Mary's arm.

"Mom, are you okay?" Sara spoke in a hushed voice, as if she were afraid that Salem—her own father—might lay a hand on her if she dared to speak. He should not have raised his voice, but what had Salem ever done that would make his daughter fear him?

"Honey, we're just fine," Mary said in her most soothing mother voice. "Your father and I were just having a... discussion. But I think we're all done."

Jamal glared at Salem and wrapped a protective arm around his sister's shoulder. "It sounded like a fight." He looked at his mother. "Are you sure that you're okay? I heard part of what you said. What was it he was trying to force us all to do?"

Salem's heart would not be still. "Jamal, you've got it wrong. You don't understand."

Jamal's eyes held Salem in an angry stare. "Don't you lay a hand on her! Don't you dare hurt my mother."

How had it come to this?

Mary went to Jamal and lay her hand against his cheek. "You know your father wouldn't do that. Sometimes parents disagree, and this wasn't our best night. But it's fine, Jamal. I promise."

Sara was weeping now, and Mary wrapped her arms around her. "Everything is good," she told her softly as she stroked her hair. "Shall I get us both some ice cream, and we'll watch some TV?"

Sara sniffed and nodded.

With one final glare at Salem, Jamal left the room.

Salem sunk down into a kitchen chair, his head in his hands, and blinked away a tear, but the frustration and the shame were things he couldn't blink away.

Chapter Eleven

A pall fell over all of them in the days that followed. Sara seemed to be afraid of Salem, and Jamal was very watchful when it came to his father, as if Mary and his sisters needed his protection against Salem.

Salem suggested any number of activities they could do as a family: movies, game nights, walks. But Jamal and Sara were having none of that, while Maryam tried to intervene on her dad's behalf. Once, Salem had listened in at a closed bedroom door as the sisters talked.

"Of course he wouldn't hurt us," Maryam insisted. "So what if he shouted? Don't you get tired sometimes and say things that you shouldn't? He's a great dad and you know it!"

He felt two things at once. His sense of shame was deep. A man should control his temper! But he was angry too. The whole thing had come about because of his insistence on doing something good to improve their lives.

More and more, he found himself working late to avoid as long as possible the bad feelings in the house. It didn't feel like home; maybe Yemen would. But he had come to fear that if he made the move, his wife might refuse to follow and try to keep the children here.

After that night in the kitchen, neither he nor Mary had said a word about the move. But she didn't look at him the same way now, and she never touched him. Her words were polite, as if he were a stranger and not a beloved husband.

One night as they sat on the couch, he reached for her hand. "Do you still love me, Mary? Or is that part of our life just gone?"

She sighed. "Oh, *love*. What does that word even mean? I'm too tired to know. I've been so tired for so long."

"You don't know if you love me? Has it really come to that?"
She paused before she spoke. "I love the man I built a life with—when we decided things *together*. Because he loved my mind. So Salem, you tell me. Is he still here, that man? Or have we lost something big?"

"More than anything, I love you."

"Or is what you love instead your *vision* of our life together? And the future that *you* planned? I won't follow you to Yemen. If you'd cared to ask, I would have told you that I have my reasons—important reasons, Salem—that I need to stay right here. But you didn't ask me, Salem. You didn't even ask."

Yemen. It was home. But it could not be home if Mary wasn't there. "Tell me now," he told her in a quiet voice. He put her hand to his lips. "Tell me what it is that holds you to this place." He'd never really tried to delve into deep discussions about the things that kept her busy. He'd ask her where she'd been when she came in late. But those questions were always thrown at her in anger, not out of any interest in her life. They were aimed at where she *wasn't* and not at where she was.

She leaned toward him eagerly. "We're making some real progress on the environmental issues. With new initiatives whose impact could be huge! People need to pay attention now—before it gets too late. And I've found a group of new friends from Northern Ireland. They feel like my people, Salem, because of where they're from. And we talk into the night about the Troubles there. I don't know how to fight it, the horror in my country, but somehow, we must. We have to fight it, Salem! It just hurts my heart."

An unease filled his chest. "Are they IRA?" he asked.

She shook her head. "Oh, no. Not that!" she murmured. "Well, maybe some of them. Some of them might have gone to meetings, but you have to understand that I'm not about the violence. I just want what's right—what's fair for *all* the people. Is that too much to ask? And it's not just the IRA when it comes to violence. It's on both sides, you know. I've heard stories, Salem . . . Oh, I just can't stand it, the stories that I hear . . ."

"Be careful, Mary. Please." Salem didn't like this. "In seventy-four! Those bombs. I don't think anyone who lives here will forget that day."

"They talk about that some. Not that anyone I know was in on a thing like that. But it's not just the IRA who cares about the cause. Peaceful people, Salem, are working for a change—or hoping one will come. We *need* a change to come. And Salem, here's the thing: there was supposed to be a call, a warning on that night so civilians wouldn't die. That never was the plan."

"But they did die, Mary."

"And so do Catholics! The things the British soldiers do, what goes on in Northern Ireland—

you would not believe."

"It's not a kind world, Mary." Salem closed his eyes. Catholics die, he thought, because of their religion, and couples die because they just need to have a night out, a few laughs at the pub. Innocents in Yemen die as vengeance for acts they played no part in. Would hate win every time? Sometimes he feared it would.

The atmosphere at home seemed very close to hate whenever Salem and his son were in a room together. And in Sara, he sensed fear whenever he was near, as if he were a monster in his daughter's eyes. That broke his heart most of all. He longed to be a father to his children.

Mary tried to reassure him. "It will just take time. But they sense the tension, Salem. Next time, take a walk — do anything but yell."

The idea of a move to Yemen was put aside for now, adding to his angst.

While Maryam seemed to be doing better, immersing herself in her at-home studies, Sara and Jamal were responding in disturbing ways to the tension in the home. Mary had overheard some conversations that made her suspect that Sara had tried some illegal drugs — which ones she wasn't sure. Every day she checked her daughter's drawers and the pockets of her clothes when Sara was at school. At night, she checked her backpack.

One night, Salem and the girls were home alone while Mary was out at a meeting and Jamal practiced with his band. With the girls in bed, Salem watched the clock. 11:10. 11:22. Then it was past well past midnight. There was still no Mary — not so unusual these days. But also no Jamal. His curfew on a school night was nine.

Salem couldn't sit still. He walked from the window to the phone, wondering what to do. No way was his son still at practice. No parents would allow music in their home this late. Now Salem questioned where his son had really gone on those other nights when he said he was with his band.

Mary came in at twelve thirty and let out a deep sigh when she was told about her missing son. "Twelve thirty! On a school night! What is that boy thinking?" she cried out. "He will be the death of me." She sank down on the couch.

"Should we call the hospitals? The police? Or the parents of his friends?" asked Salem. "I was just about to pick up the phone when you walked in the door."

"Let's wait just a bit. My guess is that he's just out somewhere with his friends. Up to no good, no doubt. But I imagine that he's fine."

So Salem sat with her and waited, and not ten minutes later, they heard footsteps and a key in the door.

Salem leaped up to confront him. "Where have you been?" he yelled. Then he felt Mary's hand on his; he understood that was her signal to take it down a notch. Salem breathed in deeply, knowing it was vital to stay calm—always calm.

Jamal mumbled his reply with his back to Salem as he headed to his room. "Just out with Seth and Michael. No need to have a fit."

"Don't you walk away from me. You get back here. Now!"

Jamal wheeled around. "I was just out. Okay?" He stared at Salem with defiance.

As he got closer, Salem smelled beer on his son's breath. "Did you drink and drive?" he asked.

Jamal rolled his eyes. "Well, I suppose I didn't fly in on a magic puff of air. So, yeah. I guess I did."

"Jamal! What in the world?" Mary walked closer to her son. "We've had this conversation when we gave you back your guitar. And we chose to trust you. Were we wrong?"

The boy looked down at the floor, ashamed. "Mama, I'm so sorry. I won't do it again."

"You're grounded through next weekend," Mary told him. "And then after that, I'll talk it over with your father, and we'll decide what's next."

"Where were you tonight?" demanded Salem.

Jamal's answer was a glare.

"You've disappointed us," Mary told her son. "What were you even thinking?

"I promise, Mom!" He told her earnestly. "I won't do it again." Then he glanced at Salem. "It's enough that he mistreats you. I've seen him when you argue—all up in your face. Your *son* won't disrespect you. You won't get that from me."

Mary put her hand on Salem's arm against the rush of fury that was building up inside him. "This is not about your father. And you're disrespecting *him*—which I will not allow. Do you understand me?" In her voice, he heard a quiet fury.

Jamal nodded, but just barely.

"Now, you go on to bed," she said, and they

watched their son disappear into his room.

All out of words, Mary glanced at Salem then embraced him before heading off to bed herself.

Salem stayed up late that night, just trying to breathe steady and calm his beating heart enough to fall asleep.

The next weeks were filled with quiet—and not the peaceful kind. It was an empty silence that formed the background now of their time at home. Gone also was the music from Jamal's guitar. The instrument was locked up in a closet now, where it would likely stay.

On one late night—a Saturday—Salem was sitting on the couch, staring at the TV screen but not really watching. It was after 2 a.m. and nothing good was on, but he couldn't fall asleep. Might as well stay up. After a long week at the restaurant, he'd wanted to go out and see a film. But he and Mary didn't dare be away from home too late. Jamal might well attempt to sneak out past his curfew. He was allowed to go out now on weekends but had to be home by ten and let them know where he was. And he was now allowed to practice with his band.

Sara, too, was on restriction. She'd been caught at school smoking in the restroom, and then two days before, Mary had found a bag of clothes stashed in Sara's backpack. Apparently, their daughter had formed a new routine. She would leave the house, it seemed, in a modest outfit and then change into a short skirt and a low-cut, too-tight blouse.

She had rolled her eyes when confronted by her mother. "Is this about what Dad wants? No one's dad but mine just goes on and on and on about *dressing modestly,*" she said. "It like he wants us to be covered up from head to toe."

"Well, neither of us thinks that *this* outfit that you've chosen is okay." Mary held up the bag. "I don't know where it came from, and I'm shocked they didn't send you home from school if they saw you wearing this."

"The boys all seemed to like it."

"I bet they did," said Mary, frowning at her daughter.

Sara smiled. "I got compliments all day. "

"I'd best see some remorse for what you did, young lady," Salem told her firmly. "There will be no more of this. Your backpack will be checked each day before you leave the house."

"Dad! I'm not a baby!"

"Then don't give us reasons not to trust you," replied Mary as they watched their daughter flouncing down the hall.

Now, as he sat up of late, Salem flipped the channel from some fishing program to a show about detectives. "All that's on is trash," he grumbled to himself. Then he flipped again. Every station now seemed to be on commercials.

On the screen, a girl with long and lustrous hair talked about her new shampoo. Her sparkly, very tiny dress showed off her long legs as she ran toward a boy. Her date leaned in to kiss her as she winked at the camera. It was no wonder, Salem thought, that Sara thought short skirts could work a kind of magic. The TVs and the magazines taught her it was so. He sighed and shut his eyes against the offending picture. Toxic media! Perhaps that should be another cause for Mary.

He picked up the paper and glanced at a story that he tried to read three times. But he was distracted by some noises down the hall. Was Mary also up at that late hour? Or perhaps one of the children? He headed down the hall and heard some whispers and some shuffling behind the door to Sara's room.

He was about to knock and ask if all was well when he heard a deeper voice, a male. She must be talking to Jamal. Mostly likely whispering about how unfair their parents were with their restrictions.

Then he heard giggling and more shuffling, and he heard Sara whisper, "Shhh. You never know about my dad. He's always up and watching."

Salem moved a little closer.

"I should go," the male voice said, "before I get in trouble. But come here one more time." More shuffling. A sigh. "That's really, really good," the young man said to Sara in a murmur.

A long silence followed that, and Salem froze, incensed.

"You make it hard to leave," the boy said to Sara softly. Salem couldn't hear his next words because of Sara's giggles.

Salem rapped furiously on the door. "Who is in there with you, Sara? You both come out right now."

A silence filled the hallway.

When they didn't answer, Salem opened up the door. Sara and her paramour were trying desperately to open up a window to allow him to escape. They turned and stared at Salem, both of them wide-eyed and afraid. Sara's hair was mussed. and the top buttons of her blouse were undone.

Salem could barely breathe. He grabbed the arm of the young man. "I demand to know your name."

"Dad, please don't," Sara pleaded quietly.

"Scott . . . Scott Evans. Sir." The boy's face was a dark red.

"You are not to see or speak to Sara. Ever. Not at school, not at the mall, not at her games. Do you understand me?"

"Yes, sir. Sorry, sir."

"*Sorry* doesn't cut it" He prepared to begin a lecture on women and respect, but that wasn't Salem's job. That was a job for other parents— who'd obviously failed to instill a proper set of morals in their son. "Just go," he told the boy.

The boy scrambled toward the front door, exchanging looks with Sara.

Salem stared at her, his heart beating wildly. "Do you have no respect at all for yourself, young lady? I cannot believe my daughter would allow her body to be used in such a way."

"Dad, just stop! Okay? You embarrassed me with Scott! You treat me like a child."

"You do not behave this way! It's not proper! It's not right! This is not okay. This will not happen in my house again. Do you understand me, Sara?" Had Mary not talked to their girls about saying no and boundaries, about having self-respect?

He noticed Maryam and Mary now, standing in the hall.

Sara noticed too. "You know," she said to Salem, "it's *my* body. It's *my* life. You need to cool it, Dad."

"I need to . . .?" In one awful moment, he felt his hand being lifted toward his daughter. He quickly pulled it back, but Sara gasped and moved away.

Salem took a deep breath to regain control. "I'm your father, Sara. And while you're in my house, at least, I get to make the rules. And I will not have you bring dishonor to our home."

"Well, maybe I should leave!" she said, tears forming in her eyes. "You think I'm not a grown-up? You think I don't understand how to take precautions when I spend time with a boy? I might be a whole lot smarter than you give me credit for."

"What precautions do you mean?" He couldn't even think about things going any further than an unbuttoned blouse and whispers in the night.

"The pill! I mean the pill! Everybody takes it. Welcome to the eighties."

Now, he was afraid his heart might thump out of his chest. "Not in my house, they don't!" he boomed.

The outburst brought Jamal, who flew out of his room. He held Salem in a stare that seemed to say, I'm watching. Don't you hurt my sister?

Ridiculous! thought Salem. As if he'd hurt his baby girl. Now, Sara on the other hand—*she* had hurt *his* heart. He leaned against the wall, trying just to breathe, as one by one, his children crept back into their rooms.

"The pill?" he said to Mary. "How would she get the pill? She would need a parent's . . ." Then he gazed at his wife, who was staring at the floor.

"She came to me last year, and I thought about it, Salem, and I took her to the doctor. I made the best decision for our daughter that I could."

His heart was racing harder. "The best decision, Mary? And why would you think that? Just because she asked? What about purity? And values? Were those not the things that we agreed we'd teach in our home?"

"I've had long talks with Sara about self-respect and boys, but I can't watch her every second, and neither can you, Salem. I don't like her attitude, her ways, and I'll talk to her again—and ground her on the weekends. I will demand of Sara that she respect us and her home. But I did what I had to do to protect our daughter and her future."

"Behind my back, you did it," he said as he stormed off.

He was mad enough that he slept on the couch that night; he couldn't look at Mary.

With a pouting Sara home now every night, not allowed to go out with her friends, it was Jamal who was often absent from the dinner table. He would come home after curfew, marching in, defiant, as if he were daring Salem to ask him where he'd been.

"Where does that boy *go?*" Salem asked one night as he and Mary lay curled up in their bed. It was at that point in the night when sleep was very close, but bits of memory and worry still bubbled to the service to escape in murmurs between a husband and a wife. Salem had come to rely on Mary for information on his son. Jamal talked to her, while he'd only glare at Salem.

He was still out that night when his parents went to bed — past curfew once again.

"I'm worried," Mary said. "He tells me he's just out with the other guys he plays with in the band. But I'm worried that he's lying."

"I wouldn't be surprised."

"Until recently, I thought things were okay," she said, "even though I'd rather that he not stays out so late."

Salem's sense of apprehension sharpened. It seemed as if Mary's mother-radar had picked up on something new.

She turned over on her side, facing Salem. "I thought that we were right to pick our battles and let him go out with his friends. I thought that might somehow help him with the anger that's eating him alive. I thought that it would help — getting back into his music, talking to his friends. I do think we were right to give back the guitar."

"You coddle him too much."

"But I think he's lying to me. Because here's what happened, Salem: Last week, he went to 'practice,' but when I went into his room to leave some things on his bed, I found his guitar still there. So, did he quit the band? I don't even know. And why would he do that, Salem? His music was the only thing that brought him any joy."

Salem sat up straight in bed. He could feel the blood rushing to his face. "If we don't know who he's with, if he's lying to us, Mary, some things will have to change. He must be made to come home now directly after school. Why was I not told this when the problem first arose?"

His voice rose to a high pitch, and Mary placed a hand firmly on his arm. "Let's talk about this calmly and not wake the girls up with your shouting. Salem, please! Be calm."

"Don't you shush me, Mary! I am not the problem here!" He would *not* lower his voice to a pitch that suited Mary; she was not in charge of that. Each day he made a living dealing with a thousand details at The Rose and Palm while he trusted her to manage things at home. And now he discovers this.

"I do think there's an issue that we have to deal with. We're in agreement, Salem." She twisted her long hair away from her neck in the heat of the room. "And so I'll tell you what I did. I talked to Sara, Salem, who didn't want to say a lot. Because, of course, no kid is eager to go squealing on her brother. But the thing is that I think Sara's worried too. She did say that Jamal was hanging with some kids who aren't good news at all."

"So are we agreed? That we make Jamal stay at home except for school? Until something changes with him and he tells us the truth about who he's with and what he does."

She sighed. "*That* will be a battle, but I think you're right; it's for the best now that I've caught him in a lie. I was not naïve enough to think he was not involved in the normal teenage trouble. Oh, you know what I mean—a few beers with his mates. But I thought he and I were good, that I could trust Jamal not to look me in the eye and lie." She brushed her hair from her eyes. "Oh Salem, I'm so worried. He is just so angry—angry all the time. Where did we go wrong with that little boy who used to be so sweet? Do you think he'll be okay?"

"Mary, I don't know. But what I know for sure is that he needs a firmer hand. By his age, I had my work, I had a wife, I had responsibilities. There was none of this teenage nonsense, *glaring* at my parents, eating meals in silence. He gets away with too much, and, Mary, it stops now. It is well past time he learns to be a man." And it was time for Salem to take more of a role in that.

The next day it was Mary who told Jamal the news about his new restrictions and the reasons why. But, of course, it was Salem who received the brunt of his son's anger. When Salem tried to tell the boy about what kinds of new behaviors would be expected of him, Jamal had lashed out. "Who are you to tell me how to be a man?" he had yelled at Salem. "You're more of a bully than a father. Do you think that bullying's the way to be a man? To yell in people's faces like I've seen you do with Mom and Sara?"

"Jamal, that's enough." Mary tried to run interference. "Your father's a good man, and someday you'll understand all he's done for us."

Jamal moved closer to his father. "Only Maryam, your favorite, is free from the wrath of Salem. And Ahmed and Omer! Lucky, lucky them with a great big ocean between the two of them and you."

A silence filled the room. Even Jamal seemed to know that he had gone too far.

This time it was Mary who was in Jamal's face. "You apologize right now to your father! What a hateful thing to say. You have no idea, Jamal, about the reasons that your father had to leave his country—and the things that he endured."

Jamal appeared to think about it, watching Salem with a mixture of wariness and perhaps regret. Then he simply walked away.

Salem could not stop shaking as Mary wrapped her arms around him. Such ungratefulness! Such hatred in his own house—and from Salem's *son*. But the darkness that engulfed him now was focused on his own behavior. His role as a father was his most important work. Had he failed miserably?

He'd bought a good life for his children through hard work, sweat, and aggravation. In opening his business, he'd modeled for his children the things that were important: ambition, diligence, and self-reliance too. He'd tried to show them how to make their own way in the world. And he'd come around to the idea of Jamal and his music, with the help of Mary—who'd been right all along. Salem had not been afraid of bending, to allow for dreams that might be different from his own.

But had he been too harsh? He hated to remember the times that he had yelled. But always, within minutes, he had tamed the storms within him until he could speak more softly. And was that not, after all, the real mark of a man, who was only human? To recognize the darkness in himself and turn the thing around, to gain control?

"Am I a good man, Mary?" It was what he wanted most.

She held him even tighter. "You love your children, Salem. There are fathers in the world who don't even care. But you *love* them, Salem, and that's the greatest gift." They sat for a moment in the silence while Jamal's words and Mary's echoed in his head.

"Hey, I know it isn't easy." Mary spoke soothingly to Salem. "It's been hard with Sara too. Sara is our rebel, which she gets from me, I guess. But she has the privilege, Salem, of walking through the world as someone who is treasured by her father. Because of you, our girls know without a doubt that they have value in the world, and that is major; that is huge. Jamal is our challenge now, but we'll make it through. We will!"

Peace. That was the thing he craved. He immersed himself in prayer and spent more time at the mosque, where the very atmosphere could soothe him. He drew comfort from the cadence of the voices of the older men as they discussed the hope found in the holy book. O You who believe! Enter absolutely into peace.

Some of the older men became like fathers to him.

So many things that Salem longed to talk over with his dad! Families were never meant to be separated by vast oceans, even time zones. He sometimes felt as if his loved ones were living out their lives in another world. It was a lonely feeling to look up at the setting sun and understand that darkness had already settled over Yemen. He thought often of his sons there. In letters, Yasmine had assured him that they were doing well, but Salem longed to see them and be sure. It was important to him to look into their eyes and see that there was no darkness there to match the torment that was brewing in Jamal.

While there was comfort at the mosque, there was no peace at home.

Jamal began to sneak out, and it was often Salem who had to deal with that. More and more, it seemed, Mary was absent from the home. She'd sweep in close to bedtime, livid over some atrocity somewhere that *must* be fixed. Right now!

Sometimes he and Mary would sit alone at night, each one lost in his or her own fears. His were focused on the home and hers on the world outside it. Sometimes on those nights, he'd have to work to tamp down his irritation toward her. Her energy should go instead to teaching Sara to set boundaries when it came to boys. She should be talking with Jamal about his attitude, his future.

Salem would admit that he'd lost any influence over his youngest son, but Mary still could reach him—if she'd just take the time.

There were other times when he could easily let his anger go. He'd reach out for her hand, and each would take some comfort in the other—although the things they grieved for didn't touch.

One night his eyes were heavy as he and Maryam and Mary watched the evening news. *Way past time for bed,* he thought. Tomorrow was a big day with new menu items being rolled out and a full list of reservations—with a waiting list to boot.

Jamal had snuck out (again), but Salem wouldn't wait up as he had on other nights, which made it hard for him to function at his peak at work. The Rose and Palm would *not* suffer once again because of Jamal's selfish disregard of his parents and their rules. Salem had decided!

He had just brushed his teeth and was reaching for the lamp switch when the shrill ringing of the phone sounded through the house. He looked at the clock: half past eleven. This could not be good. *Jamal.*

Warily, he picked up the receiver as his heart thumped in his chest. "Hello?"

An official voice boomed out. "West Midlands Police."

Jamal and two other boys had robbed a liquor store, it seemed. One of the others had a gun, which had not gone off, at least, but they would not be given bail because of the involvement of a weapon. Salem was assured his son would not be housed with adult offenders but would be held at a youth center until a hearing could be set before a magistrate.

Feelings of sorrow for his son warred with Salem's rage. Jamal had lived a privileged life with everything he needed to succeed. And this is what he does?

Salem held onto Mary tightly as she wept. More than anything, he wished that he could just let go and weep along with her. But he'd be strong for Mary; there would be more long nights of sorrow to get through after this. Of that, he was very sure.

Chapter Twelve

Empty Places at the Table

In the daylight hours, he held his emotions in. For Mary, he could do that; Mary seemed so fragile in the days that followed the disturbing call. Since Jamal had been arrested, her eyes were either blank or swimming in her tears. So he'd make time to hold her or to heat some soup for the four of them to eat on those nights that he came home to find his wife catatonic on the couch.

And so the nighttime hours became his time to mourn and drink. While the others in the household slept, he needed that relief to try to ease the shouts that reverberated in his mind. *Tell me why!* the voices yelled. *No!* They burned through his insides.

He feared his son was lost to him—irretrievably—and the utter loss of Jamal left a gaping hole in a long and vital chain. From his father, Salem had been given a way of being in the world. It was fairly simple, although often hard to do: respect yourself and others, do the right thing, and take care of those you love, who have been entrusted to you.

Through many generations, his family had continued to stay strong as this essential wisdom was passed from man to man to man . . . until it stopped with Jamal? After all that Salem had accomplished—his flight to England, the building of a business to support his two families—he had blown it in the end. He had crashed and burned in his attempt to carry out one of the most solemn duties a man has to the world.

A son. The careful grooming of a son was a man's gift to the future.

And Ahmed and Omar! How were they doing really? The four thousand miles between them left Salem feeling helpless. In his current state, he felt the distance even more. He *had* to get to Yemen, but with a son behind bars here in England, that seemed near impossible.

Mary barely even seemed to have the energy for her beloved causes, although there were still some scattered nights that she would disappear. Salem was too tired now to even try to question where she went. *Let her go,* he thought. Fighting for a better world was her attempt at coping, just as a glass of whiskey had become the way for Salem (and then another glass and then a third when the first two failed to obliviate the world). He should stop; he knew it. But he couldn't take away the one thing in his life that, on the nights that he was lucky, gave him a few minutes— just a precious few—of sweet relief.

In addition to seeking comfort in her sporadic outings and her friends, Mary, much like Salem, looked for solace in a bottle. As he had before, Salem would come home to find half-empty glasses and open bottles of her favorite red wine scattered throughout the bedroom and the kitchen.

Several times a week, he knew that Mary went to see Jamal, who had requested that she come alone. Salem hated the idea of Mary in that place, and she didn't say a lot when she returned. "He's okay—I think," was all that she would offer. It seemed to break something in her to have to see him there.

Through some patrons at the restaurant, Salem had found and secured the services of a local barrister, who let the family know what they might expect in the coming weeks. Jacob Adams strongly felt that with a guilty plea, Jamal might, if he was lucky, avoid a prison sentence once he got his day in court. He had not held the weapon and could make the argument that he didn't know about the plan to rob the liquor store when he set out with his friends. Adams would also remind the court this was Jamal's first offense.

Two things could happen next, Salem explained to Mary after his meeting with the barrister. Jamal could be released under the Crown's conditions. Service to the community might be one requirement, the barrister had said. Stricter supervision in the home might be required as well.

"But we must be prepared as well for the worst scenario: that they won't go easy on him, that he'll spend some time in prison," Salem said to Mary.

The barrister was pushing for the hearing to come quickly, and he felt hopeful that It would.

Meanwhile in the home, Sara took advantage of the fact that her parents were distracted, and she was often out with friends until nearly time for bed. When Salem would occasionally pull his thoughts away from Jamal, locked up in *that place,* he would look around frantically for Sara. He could not lose Sara too.

"Where is she?" he'd ask.

Maryam would jump in with attempts to soothe his worries. Sara was just fine, Maryam would say. She had so many friends, so many invitations, and she was involved in so many things: cheerleading, clubs, and planning groups for discos at the school.

"Who are these friends?" boomed Salem. "Is Sara out with boys?"

"I don't know, Dad. I don't know." Maryam backed away. "Why are you yelling at me?"

Friends! The wrong set of friends had been the downfall

of Jamal. They should meet Sara's friends. Better yet, they should just keep Sara here at home, except of course for school. He thought about that awful night with Sara and the boy. No way could they trust their youngest daughter to be honest about where she really was—or who she was really with.

"Except for school, she's home, and that is that," he said one Saturday to Mary after Sara had snuck in close to one a.m. Even worse than that, the girl had seemed drunk or high as she stumbled to her room.

"Did you see that, Mary?" Salem asked, alarm bells clanging in his mind. "She'll end up like her brother. She has no respect at all for us and our rules. Absolutely no respect!" After they'd discovered the boy in Sara's room, she had been kept at home on weekends for the next five weeks. Now, her curfew was at ten—and nine o'clock on school nights. But her curfew was a thing that often went ignored.

"Let's talk about it when we're calm." Mary laid a gentle hand on Salem's arm. "She's out of hand. She is. We need to watch her closely. I need to talk to Sara. I've fallen down on that because I'm just so sick about Jamal. But let's don't take it too far with her now, my love. If we take away her friends . . . well, I think she *needs* her friends. She's hurting for Jamal the same way that we are."

The next day they made a plan. Sara would be

grounded for the next two weekends in response to the missed curfews. After that, she had to let her parents know where she was at all times.

"If you say you're at a friend's house, we want the parents' number," Salem told his daughter. He and Mary had summoned her to sit with them at the kitchen table so they could lay out the new rules. "And if you say you're at cheerleading, we might drive by the school to make sure that's correct."

Sara's face turned red. "*What?* Dad! This is insane. It's like I'm two years old." She flew up from her seat, tears forming in her eyes.

Mary tried to ease the tension. "Oh, Sara, don't you see? We *want* you to be with friends and do all the things you love. But we need to know you're not out doing things that could hurt you—or your future."

"Sara, sit down, please," said Salem, who longed to make things work—with *this* child at least.

"I will *not* sit down! So now, in your all-knowing ways, you've put yourself in charge of *when I sit and when I stand?*" She slammed her chair hard against the table.

"I'm your father, Sara." He kept his voice calm but strong. "This is my house and your mother's. We get to make the rules."

"Well, then, maybe I should leave." She brushed a long blonde strand of hair off her shoulder, staring at him in defiance.

Salem felt a chill. She could really leave; she might. He watched his youngest daughter as she stared him down. Belying the fury that engulfed her, she was delicate and small, and she was a beauty too. There were so many dangers for a girl like her.

"Of course you shouldn't leave," Mary told her calmly. "Where would you even go? We're not saying don't go out. We're not saying don't have fun." She paused. "But your father and I fear you're not making good decisions about the way you spend your time."

"Like what do you mean exactly?" she asked sarcastically. "A boy in my room? Oh no! Boys have been with girls since . . . when? Since Adam and Eve, maybe? I am only doing what kids have done forever. What a stupid reason to lock me in my room! Plus, how would you even know, Mom? It's not like you're ever here."

Salem bristled at her words toward Mary.

"And it's more than just the boys." Mary continued calmly with her explanation. "Last night you were drunk or high. I'm not sure what's going on, but you could get addicted, and that is not a thing any parent should ignore. With drugs, you lose control, and all kinds of things could happen." A fear crossed Mary's eyes. "I've asked you this before, and I'll ask again. Have you been taking drugs?"

Sara strode across the room to pick up a glass that still bore the red stains of Mary's wine. She gave her parents a hard stare. "Drunk or high? My goodness. Did you say that was bad? But I don't understand!" She put the glass in front of Mary. "Oh, wait! I think I get it. It's just bad when I do it—but somehow it's okay for the two of you to sit home and get wasted every day."

Mary's face turned white. "Sara, we're not perfect. But it's *our* life. We're adults."

"Wake up, Mom. So am I! Or have you failed to notice?"

 "When I was your age," answered Mary, "I thought the same thing too. I thought I was all grown! But, you see, the thing about it is that . . . "

"That it's okay for Dad to drown himself in gin and for you to drink all day?" The emotions on her face seemed to be at war: fury versus heartbreak over what their life had become. "How early in the morning, Mom, do you start getting blasted?"

It was Salem's turn to leap up from his chair and yell. "How do you even *dare* say that to your mother? Sara, I'm appalled." He moved closer to his daughter. "Do you have any clue how much your mother has been hurt, how much it kills your mother, what's happened with Jamal? And this is how you treat the woman who loves the three of you *more than her own life?*"

He cut his eyes to Mary; tears were streaming down her face.

Still, Mary tried to take control. "Sara, please believe me. If we didn't care, we'd just ignore your curfew and let you do your thing. But we can't do that, Sara!" The tears fell harder now. "Because you're way too precious to us! Don't you see that, Sara?"

Some of the fight now seemed to have drained out of their daughter. "Oh, Mom." Sara watched the floor, speaking in a voice they could barely hear. "I should not have said those things." Then her voice returned—almost—to its normal tone. "The rules are stupid—rules for babies, which I'm not." Then she whispered softly, "But that thing that I just said? I hate what I just said. I never should have said it."

Mary's eyes were red and splotchy. "All I've ever wanted was for the three of you to have, well, to have *everything.* I know that I'm away more than you might like. And I'm sure that there are times when it would be beneficial for your mom to pay attention more, to be more present in the home. But it's for you and Maryam that I do what I do. It's *your* faces that I see when I get up in some bigot's face to try to make the world a little fairer for those of us born as women." Her eyes went to the wine glass. "And some of the things that I do—some parts of my life—aren't things that make me proud. They aren't the things I want for the three of you."

The thing that hurt Salem most was the way that Mary was trying to be strong, even as her immense love for Sara was being met with stubborn hate.

After Sara, quiet and abashed, had disappeared into her room, Mary gathered three wine glasses from the counters and rinsed them in the sink. Then she moved into the den to find another. She glanced up at her husband with new tears threatening in her eyes. "Stupid alcohol. I hate that I'm so weak."

He put his arm around and pulled her to the couch, where he held her in his lap as tightly as he could. "With all the ugliness she was spewing out at you, you answered her with love—when I was about to lose it." That kind of love amazed him. Despite the way his family's world had been rocked to its core, his children had the comfort of that kind of mother love. He leaned in to gently kiss her. "You were strong—so strong in a way I couldn't be, and I thank you for that, Mary."

And so the new rules were decided, and Sara fell in line, at least in the next few weeks. But the confrontation with their daughter had brought Mary even lower, and Salem was distracted as Jamal's date for court grew near. Sara began to come in a little later and then later still. And there were times that neither he nor Mary even glanced up at the clock when they heard their daughter's keys jingling at the door.

Sometimes he'd hear Maryam taking on the role of pseudo-parent. "I'm watching you," he overheard her say to Sara once. "Let me see your backpack, or I'll tell. And I'd better not be finding any drugs."

"You sound like Mom," said Sara.

"And don't think that I don't know there are other places to stash that stuff away."

Keep her safe, said Salem in a silent plea to Maryam. It just seemed too hard for him or Mary to reach their youngest daughter.

Throughout that year of struggle, Maryam stepped up in other ways as well. Since she was quick with her studies, she had time to cook and shop. Some nights, Salem came in tired from work to find that Maryam had prepared some of his favorite foods from Yemen. She used techniques and recipes she'd picked up from Sadeq, and she really proved to have a talent in the kitchen.

Those meals were a bright spot in a bad time for Salem. The smells and tastes of home—cardamom, ginger, chili peppers—warmed and comforted him. He hoped he did the same for his beloved expat patrons at The Rose and Palm, where he had always felt that food was more than a simple meal. It was part of a place they missed— just a tiny part—covered up in honey, mixed with lentils, or served up in a fragrant stew.

Then came a major day in the family's life.

It was the day they welcomed back a very sullen, unrepentant son after his day in court. He had been fined and released on restrictions, including limited activities as well as closer supervision in the home.

Once again, the mood in the house was changed. Often, the three children would talk late into the night. But Jamal had hardly anything at all to say to Salem. There was no *I'm sorry* and no word of thanks for the hiring of the barrister who had seen to his release.

Salem found it shocking that the boy would walk around disgruntled. As if it were somehow *Salem's* fault that a buddy of Jamal's had held a gun to some man's head, landing all the teens in jail.

But Salem held his tongue, hoping that a little time might start to ease the tension that had cast a deeper pall on the family home. He was tired of fighting now; what he wanted was his son.

But he had little hope that he would get him back. Even in those first days, Jamal was making plans to move in with a friend; the friend's parents had okayed it. As soon as the Crown lifted its restrictions, Salem knew Jamal would be gone from his house.

As proved to be the case.

And then, unexpectedly, there was another empty place at the family table, another empty bed.

Events were set in motion on a day that had been all wrong from the start. There were complications at the restaurant almost from the time they opened up the doors. Orders were mixed up. Reservations had been lost. Two waiters called in sick, meaning that some diners experienced long waits, despite the fact that Salem pitched in as he could to help with tables.

When he came home at last, exhausted, he was greeted right away with the sound of yelling coming from the kitchen. He hurried toward the confrontation and found Mary nose to nose with Sara, both of them close to tears.

"What on earth?" asked Salem.

"Well, the *dictator of my life* has now decreed I have no life at all." Sara stared at Mary. "And what she's doing is unfair, Dad! It is so unfair! Why should I have to stay here—in this sad, sad house—and miss the disco I've been looking forward to for months? The disco I helped plan?"

Salem looked to Mary, who held out her hand to show eight or nine colored pills. "She's been taking Ecstasy, which can really do some damage. This is bad stuff, Salem. I found it in her room."

"Where you had no right to be! Why don't fix your own life?" Sara asked, indignant. "You mope around all day and drink with nothing else to do but snoop in my belongings, and then you give me hell if take a stupid pill."

Salem stared, incensed.

"It's a hallucinogenic," Mary told him, looking shaken. "It can be addictive, raise her heart rate, and, of course, these little pills are nowhere close to legal. As if we haven't had enough law breaking in this house." Then she turned to Sara. "Do you even have a clue how many problems this can cause?"

Sara fixed her eyes on Mary in a derisive stare. "Do I *look* addicted, Mom? And my heart is beating fine, just like it always has, thank you very much. And now if you'll excuse me, I'm going to Danielle's to pick our dresses for the dance."

"Did you not hear your mother?" Salem grabbed her arm. "There is to be no disco. Not tonight for you—or anytime real soon." How dare she speak like that to Mary? How dare she put herself in danger with a bunch of stupid pills?

"Get your hands off me!" she yelled, jerking her arm away from Salem.

Salem tried to catch his breath. He tried to calm his nerves.

"Get to your room, young lady," Mary said to Sara. "We'll talk some more tomorrow."

"Oh, go pour yourself a drink. By the time you're on your third glass, you won't remember that I'm gone. And by number four, you'll be saying *Sara who?* You'll forget you have a daughter!"

Tears filled Mary's eyes as she gazed at her daughter.

"Not another word!" roared Salem. "You ungrateful little . . ." He was too furious to finish. Speaking of heart rates, his was off the charts.

Mary sank down in a chair and began to weep.

Salem grabbed his daughter's arm. "Apologize," he screamed. "You'll apologize this instant!"

In his daughter's eyes, defiance was replaced by fear. "Dad, I said, don't touch me."

"You apologize!" he roared.

Then he felt another presence. it was Maryam; her hand was resting gently on his shoulder. Her eyes were wide with fear.

"Let's leave this for now, okay?" She looked at him pleadingly. Then she turned to her sister. "And I will see that Sara stays in her room tonight." It seemed to be half question and half statement, directed at a shaking Sara—who nodded gratefully and headed to her room.

The next day brought authorities to inquire if the family was okay. It seemed that a neighbor had grown concerned for Mary and the children after overhearing angry shouting in the house the night before. While she could not make out Salem's words, his fury could be heard across the little garden that separated the two homes. The woman, Mrs. Pinsky, thought she heard a female voice yelling something like, *Don't touch me.* The woman reported she was shaking when she turned out the lights, and in the morning upon waking, she knew she had to call.

Salem felt humiliated, but at the same time, he was certain that almost any man would have lost his cool. Such horrific insults directed at his wife—by her own daughter nonetheless!

Calmly, he and Mary went over with the man the sequence of events that had happened in the kitchen:

who said what and when.

The officer was sympathetic. "Ecstasy is causing all kinds of issues here—and all over, really." He gave Mary a small nod. "It's good that you were aware, ma'am, and stepped in to intervene." Then he turned to Salem. "And the drugs could be responsible for the kind of tone that she took with your wife. It does affect their moods. I know how hard it must have been to hear that, bloody hard to hear."

After that, he spent some time alone with Sara, and he recommended she be taken from the home and put into a residential program to help her understand the dangers of illegal drugs.

Salem and Mary readily agreed, hoping that their daughter would come back whole and healthy.

With both Jamal and Sara gone, the house felt way too quiet. To Salem, both of their goodbyes had smacked of failure—his own failure as a parent.

He threw himself into his job, often staying late, and he and Maryam spent more time at the mosque.

Mary also coped with the changing household by spending time away, doing her Mary kinds of things. She'd come back energized, filled with news and righteous fury. A new bill had passed! Changes on the way! An opinion piece was now set to be published in the *Guardian* very soon.

"Oh! And you won't believe who I ran into, Salem," she told him one evening, setting down her papers. "It was your old friend Marouf."

"You don't say. How is he?" He hadn't thought of him in years.

She gave him a shrug. "There wasn't that much time for us to really talk. But he seemed to be okay. And he looked just the same. I would have known him anywhere."

A vague sense of unease passed through Salem. As he'd grown more mature and looked back on his life, he wondered what he'd ever seen in a man like that—who had never been a true friend or a man of character. But back in those first days in Birmingham, Salem had been lonely, and Marouf was company. He'd been a diversion if not a soul mate or a friend. Plus, it had been Marouf who'd taken Salem out on the night that he met Mary. So he owed the man a lot. And perhaps Marouf had changed with time. Salem wished him well.

And then came the night that Mary wasn't home when Salem went to bed. Not so unusual as to cause him any worry. But when he awoke the next day, she was nowhere to be found. Had there been a rally or a meeting that had gone on all night with the participants all hyped up to a fever pitch? He supposed that it could happen. But he worried still.

The next night? Still no Mary.

He came home from work that evening to find a stillness in the house. He exchanged worried glances with Maryam, who shook her head, meaning that there still had been no sign of her mother.

Then Salem grabbed the phone.

"It's an emergency. Yes, please. We need you to come quickly."

Chapter Thirteen

Gone!

Ten, twenty . . . forty minutes passed. Salem punched his fist against his hand. Was this their foolish version of rushing to a scene where time was of the essence? There was also anger directed toward himself. He should have called this morning or checked in during the day to see if she was home.

If someone had snatched Mary, they could be getting further from the city as each new hour passed. And if she were laying hurt in some ditch or underbrush, she needed them to hurry, to come *now*. Salem couldn't breathe.

Then, finally, he heard a rapping at the door, and two uniformed men introduced themselves and entered. The officers and Maryam huddled on the couch while Salem paced the room.

"And she was last seen when?" The youngest officer took out a notebook and a pen. His eyes were curious, alert.

"I saw her yesterday at breakfast." Salem ran his hand roughly through his hair. He pictured Mary at the stove, scooping eggs onto three plates, keeping one eye on the bacon. "And then there was last night. She didn't make it home, and it just kept getting late, but Mary had her groups, her meetings, she did a lot of things.'

An older, bearded man kept his eye on Salem. "And that did not alarm you? That your wife did not come home?" He had introduced himself as Robert Davies.

"Well, it did, of course. It was not a thing she does, and, I have to tell you that I didn't sleep at all." He paced over to the window, his hands shoved into his pockets. "But you don't think the worst at first. It could have been a lot of things! Well, you understand—a meeting running late, so she stayed over with a friend. And some of these things she goes to, well, they can get intense. And I just thought, you know, that some of them might have started talking and talked into the night. She's had late nights before. So I tried to tell myself that surely she was fine."

Foolishly, he glanced out the window, hoping he might see her car pulling in the drive.

"What kind of meetings?" Davies asked.

With both hands on the couch, Salem leaned in and took a breath. *Stay calm, stay calm, stay calm.* But Mary was the calm one; it was only Mary who could settle

Salem's nerves. And Mary wasn't here.

"Oh, all sorts of things," he said. "Women's rights, relief for the impoverished—especially the children. Oh, and there's the stuff that's been going on in Northern Ireland, which is the home of Mary's people. The treatment of the Catholics—my Mary's all about fixing that as well."

A steely look creased the forehead of the bearded man. "The IRA!" A statement, not a question.

"Well, no. Not exactly. She just thinks there should be changes —fair treatment, all of that. She sees some injustice there—and everywhere, in fact."

"And tell us what you know of her plans for the day on the day she disappeared. That would be yesterday?" The younger officer looked from Salem to his daughter, his pen poised and ready.

"Ah, not so much, in fact." Salem sighed, frustrated with his helpful lack of information. He'd been over this with Maryam while they'd waited for the knock. "She didn't really tell us what was on tap for the day. We all talked some at breakfast, but that morning, we were rushed. There were so many causes that she jumped in to assist with, so many meetings and so on." He moved back to the window, restless. "And then there was the marketing. I think she went on Wednesdays, but she'd mentioned craving chicken—a nice roasted chicken, I think, is what she said—so it might have been that she was planning to, you know . . ." He let his thoughts trail off. Why had he not listened? They used to talk so much; he should really listen more.

Davies stared at Salem, watchful, as if Salem were the hunted and not some desperate, hurting husband begging him to find his wife.

But Salem didn't care. What Salem cared about was the lack of action, the absence of a plan. "So what's next?" he asked. He had really hoped that while one of them asked questions, the other would be busy getting something underway in the form of an investigation. "Perhaps while I talk to one of you and tell you what I know, someone could be searching? Putting out a bulletin?" *Please look for my wife.* "I have pulled some recent pictures." He took them from a table and stared down at his Mary, whose look seemed to signal that she was amused by something to the left of the camera' lens. It had been taken on a good day, when they'd been at the table playing cards with Maryam.

They were interrupted by loud static from a device that Davies carried. "Excuse me, please," he said as he left the room.

Salem's heart thumped harder. "News of Mary? *What? What did they say?*" he called.

But there was no reply. Instead, the younger man

continued with the interview. He asked about the places that Mary liked to frequent and any people that she regularly associated with.

While Salem was no help at all, Maryam proved to be a font of information. Mary and Maryam had, in fact, grown closer and indulged in some long talks since Maryam began to do her schooling in the home. Their daughter was, in fact, able to provide the names of some women who'd become her mother's friends. Maryam also knew about some projects on Mary's calendar that week, such as a meeting with her old boss at the council. They were set to brainstorm ways to help the large percentage of local children who could not afford school lunch. But was that yesterday or Friday? She wasn't sure just when.

Salem half listened to his daughter and half listened to the voices coming from the hall, where the other man was speaking into his radio. He heard Mary's name. And, very improbably, he could have sworn he heard the name of his old and not so fond acquaintance.

A coldness swept through Salem. Trouble always seemed to follow when he heard name Marouf. For his sister back in Yemen, the name had meant pure evil. The local version of the scoundrel seemed the milder sort. He was selfish and conniving, but could there be a darker side to the man as well? Why had Davies said his name? Surely Salem's old friend had not made Mary disappear!

The older officer returned. He shook off Salem's questions. "I ask, sir, and you talk. Do you understand?"

The man was harsh, thought Salem. He hoped his detecting skills were better than his skills with people and putting them at ease.

A few questions later, the two officers were heading to the door.

"What do you plan to do?" Salem followed them, frustrated. "What do you plan to do to find my wife?"

The younger officer shot him a sympathetic glance but was of no help whatsoever. "We will be in touch," was all that he would say.

Shocked and frightened, Salem's other children waited out the next two days at home with Salem and their sister. Sara got leave from her program to come home until the situation with her mother was resolved. Jamal as well wanted to be close to family.

Those days passed in a blur of lack of sleep, unanswered calls to the police, and trading theories back and forth, all of them unlikely, about Mary's whereabouts. With the help of Maryam, Salem had compiled a list of places where some of her recent meetings had possibly been held. He drove through their parking lots, looking for her car, and drove past the council offices as well. But there was no sign of Mary. He had called her sister, who said she hadn't heard from Mary for two years at least. "Please keep in touch," she told him, worried.

Too preoccupied to go to work, he left The Rose and Palm under the capable supervision of Elliott Booth, who had been his restaurant manager for the past three years.

Always close to tears, Sara seemed to cling to Maryam for comfort. Her battle with her father seemed to have been put on hold—for now. Once, as she was sobbing, he'd moved to the couch to sit quietly by her. Salem was unsure if his daughter would welcome an embrace from him, but he could at least be close, a signal he was there. Sara tearfully reached out for his hand, and her father took it, resting his head close to hers as both of them tried to cling to hope.

"Is it my fault?" Sara asked him in a small voice. "Did she leave because of me? Dad, I was so mean."

He kissed her on her forehead. "Don't you think that for a minute. She knew you loved her, Sara. Mothers always know."

Jamal, on the other hand, did not have much to say to Salem. His steely stare reminded Salem of the way the bearded officer had kept his gaze on him.

In the quiet of the house, Salem had a lot of time to think. He replayed in his mind his last talks with his wife, grasping for any hint about where she might have gone. But Mary's disappearance was inexplicable to him. Sure, she met a lot of people as she went about her days, but they were the kind of people who were out to *save* the world and not to do any harm.

Of course, he had told her often that the streets at night were no place for a woman who was out and about on her own. He'd remind her about muggers, roustabouts, and drunks who might tend to get violent and even carry knives. She'd be no match for them, but she had insisted. "I have to live my life."

"Walk with a friend at least," he'd begged, and she had promised that she'd try.

But there must have been something else that had swept into their lives and caused her to disappear. Salem was almost sure. If it had been a simple mugging, a quick rescue would have followed. Salem would have been awakened by a phone call in the night— a nurse, telling him to come.

He put his head in his hands. *Mary, where are you?*

Then on day three, there was a knock.

Maryam and Sara gasped and jumped up from their places on the couch. They were eager, naturally, for any news that might await them once the door was opened. But a sense of foreboding swept through Salem when he heard the rapping of someone at the door.

The sound of a knock could do that; it often sent a shock of fear through Salem, even on his best days. He thought of his mother's recollections of the nightmare that had ended with a brutal killing, the loss of her child. Years later, he might find her keening in her bedroom or the far corners of the palm grove as her grandchildren played together in the distance. When he would go to her, she'd whisper that she never saw it coming. She would grab his hand and tell him, "It started with a knock. I can hear it still—the knock."

Maryam ran to the door and admitted Davies, who scowled at Salem as he entered. He was accompanied on this round by a heavyset and balding man, who introduced himself as Alvin Whittington, another officer. The newcomer held out his hand to Maryam, nodding affably. Then he met Salem's eyes. "Just a few more questions, sir, if you don't mind."

"Is there any news?" asked Sara. "Please tell us you have news!"

"Where is my mother? *Where?*" Maryam was sobbing, and Salem went to her.

Whittington shook his head. "I'm so sorry, loves. We have not been able to determine your mother's whereabouts."

"May we sit?" asked Davies.

"Certainly," said Salem. "Absolutely. Be my guest."

Davies glanced around at the three teens, who were watching nervously. Then he turned to Salem. "I think this might be handled best in private—if you could ask your children to please rest in their rooms."

Salem's anxiety shot up. *What was this all about?* "If you think it's best." He glanced at Maryam, who steered Sara out with a gentle hand resting on her sister's shoulder.

Just Jamal remained. He stared at Salem in defiance. "I deserve to hear this," he said boldly. "I believe *her son* deserves to hear what's up."

"There's no news on your mother, son," Whittington cut in. "We just need a moment with your father, then we'll be on our way."

When they were alone, Davies leaned toward Salem. "What can you tell me, sir, about the status of your marriage?"

"I don't understand. What does that have to do with looking for my wife? Surely you don't—"

"I believe I asked a question," Davies interrupted, "and the sooner that you answer our inquiries, the sooner we'll move on."

A wave of sickness moved through Salem's stomach. For the lack of a better answer, try to pin in on the husband. Was that where this was going? Had they even looked for any evidence at all of what might have happened to his wife? His calls to ask about their progress had all gone unreturned.

Now, he cleared his throat. "What I can tell you, sir, is that I love Mary beyond measure, and that has always been the case."

"So you deny that there's been trouble? Between the two of you?"

Salem hesitated. "Well, any marriage has its troubles, as I'm sure you understand. Every couple has their share of things they don't agree on. Mary would have liked to have returned to work while I preferred her to be home—you know, until the kids are grown." He coughed, uncomfortable with the subject matter as well as with the accusing glare of the man across from him. "And while I admire her dedication to her many causes, I have told her I'd prefer she place a bigger focus on our family. But those are things we've worked out. As any couple does, we have learned to compromise."

What intrusive questions. But he would keep his cool. This was a man he needed; he needed him to find his wife.

"Did you ever threaten Mary or get physical with her?"

"I would never hit my wife! Of course I would never dream . . ." He stared at the other man. "Did someone tell you that I did?"

It was Whittington who answered. He gazed down at a paper in his hand. "In a previous incident report from this same address, it seems a neighbor called in to the station with reports of a loud fight."

Salem was exasperated! *This* was how they looked for Mary? He took a deep breath and began. "The 'loud fight' she reported was a situation with our youngest daughter, Sara, who's been having a rough year. My wife had just discovered some drugs in Sara's room. And what the neighbor heard was our attempt as parents to rein our daughter in, to say that under no circumstances would drugs be tolerated."

"I repeat," said Davies sternly, "did you hit your wife?"

Salem looked him in the eye. "And I repeat as well: I most certainly did not."

Whittington glanced down at the paper in his lap. "It says here that the neighbor overheard a female voice.

The female said, 'Don't touch me,' or something to that effect. And the female was distressed, according to the witness."

Salem looked down at the floor. "I will admit my anger got the best of me that day. I believe I scared my daughter. Of that, I am not proud. When Mary let me know of the abuse my daughter had inflicted on her body, I will admit my self-control slipped for just a moment. But only for a moment. And if there is anyone who's stated that I ever in my life hit my wife or daughter— or any other female—then you, sir, have heard a lie."

"Salem, is it accurate that you make a habit of screaming at your wife when you have these 'disagreements' that we have discussed?" Davies leaned forward with the question. "Is it true or false that you get in her face and yell? What is that about?"

Salem hesitated. "Well, I suppose I have. Again, not my proudest moment. But as a habit? No! It hardly ever happens. Very, very rare." He sighed, feeling sick at the turn this little talk had taken, swerving into his private life. "There have been some real rough years. But if you'd been in my house to watch, then you would have also seen great moments of support between me and my wife. It was of great importance to me to be of comfort to my wife—as she was to me. I can assure you, sir, this is a home built on love. Not a home filled with hate."

Something nagged at Salem. Where was this coming from? No one would have been in the house to see the arguments that had broken out between him and Mary. Unless . . .

"Have you talked to my children?"

"We'd love to talk with Maryam," Whittington replied. "We've talked to Sara at her school and we've spoken to Jamal already at his current residence."

Salem leaned back against the cushion, stunned at what he'd heard. Neither of his children had said a word about this; they'd kept their damning words a secret. The shock and despair seemed to well up in unshed tears that had been threatening for days. He thought he'd found a fragile kind of peace with Sara in the wake of their shared distress. And while there was no peace, of course, with Jamal, the two of them at least had been able to exist in the same space while they waited for some news. They'd felt more like a family then they'd been in quite a while. Surely Jamal and Sara couldn't think that Salem . . . He could hardly bear the thought.

"Your son and daughter both reported tension in the home," said Whittington in answer to the question he could see in Salem's eyes. "They both said you had a temper and that they on occasion worried for their mom."

Unbelievable, thought Salem. "Well, you've asked a lot of questions of both me and my children. And now I have one for you. And I will try to make this request of you with the utmost respect. Would you turn your focus *please* to the very urgent question of what happened to my wife? She has been gone for days, and I'm frankly terrified—to the point that I can't sleep—about what might have happened to her." He looked at them earnestly. "But one thing is for sure. She is not okay! If Mary were okay, she would be right here. She would have called at least."

"I can assure you," Davies said, "that these questions are absolutely aimed at discovering the answer to that question." Then he cleared his throat. "If I may continue, my next question is as follows: Are you now or have you ever been unfaithful in your marriage?"

"This is an outrage," Salem roared. Then he made an effort to keep himself in check. If he was indeed a suspect—which would be just absurd—a show of temper would only serve to bolster their case.

But Salem was incensed. "I am a man of honor, and respect for women is an aspect of my character in which I take great pride." Was this the way a man should be treated when he came to the government for help? Should he get that barrister that he'd found for Jamal to come over and advise him?

Faithfulness to Mary. He closed his eyes and took a breath. Of course, he had been tempted, but he had withstood the testing that had come his way. There are times a husband longs to be looked at by a woman in a certain way. And there are times a wife can only look upon her husband with patience and endurance. Then the two of them must wait for the passion to return. And he and Mary had indeed found their way back to each other. Not to the passion of the early days, but to a sweeter kind of love, seasoned with long years of holding on together when life had not been kind— when life had, in fact, become a tormenter of his soul.

And now, when fate had dealt the cruelest blow of all, he longed for Mary's hand as he waited for more news. He longed for her gentle touch upon his arm or shoulder when these fools of investigators dared to even question the kind of man he was. He longed for her arms wrapped around him tightly like she'd never let him go as he sobbed and cried out to Allah in the dead of the night.

Two days later, he decided that he'd return to work, partly to escape Jamal's accusatory stares, but mostly to escape the thoughts and questions that played out in his mind. Mary by that point had been gone almost a week, and he was terrified.

Elliott and Sadeq kept a worried eye on him all morning and throughout the afternoon. "Hey, we've got this, you know," his manager assured him, "if you need to take some time." His tousled hair and loosened tie were evidence that the lanky, long-armed Elliott had things on his mind.

Salem caught another pair of diners staring at him in a kind of fascination. That had been happening all day. Then they quickly looked away when they saw that he had noticed.

"I guess the word is out." He sighed and shook his head as he tried to concentrate on a stack of recent orders.

"The bloody, bloody paper! Sometimes I don't think they know the difference between a real news story and the stuff that you'd expect in some cheapo gossip rag." Elliott put a hand on Salem's shoulder. "We're all behind you, Salem. You're our guy."

Salem's heart began to pound. "What are they saying in the papers?" Surely the police would keep their suspicions to themselves. Unless they had enough to charge him—which of course, they didn't.

Elliott turned red. "You haven't seen the papers?"

Salem's chest went cold. "What do the papers say?"

Elliott watched the floor for a long time before he finally spoke. "Ah, man. I hate to have to tell you. You know, they always have to zero right in on the husband. Every single time! But in this case, Salem, all of us at

The Rose and Palm know there's just no way. If they'd just do their job and find a *real* suspect—or a theory even about Mary that made any kind of sense—it would make this silly nonsense go away."

"Do you have a paper?" His heart was beating faster.

His friend hesitated. "I have to tell you, man: I really wouldn't do it. You've already been through hell."

"Elliott, I asked you, do you have a paper?"

Elliott looked defeated. "Yeah, I've got today's. Let's head back to my office, and you can take a look."

Once they reached the small room in the back, Elliott handed him the paper. "I'll leave you alone, man. I'll be up front if you need me."

Salem stared down at the front page. Right there was his picture in the prime spot just above the fold, underneath a headline: *Still No Sign of Local Woman. Focus Turns to Husband.* The photo was a headshot that had appeared before on the occasion of awards for The Rose and Palm.

Dizzy, Salem scanned the story. He could barely take it in. One phrase jumped out at him and seemed to stab him in the heart: history of drunkenness and trolling local bars in search of women.

What was all this nonsense? Who would print such lies, and did they not know *his children* might pick up the foolish paper? What would his children think? He tried to calm his heart enough to read.

After the suspect's photo ran on the local news, witnesses have come forth.

Witnesses? What witnesses? He sunk down in the chair and forced himself to read. As he scanned the stories of the women who had spoken to police, pictures filled his head.

He saw the woman at the bar, her lips pressed gently into Salem's until he'd finally forced himself to leave.

"It got physical real quick," she had told the paper when they tracked her down. "There was a real connection, quite intense. He talked about his restaurant. He said nothing of a wife."

Worst of all, his mind moved to a scene that same night on a darkened road: two cars stopped at an angle while a child wailed in the back seat.

"I won't forget that man's face if I live to be a hundred. He could have killed my daughter. Clearly, he was drunk."

Salem dry heaved in the bathroom. He wanted to throw up, but he hadn't eaten anything since the night before, and then it was not a lot. Was he even safe here? Was innocence enough to keep him out of jail? He was not naïve enough to think that it was so.

Salem had to run! But how could he leave Birmingham? Who would look for Mary? Not the police, it seemed. They had their eyes too focused on the man who *hadn't* done it.

But he thought of his children, who might have lost their mother. If he were to be arrested, they'd lose their father too. He had to leave—for them. And they could be reunited when the time was right.

It would now be up to Jamal to keep the search up for his mother. Just as fiercely as the boy might hold a grudge against his father, he had always loved his mother with an equal fervor. If there were a trail to follow in the quest for Mary, Salem knew Jamal would go. And perhaps this would be the way his son would grow to be a man.

As Salem rushed past Elliott, he nodded his goodbye.

"You might think about a barrister," his friend said underneath his breath, "and I'd take care of that real soon."

"Thank you, Elliott. Thank you for everything." His friend had no idea this was a *last* goodbye—for a while, at least. But Salem knew this place would thrive with Elliott and Sadeq looking out for it.

At home, he found only Maryam. *Had she seen the paper?* A wave of shame rushed through him.

"The others. Where are they?" he asked.

Her face was white. "The paper, Dad. The paper." Trembling, she held on to a chair.

Salem took a deep breath. "You know I love your mother. Despite all my many faults, I've stayed true to my vows. You believe me, right?"

She ran to him. "How could you even ask?"

He took another breath for strength. "Maryam, we may not have much time. I'm thinking we should leave before they take me in for a thing I didn't do. Your sister has a place here, and your brother does as well." He reached for her hand. "But you'll come with me, Maryam?"

"Oh, yes. You should not be by yourself, Dad, and I agree that we should leave! But Dad, where we will go?"

The thought came to him unbidden.

Yemen. He'd go home.

But his thoughts were swirling. Life would be so different for his daughter if that was indeed the place they ran. *Home,* of course, had been in his plans all along, but he'd just had a harsh reminder of the way the world could treat a woman. Would Maryam be safe? He had no idea what kind of monster Mary had encountered here in Birmingham. But he knew that Yemen had dangers of its own.

For *one* fragile Maryam many years before, the toll had been severe. With his second precious Maryam, he'd have to take great care.

He gave her hand a squeeze. "Your grandparents and your brothers have been waiting for so long to meet you." He closed his eyes and squeezed her hand. "Maryam, we're going home."

Chapter Fourteen

Allah Watching

After the shock of the local headlines came more disturbing news. That same week, a patron of the restaurant called Salem with some confidential information, gleaned from his association with some highly placed officials. The info involved Mary—and Marouf.

Rather than being jobless now, Marouf was a government employee in the field of criminal investigations. He would often spend time in public places where terrorists and other criminals were thought to congregate. Unobtrusively, he would watch and listen. Then Marouf would provide authorities with names. Mary's name was one, according to the information Salem's friend obtained.

"I don't understand." Salem was confused. "On a list for what?"

"Marouf is saying that your wife is a likely member of the IRA, that she may have been involved in their activities—or at least had prior knowledge of what they were about to do," said the friend, whose name was Richard. After the bombing at the pubs, the violence in England had continued with other instances of terror.

Salem bristled. "That's untrue."

"As I understand it, this Marouf is all about filling out a suspect list." Salem's friend let out a sigh. "He has no care for the truth."

Although they hadn't told the press, some police officials had become convinced that Mary had left on her own in an attempt to run from the law.

"That makes sense!" said Salem. "If she's being hunted for a thing she would never dream of doing." He was filled with hot rage at Marouf—who had stood with him at his wedding!

The theory of Mary on the run took some of the focus off of Salem as a suspect, according to the things that Richard was now hearing. But still, Salem couldn't too be careful. Birmingham did not feel safe.

The next week was a flurry of travel arrangements and the packing up essential items.

Soon, he was strolling with his father in one of the family palm groves, breathing in the scent of the nearby water—and of home. Yemen at long last!

It seemed almost like a dream as he watched the laborers going through the old familiar motions of their work among the palms. Not that long ago, Salem had been ensconced in one life; now he was in another, thousands of miles away.

Some of the men were brothers, nephews, cousins. Some he didn't know, but their faces were familiar; they were the sons of men that he'd grown up with. Salem had come back to the place where he belonged.

But the father who walked beside him was not the man he'd left behind. In the years of Salem's absence, his father had grown frail.

Salem had to slow his pace to match the older man's. It just added to his pain to see the way his dad was careful of his footsteps. His father often stopped to grab onto a tree to support his weight while he caught his breath.

"Is he sick?" Salem had pulled his mom into a corner soon after he got home. "Please. Tell me the truth."

"It's just old age." She smiled wearily, touching Salem's face as if she were still astonished by the sight of him— her son! Right there in her kitchen after all these years. "All of us get older, and for Shaikh Naser, as you know, the years have not been kind."

Her face had changed as well with new wrinkles in her forehead, which was often creased with worry, as well as around her eyes, where they crinkled when she laughed. She seemed to laugh a lot still, he was glad to see. His mom was very playful with the grandchildren of his brothers, who often filled the house—many of them children he had never met.

Daughters-in-law were present too. So many of them scurrying through the halls and kitchen! They scrambled so his mother no longer had the work of the cleaning and cooking. She'd earned that place of honor, wearing her shimmering gray hair piled atop her head like a silver crown.

His dad, who walked beside him now, didn't seem as willing as his mom to let others do the work that he had done for years. "You have to leave," he said to Salem firmly. "I understand that England can no longer be your home, but there are dangers here as well."

While Salem had been away with troubles of his own, there had been no easing here in Yemen of the thirst for blood revenge. That meant danger always lurked in the streets and homes. With his nerves already frazzled, that reality had come close to breaking Salem; he needed to be home.

He'd known from family letters that dangers still existed, but he'd had no idea how bad the situation had become. Omar and Ahmed were settled now in Abu

Dhabi on the advice of their grandfather, as were many of the other men in Salem's family.

"I shall stay," said Salem, "and work here in the palm groves. Dad, you need your rest."

"You still have brothers here—the ones who refused to leave. Let them help me, son. You've been through enough." His father put a hand on Salem's back and gave him a tired smile. "I'm not useless yet! There is still much in me that can benefit our palms." He looked at Salem knowingly. "And here is what's important: Those who seek revenge against our clan will leave an old man alone. Now, a younger man like you might be a different story. That's why you have to go. You should go—for her." He glanced toward Maryam, who walked a little bit in front, out of hearing distance. "A young girl needs her father. In Abu Dhabi, you'll be safe. I can make arrangements for the two of you to settle there. And you'll be with your boys."

Her hair blowing in the breeze, Maryam held the hands of two little girls while a sea of children swarmed around her. The youngsters were all charmed by this new aunt and all her stories of the place called Birmingham that lay beyond the sea. Her studies of the language now served her very well, and she had little trouble talking to her extended family here in Yemen.

The first time that he'd proudly introduced her to his parents, Salem's mom had gasped, and tears came to her eyes. He should have prepared her, he supposed, for the startling resemblance to his sister. Now, his mother and his daughter had formed a special bond, often spending time just sitting quietly and talking.

Once, he'd caught his mother staring as Maryam spent time in a palm grove chasing nephews and teaching them new songs.

His mom had grabbed his hand and smiled. "It's like she's come back to us. Once more, she walks among us. Oh, Salem, what a joy."

With the great pleasure that his mother took in Maryam, how could Salem leave? He also felt compelled to stay as he watched his father's slow, proud steps across the beloved palm groves he could no longer manage with the ease he had before.

Now, he teasingly told his dad, "I have only just arrived! And now you say to leave. For the moment, we shall stay."

His father stopped to rest again. He lay a hand on a tall palm and looked up into its branches. "Oh, that we were as strong as the palms we cultivate so carefully. The storms come, and they hang tough! This old man? Not so much. And some families here in Yemen, they have more storms than most."

"I know, Dad. You are tired," Salem told him gently.

"But your son is here to help."

"It does my eyes good to see you! But I will tell you something, son. The things that make a father weary don't have to do with harvests. They don't have a thing to do with trimming trees or with an old man's aching bones. The thing that makes a father tired is worry for his son. But I suspect you understand that. I expect your heart's the same." Salem had filled him in—but just a little—on Jamal.

"Yes, a father worries, but I tell you: we will stay. At least, we'll stay for now."

Over the next days, he found solace and forgetting as he labored in the groves and urged his dad to rest. "I will manage things out here. You spend some time with Mom and get to know my daughter."

He loved the way the work could take his mind off Mary for a while. But the forgetting didn't last for long. When he sat down to rest or closed his eyes at night, he'd wonder where she was and if she was safe and warm. He'd think of Jamal and Sara. He'd sent them a note before he left, figuring the simpler, the better: *We love you. We're okay.* By that time, Jamal had returned to his friend's house and Sara to her program. He had dropped it in the mail while he was still in England. Postmarks, after all, can tell tales on wanted men.

Would Salem's children understand why he had to run?

Jamal, he suspected, had now begun to think that his father was a killer. Was Sara thinking, *Maybe . . .* He and Sara had made progress on getting to a better place in their relationship before their world had exploded, but that peace had seemed so fragile. He hoped that it would last.

More than anything, he was terrified for Mary and lost without her there. When he'd dreamed about these palm groves and being here again, he'd always seen himself walking hand in hand with her.

She'd opposed a family move here, but she'd always longed to visit. They'd made a lot of plans about the things they'd see together. More than anything, she'd been excited at the prospect of meeting Salem's family. Somewhere inside of Mary was the lonely little girl enchanted by the thought of a big and boisterous clan.

He closed his eyes and saw her face. *I'm here now. Where are you?*

He begged Allah constantly as he went about his work, "Please let her be okay."

On some days, the frustration overcame him. He should not be here at all! He should be looking for his wife! If she tried to send a message to the restaurant or the house, Salem would be utterly out of reach. But how could he look for Mary if he was locked away in jail? There were no easy answers.

All day long, he ached for the loss of Mary. Despite all their differences, something deep between them had managed to survive—and thrive—despite the difficulties they'd gone through in their marriage. She was a part of him now. So surely he would know it if she'd slipped out of the world. She *had* to be okay, he tried to tell himself. And as soon as it was safe, he would go back and find her.

But other times, he lost hope. He'd wake up in a sweat with a desperate need to touch his wife and pour out his heart to her. In the middle of some simple task—putting on his shoes, lifting a cup of tea—he'd begin to sob.

Every now and then, Salem's father would head out to a newsstand in a nearby town in search of news from England. He knew of one that carried papers from around the world. But there was no news to be found of a missing wife in Birmingham and her now-missing husband, suspected of foul play. Salem longed to reach out to Sadeq or Elliott to find out what they might have heard. But he dared not involve his friends—whom police might well be watching closely.

"You're losing weight," his mother said one day when he came in from the palm groves. She stared at him intently, as if she could somehow find a way to take away the sorrow that lived in Salem's eyes. "You're not sleeping, Salem, and you need to eat to keep up your strength. Your Mary will need you to be strong when all of this is over." She gently squeezed his arm. "And it *will* be over, son—with all of you together. Salem, you must believe." She gave him a small smile. "Then you must bring her to your mother, so I can meet this special Mary that I've heard so much about."

Someone else as well had been waiting for a long time to welcome Salem home.

She'd been standing by the front door on that first day as Salem and his daughter made their way into the house, exhausted from their flight. Small wrinkles were now visible around Yasmine's mouth. But the new soft roundness of her face only enhanced her beauty. She was a woman now. But somewhere in her dark eyes, he saw the hint of fun that had always been on display when they had hidden from the grownups in the palm groves or raced each other to the water's edge.

Now, he also saw a shyness in those eyes as his former wife stepped forward. "Welcome home," she said. Having raised the boys in Salem's father's household, she had continued to live there, helping with the cleaning and the cooking.

He smiled at Yasmine warmly and took her hand in his.

Soon after he arrived in Yemen, Salem took a stroll with Yasmine.

They sat beneath the trees as the moon spread its silver color on the palms, and they reflected on their lives. They spoke in detail of the lives they'd lived apart, and they spoke of the boys. Salem found himself ravenous for the smallest details about Omar and Ahmed. They now were men, not boys. And they were also strangers to their father.

Through Yasmine, he now knew that Omar loved to talk and had a gift for friendship and for humor. Ahmed was the silent, thoughtful brother who'd been gifted with a thirst for learning that was much like his father's.

"I've missed so much in those boys' lives," he said to Yasmine softly. "I've wanted to come back and fix that. A dad should know his sons."

She smiled at him shyly. "Two things you should know: they are good men, your boys, and they are happy men as well."

"You raised them into fine young men, and you did it by yourself. I thank you for that, Yasmine." While the son he'd raised had struggled, these two boys had thrived while growing up without him. There must be something mighty and determined— something strong and fine—in this petite and long-haired beauty who sat beside him in the breeze.

In the coming days, as requested by his parents, she became his wife again. He could honor her and Mary both as wives. And at night, the feel of Yasmine next to him would bring Salem a sweet comfort.

On the night that they were wed, he could feel in her touch the wanting of the thing for which neither of them had been ready when they were a young bride and young groom, more suited for the games of childhood than the marriage bed. Back then, there had been much waiting for the sign of blood, at which point the family would raise their guns to the sky in celebration. The bed sheets would give proof the bride had been a virgin, giving honor to her husband as they first lay together.

But now Yasmine gazed at him with a woman's eyes rather than a child's. And she reached out to press his cheek with a woman's touch.

For him, the kiss that followed was a search for refuge from his pain; the kiss was full of missing Mary. But the kiss also felt to Salem like a kind of coming home. This was a woman that he cared for—and perhaps could have loved had there been more time.

And this time she leaned into his touches with desire rather than a sense of duty. "I have been dreaming so long of this moment," she whispered into his neck.

And so his days in Yemen passed, filled with aches and comfort.

Sometimes he caught Maryam in a pensive moment. He would put his arm around her, and they wouldn't need to speak. He knew that Maryam must be missing the same things that he was: the sound of her mother's voice when she got excited, the way she'd up sneak from behind you and catch you up in a fierce and quiet hug. He knew that a certain way the breeze blew must remind his daughter of the flowery perfume that had always meant Mary was close by.

And for them both, he knew, the sadness they brought with them was now mingled with the other sorrows that the house had known.

One day, she leaned against his shoulder and asked in a quiet voice, "Will you please take me there—to the place it happened?"

He knew what she was thinking. She and his mom had talked a lot about the first girl in the house who had borne her name. He had seen them smiling over the old photo albums.

Now, he knew that her collected pain had mingled for the moment into a single ache. She was thinking of the aunt she would never meet and the people at her old school who had told her she was nothing. Her thoughts were of the boy who'd seemed to cherish her then crushed her with his *no*. And most of all, she mourned the mother whose gentle arms were now so far out of reach, who had served her a plate of eggs one morning, kissed her on the forehead, and disappeared with no goodbye.

And so he told her yes; he would take her to the well.

The next afternoon, they set out when he had finished work. When he told her he was ready, she grabbed a basket from the corner, and soon they reached the well and the tree that sheltered it.

Almost all at once, he was filled with sorrow and, at the same time, with a sense that things would be okay. He seemed to hear his sister's voice reaching out to him in comfort. After all, this was her place. *Do you know who Allah's watching? He's watching over* Salem, she would say each night when she tucked him into bed. And perhaps that was the last time that he'd felt truly safe.

And then she was gone, and if Allah wasn't watching a girl as perfect as his sister, might he take his eyes off Salem? A devastated little boy had begged his mother for the answer. She was too lost in her sorrow to answer Salem then, but he found his answers later in the holy book. In that way, he grew to trust once more in Allah's goodness. But the sense of joy—pure joy, that no one could take away—never came again.

"This is a tragic place," he told his daughter now, "but so much happened here. She found a man who loved her. Maryam, I'm so glad she got to know the way that feels." He put his hand against the trunk of the sacred palm. "This tree has stood witness to some defining moments in our village life. So much love. And hate." He felt tears rising up behind his eyes. "They shouldn't go together, but in this case, they did."

Maryam grabbed his hand. "She'd be glad you came here, and she would be so proud of all the things you've done." She leaned against her head against his chest. "And that you named me for her. She'd love that you did that." She paused. "I should have met her, Dad. She should be here with us."

From her basket, she took out handfuls of white candles and placed them carefully to circle around the tree

As Salem watched her light them one by one, tears of pride and thankfulness mingled with the tears of sorrow that had begun to form already in the corner of his eyes.

Yemen had brought changes in his daughter, who now seemed even more determined to be there for the people that she loved. She'd often walk with Salem in the evenings when she sensed that her father was feeling overwhelmed. She'd listen patiently as his mother told old stories that Maryam had surely memorized by now.

Every now and then, he'd see her turn her head when

she saw him standing close to Yasmine as the family gathered for a meal. But she'd known since she was little that her father had an ex-wife, and she and Yasmine had developed a kind of rapport. They liked the same TV shows, and Yasmine would often take the time to make Maryam's favorite *ka'ak,* a sweet treat that was crunchy on the outside and soft and flaky in the center.

Although she was fond of Salem's daughter, Salem understood that this was mostly Yasmine's way of proving herself to a husband from whom she had been long absent. "I know that you are hurting for your Maryam," she said to him one night as she rubbed his back, which was aching from a day of work.

Always a clever one, she also understood when to back away when it came to holding Salem's hand or touching him in front of Maryam. Girls from the West, she knew, were used to seeing love as a thing a man reserved for one woman at a time—in this case, a beloved mother who was gone.

One night, a month into his time in Yemen, he was sitting on the back porch with his mother after they'd had dinner. "I took Maryam out to the well," he said. "She asked if she could go—about ten days ago, I believe it was."

His mother watched him closely as she sipped her tea. "And every day since then, your Maryam returns to the palm and spends time at the well. As the sun sets every day, off she goes with her bag of candles— between her chores and dinner. Did she tell you this?"

Salem shook his head.

"She's a special one, your daughter. She feels things deeply, as your sister did. There's a whole lot on her mind, and I think that it runs through her, the sacred spirit of the place that she is drawn to. Your daughter feels the beauty, but she feels the loss as well."

"So much loss," he said. In his mind, the sorrows ran together; the sudden loss of Mary merged with the death of his sister, who should be here, giggling and whispering with his daughter. She would have been a kindred spirit to his Maryam.

The deep connections that his daughter now had with his mother and the village were just another reason that they had to stay. His father had informed him of arrangements he had made for Salem, Maryam, and Yasmine to go to Abu Dhabi, but Salem told him no.

"Maybe soon," he said. "I want to see my sons! But for now, the time is right for us to remain. We have been away too long already from you and from Mom." What a gift was Maryam to his aging mother! Hardly ever did a grieving mother get the thing she longed for most: the chance to hold their child once more. But Salem understood that when his mom looked at Maryam, it was as if another girl had returned to her—if only for a second and only in her mind.

And just as his mother needed her, Maryam increasingly seemed to need Salem's mother. Changes he could not explain were brewing in his daughter. Maryam still wept—more than she had before—but the sorrow now was interspersed with dreamy, happy spells. Sometimes, inexplicably, he looked into his daughter's eyes and saw a kind of joy he'd never seen in Maryam before. Did she have her eyes on one of the young workers in the groves? He wondered.

Then came the day things changed, and he knew he had to run—again.

As he headed off to bed that night, he could hear the voices of his daughter and his mother, who often stayed up late, talking well into the night. This time, Salem paused to listen. There was something different in his daughter's tone. He stood just outside the door, where he could hear but not be seen.

"I've only seen him three times," Maryam was saying. "I barely even know him, and yet the things I feel are so intense that I just want to weep. Is that crazy, *Jedda?* Is that even normal?"

"You are lucky, Maryam. "His mother's voice was gentle. "What you feel, my sweet, is love." She paused. "And like my other Maryam, you found it at the well—

underneath the palm, the enduring witness to the story of our family."

A cold fear rushed through Salem. Love found at the well: it was not a story he wished to see repeated with another Maryam he loved.

"But now something just feels wrong," Maryam whispered to his mother. "You see, when he and I . . ." She was now too choked up to speak. "I don't understand exactly what the danger is, but things felt, well, *so different* at the well today." Salem heard his daughter take a deep breath. "Oh, Allah, keep him safe," she whispered. "He's so beautiful, the boy."

Fear had made its way into his mother's voice as well. "Tell me. Please! What happened?"

Salem's heart was pounding. Beneath that ancient palm, things always seemed to take on a deeper meaning. What was about to change in his daughter's story?

"Oh, Jedda, it was magic. At first, at least, it was." Maryam paused to find the right words for what she had to say. "I've started feeling things that I've never felt. You see, at home, there was a boy that I *thought* I loved, but this is so much more. It's like there's a part of me that only he can see—like we're meant somehow to be together." Her words came in a rush. "And what if we had never come to Yemen? What if we'd stayed in

England, and we had never met? What if the world is filled with tragedies *that we never know have happened*—people you're supposed to meet but never get the chance? Perfect, perfect boys who live for their whole lives on one side of an ocean while you live on the other?" She sighed. "A part of you would always love him—although you'd never know his name."

"Oh, child, you take me back. Young love—it's so intense. But there will be other boys if things do not go well with this one. Yes—perfect, perfect boys. The world is full of those for a young and pretty girl." His mother's voice grew soft. "And for an old woman like myself? I can still remember how it felt to know one of those perfect boys. Tell me more about him. How did you meet this boy?"

Maryam's voice was hushed. "He first came last week. I was lighting candles. as I always do—to remember *her*. One night I felt him watching, and then gently—oh, Jedda, *so, so gently*—he put his hand on mine to help me light the candles. It was such a simple thing! But I can feel it still, the way he touched my hand." Her voice became a whisper. "Sometimes I almost feel like I'm in some kind of trance when I think of how it felt, his skin touching mine. Sometimes I just need to find a place to be alone, so I can remember that."

"And you say that he came back?"

"Oh, yes! Almost every night, he's there, although not

for very long. He must get back, you see, with the water for his family that he takes from the well. Oh, Jedda, he's so strong, but in his eyes, there's such a softness. And Jedda, do you know what? He calls me *beautiful*— his beauty from the well."

The anxiety had now risen to a peak in Salem. Young love at the well? In his family, that meant terror. It was all too much. He took a calming breath. Somehow, he knew exactly how Mary would react if she were here to talk this over with him, a calm hand on his arm. *Young love!* She would tell him. *Don't you remember, Salem? A certain pub, a dance. Let her enjoy her turn.*

But Maryam had gotten to the point where the story had turned dark. "Today was different, Jedda. Someone else was there, someone who was watching. And something changed in Mohsen. I could see that he was scared."

Mohsen. A chill filled Salem's body. *Just a coincidence,* he tried to tell himself. *It's such a common name.* But a part of him was ready to burst into the room and forbid his daughter from returning to the well.

His mother's voice was trembling. "Maryam! Did you say Mohsen was the name of the boy?"

"Mohsen Al Harithi is his name." Some of the old dreaminess returned to her voice.

Salem put his hand against the wall for support. Maryam's new love was from the same clan as the boy who had loved his sister.

His mother's voice was quiet with fear. "And did you say someone was watching? Do you know who it was, child, who was there with you and him?"

"Mohsen said he knew of him and that he was a person who loved trouble. Someone named Marouf." She paused. "Jedda! What's the matter? Should I call someone for help?"

"Get your father, please," her grandmother told her weakly.

Marouf. The very name made Salem rage. *Marouf*—with his evil eyes on Salem's sister at the well. *Marouf*—who had told lies about his Mary just before she'd disappeared. And now someone by that name had been following another of the women who made up the very essence of his heart. He wanted to grab Maryam and never, ever let the girl venture from his sight.

It was decided then. They would leave—and as soon as possible. But Maryam was inconsolable when she heard the news.

"Why must it be this way?" Salem asked his father in frustration. "Why must she run from love in order to be safe?"

Early the next morning, Salem's father, as the sheikh, went to the sheikh of the Al Kindi clan and came back with good news. He had offered reconciliation to the other clan to pave the way for a peaceful union between Maryam and Mohsen.

"Just as I thought, he was more than happy with the plan, "Nasser told his son. "This way is best for all of us, his clan as well as ours"

A sense of joy welled up in Salem, but also something else. Why had someone not stepped in long ago to protect his sister and the boy she loved? He had come to understand that the troublemaker in his sister's case was highly connected and very motivated to bring back reports such as the one that had put an end to young love—and to his sister's life.

The next day Salem, Maryam, and Yasmine left for Abu Dhabi, where his father had already made arrangements for the three of them to live. Still shaken from Maryam's encounter, he felt the time had come.

Not knowing yet about the plans that were being put in place for her, Maryam grew tearful, taking one last look toward the well as they left the house.

"It will all be good, my darling," Salem whispered to her as he held her close. "Things are such in Yemen that we

have to go. But my family will send word to your
Mohsen through his father, and he'll know where to
find his beauty from the well."

361

Chapter Fifteen

Interlude

After they had settled in at their rented house, Salem was more than anxious to be reunited with his sons. They came over right away for a family dinner and to greet their father and meet Maryam.

Both boys now towered over Salem and spoke in the deep voices of grown men. As they enjoyed a feast that Yasmine and Maryam had worked all day to prepare, Omar proved to be quite the storyteller with long and entertaining descriptions of his life.

Salem's favorite story was about Omar's boss at his accounting job: a kind man but forgetful.

"He set out for lunch one day, and I had to call him back." Omar shook his head in disbelief. "He was almost out the door. And I had to tell him, 'Sir, you must come back! You aren't wearing any shoes.' He likes to kick them off while he works at his desk."

Once, Salem caught Maryam with a big smile on her face as she turned to her brother. "Look at you!" she said. "You made our father laugh, which he hardly ever does."

Salem smiled and nodded. "I've needed that—to laugh." He reached for Omar's hand. "Thank you for that gift."

Unlike Jamal at home, Omar seemed to hunger for his father's wisdom. It seemed he was at a crossroads: he enjoyed his work, but now he wanted more. "Numbers are just numbers." He shrugged. "They don't bring me any joy, and yet numbers are the things I have to look at every day."

"Your calling may surprise you," Salem told his son. "When I was a young man, I never thought about a restaurant. But then I found myself living among expats who I knew must hunger for a taste of home. And the British loved it too, once they finally decided to break out of their routine, to try a little something new."

"That worked out great for you," Omar said as he dug into his rice.

Salem watched his son. "So what I'd say to you is to find the thing that will bring you joy." He shook his head and laughed. "Now, if I could tell you what that was, my advice would count for something."

Omar smiled. "No, Dad. That makes sense! Find a need and fill it. I'm just not sure I have a talent for any kind of job that would get me all excited."

"Well, I'm no cook," said Salem. "You don't have to be an expert at everything, you know, to open your own business. You just have to be good at finding talent—extraordinary people—and building a strong staff."

Omar thought about that. "Interesting," he said.

Yasmine had confided that Omar had begun to feel somewhat overshadowed by his brother, who was a rising superstar in the world of engineering.

Like his brother, Ahmed loved to spend time with his father. He would often stay late into the night, asking Salem questions about England and the life of an expat. Salem loved the way that his son thirsted for more knowledge. *This boy will go very far,* he said to himself.

As he got to know his sons, his bond with their mother was deepening as well. She would often come to Salem with a shy smile and take hold of his hand, her signal that she craved some closeness with her husband. And he was filled with gratefulness to have her in his life. He'd come to love her in a way that was shaped by years of their growing up together, telling secrets, playing games, and growing into a man and woman long before their time. He loved the easy way that she had with their sons, the way that just a word from her could seem to calm their fears or bring quick smiles to their faces.

And yet he knew that he could never feel for Yasmine the deep, abiding love that coursed through him every time he thought of Mary.

After his years with Mary, he'd come to see women's lives in a different way, and he wished Yasmine could somehow know the feeling of being loved with that same intensity. Surely Yasmine knew that it was for another woman that he sometimes sobbed so hard that he could barely breathe. But she loved him through it and held him in the night when he woke up to weep.

After a week or so into their time in Abu Dhabi, someone new appeared: a muscular young man with a shy smile and kind eyes that always seemed to focus on a bashful Maryam. Ahmed was quickly able to find a job for Mohsen in his engineering firm, and the boy settled into a rented home close to Salem's family.

It was a gift to Salem to watch Mohsen with his daughter. Maryam, he thought, would always know the joy of being cherished. She loved to keep her hand in Mohsen's, and when Mary's name came up, Salem saw that Mohsen would pull his daughter close or stroke her hair in comfort while she quietly missed her mother.

Often after dinner, the boy would sit with Salem, Ahmed, and Omar over coffee, and Salem grew more pleased with fate's choice for his daughter. Although it had been a spark of magic that brought the two together, they had things in common they could not have known when they met beneath the palm. Like Maryam, the boy had a love of learning; he dreamed of a house with a big library where he and Maryam could spend time every night.

"I'm so happy, Dad," Maryam said to Salem one night as she returned from a walk with Mohsen. "Do you think the other Maryam sent *my* Mohsen to me—since I met him at her place?"

"I think she'd be glad you found him."

"I think of her a lot, how she must have felt the same things that I did." A shadow crossed her face. "But then her story stopped."

He gently kissed the top of his daughter's head. "And yours has just begun."

Something felt completed that had started long ago. Love had blossomed at the well between a Maryam and a Mohsen—and this time, the evil was defeated. Love had won. Not hate.

Before too much time had passed, Maryam and Mohsen became man and wife.

With his family safely settled, Salem now turned his mind to Mary. Ahmed told Salem of a place to find news from around the world, but the investigation was not mentioned in any of the papers that were available to Salem.

One day, though, he did come across a name that was all too familiar to him. Marouf was singled out for giving information on a number of suspected accomplices in matters dating back to the seventies.

"It is important that no one go unpunished who played a hand in this," the article went on to say, quoting a top-ranked law-enforcement source.

But it also seemed Marouf had his share of detractors, with some claiming that he was overeager to see suspects jailed, to the point of naming suspects with little proof of their involvement in the violence. It was just as Richard said.

Scenes rushed through Salem's mind:

Mary, returning from a meeting: "You won't believe who I ran into . . . It was your old friend Marouf."

A short while later, she was gone.

Another memory crossed his mind: the reaction of the officer when Salem mentioned that his wife had an interest in the plight of the ill-treated Catholics in Northern Ireland.

He had asked, alarmed, if she was in the IRA.

And yet another scene: Marouf, many years ago, urging a young Salem to come out with him to the pubs: *Girls like you've never seen!*

He had been the one to bring Mary into Salem's life.

Had he taken her away as well?

Salem paused to think. She couldn't be in jail. If Marouf had been successful in getting Mary locked up, the police would have let him know when he'd reported she was missing. (And they would not be eyeing Salem for her disappearance.)

So she must indeed have fled! Mary had a keen eye for what was going on around her. She could have had an inkling that Marouf had set his sights on her. Perhaps she'd seen what was coming: Marouf reporting to officials that she'd been in attendance when "suspicious" gatherings were held.

A hint of relief—or at least a sense of hope—was sparked in Salem. Would that mean that she was safe? Not necessarily, he guessed. If others were convinced she was in the IRA, her life could be in danger—or they could have taken Mary's life.

He blinked back his tears. She was fine; she had to be. Surely, she was waiting somewhere to get word to her family that she was okay. But how would she find them now? If she found out that he had fled, perhaps she would leave word at The Rose and Palm when she felt the time was right. But for now, he didn't dare reach out to Elliott or Sadeq. Too many eyes were watching.

And what of Sara and Jamal? *They both must be so frightened; they must feel so alone,* he thought. But surely, the others at the restaurant would reach out to the children to see what they might need and offer their support. Plus, Sara had the leaders from her addiction program, where he had paid for her to have a room for as long as she might need to stay. Since the program housed young people with a variety of needs, some stayed quite a while. And Jamal had the family of his friend who had opened up their home to him.

He pondered going back. The police had seemed intent on looking at him with suspicion, but very rarely did they try a man for murder if there was no body. But he could not forget the way the officer had watched him, as if he was almost certain Salem was a guilty man.

Soon, he thought. But not yet.

Salem vowed that he'd stay positive and make the best of this time with his oldest boys. While he was here, he thought, he needed to find something to occupy himself and perhaps make some extra money. After all, an idle mind has more time to worry. That's what his father always said.

"I guess I should find a job," he said one evening as he sat out on the porch with Yasmine, Mohsen, and his children.

"You do look kind of lost," said Maryam, "without recipes to think about and reservation lists. She turned to her brothers. "In Birmingham, my mother says, he'd wake up in the night, talking in his sleep. Shafoot topped with minced meat! Bread to table four!

"There are lots of opportunities here in Abu Dhabi." Ahmed picked up his glass. "What did you have in mind?"

"Find your joy," said Omar. "That's what you said to me."

Salem thought about it, but nothing felt quite right.

"You know, I'd love a Mandi restaurant that's close enough for lunch," suggested Ahmed. "I know my mates would too. And that way, you'd be sticking to the thing that you do best."

"But this is just temporary, my time here in the city. I just need a job, not a business of my own."

"Well, you said you're good at hiring," Omar reminded him. "If you hire good people, they can keep it going when you leave."

Omar had a point. He hoped that's what was happening at The Rose and Palm: his great idea still thriving in his absence.

"Plus, Omar and I will be here to keep an eye on things. I think you should do it," said Ahmed.

And so Salem did. He called his restaurant Interlude since it was begun to fill the days between his time in Birmingham and whatever might come next. To his patrons, he hoped the name would come to stand for something else: a pleasant break within their day for nourishment and friends.

Luckily, a good site had opened up near the popular Hamdan Centre, which he took as a sign of luck. Ahmed, through his local contacts, helped him find a chef with talent who understood the local taste. Salem threw himself into the day-to-day management of the place, finding a familiar comfort in the old routine. The restaurant served gourmet variations of the traditional Yemeni Mandi, made with spices, rice, and meats.

After the first few nervous weeks, the tables stayed mostly filled as word got out about the authentic new addition to the dining scene.

Omar came in often with his friends and offered up suggestions to draw in the younger crowd. Omar knew the kinds of drinks the twenty-somethings liked, and he urged his father to keep the doors open late on weekends. Young people, he explained, were often ravenous after shows and concerts. Pleased, Salem found that he was right, and the young people filled big tables when they'd come in late.

He slapped Omar on the back. "You are a businessman! This might be your calling."

With her studies now complete, Maryam worked with Salem at the restaurant. She mostly acted as the hostess, greeting and seating guests and taking reservations. But there were also times he found her in the kitchen. Just as she had done at the Rose and Palm, she loved taking in the smells and bustle of the kitchen, watching how her favorite dishes came together.

When it came time for her break, Mohsen often would appear, and the two of them would sit quietly at a table in the corner. Salem liked the way the boy would listen so intently when Maryam would talk. He had prayed each of his girls would find such a boy who recognized their worth, and Allah had sent Mohsen.

Despite the busyness brought on by Interlude's success, anxious thoughts of Mary were never far from Salem's mind, especially at night when she came to him in dreams. In some dreams, she was happy, planting tiny Mary kisses on his face, whispering to Salem how proud she was of him. "It will be okay," she told him, and the dreams would seem so real that he could almost feel her soft hair brush against his chest.

Those would be the mornings that he'd curse the alarm, trying desperately to ease back into the dream.

In other dreams, she'd cry out, "Salem, help me, please!"

And he'd wake up in a sweat. "I don't know where you are."

After four months in Abu Dhabi, the dreams grew more intense. He had trouble sleeping and would wake up late, finding it increasingly hard to concentrate at work after his sleepless nights. To quiet his bad thoughts, he'd sit up late and drink—which just made it harder for him to fall asleep.

"I worry for you, Salem," Yasmine told him one night after dinner as Maryam was in the next room cleaning up the kitchen. On the table was his plate with the food left almost untouched. "You don't sleep, and you don't eat." Yasmine touched his hand. "You should see a doctor—soon."

Salem rubbed against his temple at the spot where the pain had begun to throb. "No doctor needed," he told her. "The diagnosis: stress. Too many people that I care for are unaccounted for. And here in Abu Dhabi, I am absolutely helpless to even try to help."

Yasmine stood and rubbed his back. "You can't go on

like this. You must be kinder to yourself," she said in a gentle voice. "You are a good man, Salem, and it is not your fault that you had to flee."

Salem had a good idea that Yasmine had gone to their sons with her worries for their father. The next night, they showed up for the evening meal and said they'd like to sit with him out on the porch after they'd had dessert.

Salem nodded as he stood up from the table while Maryam grabbed his plate. "That sounds very pleasant. Yasmine?" He nodded at his wife. "Pour us some coffee, please."

Once they had settled in their seats outside, Ahmed hesitated then looked down at the floor. "Dad, I hate to say it, but you're drinking way too much. And, hey, I understand! I know what's on your mind. But it's not good for your health. Plus, you need to eat."

"We need you to be healthy." Omar put a gentle hand on his father's arm. "You need to keep your strength up—for Mary, Sara, and Jamal. When it's time to go find Mary—and you *will* find Mary—they'll need you at your best."

Although he'd learned to calm his temper, Salem felt the old rage begin to twist inside him, fueled by exhaustion. With the nightmare he was forced to live, the last thing that he needed was a talk like this.

Then he looked up at his sons. They looked uncomfortable with the message they'd come to deliver, but they'd said it anyway—for the sake of Salem. For them, he would make an effort to ease up on the alcohol and look at the world clear-eyed. But he wasn't sure that he could do it. Even blurred by vodka, the world was sharp enough to sting.

"Very well, then," he said. "I will try my best. I do appreciate your concern for me."

"You also need to find a way to get some sleep," said Omar. "What can we do to help?"

"Aside from finding Mary, there's nothing you could do to make this any better," Salem told him with a sigh. "I am just frustrated. It seems the longer I'm away, the harder she will be to find. And I also worry for your brother and your sister." He closed his eyes against the awful truth and a brand-new headache coming on. "And the more they will have changed, the less we will feel like family when we all come back together." *When* or maybe *if*. But he did not say that out loud. He looked down at the ground. "I missed out on time with you, so I'd love to bring them here. So we all can be together. Here or perhaps in Yemen— if the blood revenge will stop." He stopped to shake his head. "Have they not had enough of hate in my beloved Yemen?"

They talked long into the night, with the boys asking for more details about Mary's disappearance.

Ahmed at one point leaned forward in his chair. "You say that Maryam has names—of some of the women that her mother used to do things with? That's a place to start."

"She made some calls in Birmingham, but mostly no one answered."

"And Sara and Jamal won't be hard to find," said Omar. "You know the family Jamal stayed with and the name of Sara's program. Even if they've moved on, you'll have good contacts there."

With no parent to have signed her out, Sara should still be living in the program housing. But if she had left on her own, run away perhaps, the administrators would have had no way to get word to her parents.

"I need to be in Birmingham!" said Salem. "And yet I just can't go. Although I think most of the police force believe that Mary fled, one officer at least seems convinced I hurt her. I never will forget the way that man stared me down. "

"Do you know a good barrister in England?" asked Ahmed.

Salem nodded.

"There's no evidence at all that you did something to her!" said Omar. "What rubbish that all is."

Salem shook his head. "The papers have a way of making men look guilty for things they didn't do." The thought of the news stories and their sordid details made him cringe. He fervently hoped his sons never saw those stories.

"We could go, the three of us, and you could lay real low while the two of us investigate," said Omar. "You could stay in some hotel—and not under your own name."

A sense of hope filled Salem. "You boys could take the time off to go with me to England?"

"How could we not?" asked Omar. "Our brother's there! Our sister. And they need to see their mother and make sure that she's okay."

"I don't know how to thank you," he told them, now near nears.

Ahmed put his arm around Salem's shoulder. "Tell us more about this brother and this sister that we're setting off to find."

"They're troubled, both of them, but I think meeting

you will help. I think that you're the family that they've needed all along. And Mary—you'd love Mary. She's heard so many stories about the two of you."

And so it was set. As soon as the travel papers and work considerations could be put in order, they set off for Birmingham: Salem, Ahmed, Omer—and Maryam as well.

When Salem had told Maryam about his plans to go back and search, she'd burst into tears. "I've been holding it in for so long," she said as she clung to Salem. "But the thought that soon, I might get to run to Mum—I just miss her so much. And Sara and Jamal!"

He had kissed her cheek. "Sweetheart, I know you do. Your brothers are smart men. With their help, I will find her."

He heard Mary in his head. But it might be your smart daughter who unlocks the mystery. Women's brains are every bit as efficient as your own."

"Come to Birmingham?" he asked her.

And then there were four.

Chapter Sixteen

Answers

After endless hours of travel, they arrived in Birmingham, exhausted.

As he had done so long ago when he'd first seen the city, Salem stepped into the fog and cold that was Birmingham, but this time it felt familiar, almost welcoming. Somewhere in that fog might be news of Mary.

They settled into a Travelodge with one room to be occupied by Salem and his daughter and another, one floor up, by Omar and Ahmed. Briefly, Salem had considered having the boys and Maryam stay at his house, but he knew there was a good chance that it was being watched.

After a quick dinner at a steakhouse across from the hotel, they settled into their rooms. He longed to show his sons the places in the city that meant the most to him. They'd heard so many stories of the factory, and, of course, he'd love for them to be treated to a meal at The Rose and Palm. But he felt Marouf's eyes on almost every place that he'd want to go. He might squeal on Salem as he had done with Mary. All of the old places were off-limits to Salem now.

Salem reflected on the fact that Mary's story had some similarities to the tragedy that had ended with his sister's death. The Marouf who had brought about the evil that took the life of Salem's sister had worked for the Sultan — much as the modern Marouf worked for the government in England.

The next morning, they began.

Maryam worked the phone, first searching for the numbers of the friends she remembered her mother speaking of. Not that it was easy. With last names that were common, she would often have to try several numbers before she was successful at reaching the right house. And in many cases, the woman wasn't home. She'd even reached one woman whom she'd spoken to before as she'd frantically looked for information in the first awful days of her mother's disappearance.

The woman said to Maryam that she thought of the family often and worried so for Mary.

Armed with names and addresses, Omar set off for the

treatment center while Ahmed took the job of searching for Jamal.

Salem longed to jump into the fray as well, but all he could do was wait and listen in as his daughter made her calls.

At first, they sounded fruitless.

"Do you know when she'll be home?"

"No, I was looking for Clarice."

"Okay, I understand."

After a quick break for lunch, Salem dozed a little as Maryam got back to work. At one point, he woke up from his half-sleep, catching a new, more energetic tone in his daughter's voice.

He sat up to listen as she talked.

"How long ago was that?" he heard his daughter say.

With every question that she asked, her voice rose in excitement:

"And you're sure that it was her?"

"And on what side of New Street?"

"Thank you so, so much!"

When she hung up, she was breathless. "She's here! Or at least, I think it's her. Oh, Dad, we may have found her."

Salem's heart was pounding as he stood up from the bed. "Oh, Maryam! Do they say that she's okay?"

"I think she is, at least. There's a little coffee shop." She looked down at the notepad that she'd been writing in. "It's called C and D Café. They say she's there a lot. There are other people who hang out there who are working for the cause—you know, the Catholics, Northern Ireland, like she used to talk about."

"But when did she come back here? Did she even leave the city? And where was it, Maryam, that she went when she left?" A nagging worry had begun to creep into Salem's head: was it possible that Mary didn't even *want* to be found by him? If all this time, she'd been in right here in Birmingham, she could have sent a message before he left for Yemen.

But he swept the thought away. Something had frightened Mary; something had made her flee. She would not have left her children if it had not been so.

"How does she seem?" he asked. Frantic, he glanced around the room for his keys—until he remembered that his car and keys were far away in Abu Dhabi.

"Oh, Dad, I don't know. But hurry up! Let's go. And maybe you can ask her." Maryam already was putting on her coat. "Maybe she's there now."

"Let me call a cab." Salem felt lightheaded as picked up the phone. They had rented a Ford Escort, but one of the boys had taken it when they'd set out that morning.

Before he could finish dialing, the door to the room burst open, and Salem looked up to see Ahmed. Salem ran to grab his arm. "I believe that we've found Mary."

"You've found Mum? Really? *You've found Mum?*" asked a familiar voice. "Where . . ."

Salem turned to see Jamal, who could not complete his question as Maryam ran to him and engulfed him in a hug.

"Dad!" All of the old sullenness was gone from Jamal's face. All Salem saw was pure relief that Salem was okay.

He moved to Jamal and hugged him, and they held on to each other for a long time until Salem finally pulled away to look into his son's eyes. "I worried for you, son, but they were after me—for a thing I didn't do."

"I was so afraid," said Jamal, breathing hard, "about what they'd do to you. How could they think that you would hurt her?"

"And you say that you found Mary?" asked Ahmed.

"Is Mum okay too?" Worry clouded Jamal's eyes as he waited for the answer.

After a brief explanation, Ahmed told them he would drive them all to the café. He was in the Escort; Omer had called a cab.

Salem's heart was beating hard as they found a parking place not far from the café. In the misting rain, they hurried toward the lighted sign.

With most of the tables filled, Salem glanced around, his heart pounding against his chest with every flash of blonde hair that he glimpsed.

Then he spotted Mary.

She was in the back, her head bent over a newspaper as she slowly sipped some coffee.

"Mum!" Maryam caught her breath, then she rushed to

Mary as the others quickly followed. Maryam and Jamal caught Mary in a hug.

Still in their embrace, Mary looked over her daughter's shoulder at her husband while tears streamed down her cheeks. The new onslaught of worries had added some new wrinkles around Mary's eyes, and she looked exhausted—but more beautiful than ever.

Salem, too, was weeping as she pulled him into her arms.

"Salem! You're okay," she cried.

"I was so worried, Mary. What happened to you, Mary? Where did you go? And why?"

Mary glanced behind her. "There's a little meeting room right there in the back. Come on. Follow me."

In the privacy of the back room, she was introduced to Ahmed, who had stood by quietly, smiling, during the reunion. Then Mary told her story as Maryam clung to her hand. After a round of new arrests, Mary said she'd come to fear that she might be next. "It was that Marouf!" she said. "He was asking questions. He was up to no good; I didn't trust Marouf."

"He works for the government," said Salem with a sigh. "But I only just found out."

"You're right. He's in intelligence these days—and he was watching me. Everywhere I went, he followed, and I was so afraid! I've been in Scotland, Salem." Mary reached for Salem's hand. She spoke in a low voice. "I hated to just leave, but I *couldn't* go to jail. The fact that I hadn't done a thing to be arrested for was no reason to rest easy. Marouf isn't interested at all in whether he's right or wrong—as long as he can give them names to make himself look good. I figured I'd come back soon—and it would be okay; they'd move on to something else. What proof did they have that I'd done something wrong? But then I saw the paper and it had your picture, Salem, and I . . ." She burst into tears. "How could they even think that? The things they said about you!" She paused to take a deep breath. "And so I came back to say, 'I'm here. My husband's not a killer.' But Salem, you were gone. Gone from the old house. Gone from The Rose and Palm."

"I ran as well," he said. He paused to take in all the news. "But, Mary, you came back here to go to the police? You might have been arrested!" He thought about it for a moment. "For me, you would have done that." Tears rushed back into his eyes as he reached for her again.

After she returned and learned that he was gone, Mary had been staying in a nearby town in hopes of hiding from Marouf. But she came back often to search for news of Salem and to check in with her friends, who still liked to meet at the C and D to plan rallies and fundraisers for the poor and oppressed. It had also become a gathering place for Northern Irish expats who were sickened by the Troubles in their country. As were some of the others, Mary was suspected, she believed, in some recent bombings.

"But anyone who knows me understands that's not a thing I would even think of doing," she said in a quiet voice. "Of course, there are atrocities that must be addressed—atrocities committed by the British government. But I don't fight with bombs; that is not my way. And no one else should either." She glanced at Maryam; her eyes rested on Jamal. "There were other mothers' sons and daughters near the places where some of those bombs went off."

He went to her and kissed her, reveling in the smell and feel of her. He ran his hands through her hair, across her cheek, and gently down along her arm. "I can't believe you're here," he whispered.

She looked around the room, then she looked alarmed. "Sara? Is she fine? Please tell me Sara's fine."

"We've just arrived in town," Ahmed stepped in to explain. "My brother's been assigned to go and check on Sara. They might not let him sign her out, but she'll know that we're here."

She nodded, understanding. "What should we do then, once we have our Sara? And where can we go?" Mary looked a little lost; Salem could tell she was exhausted. "We can't go back to the house!" she said. "I hear Marouf's still watching all the pubs and the neighborhood. Although we've managed to keep this coffee shop as our little secret. All the friends of the cause like to come here often, along with some other groups. But the government, so far, never comes to look."

"Come back with us? Please, Mum?" Maryam took her hand. "There's a great new restaurant that we've opened, and you'll love it."

Mary looked surprised. Then she smiled and nodded. "Oh! But where . . . and when . . .? As long as we're together. But Sara!"

Salem pulled her to him. "We left her in good hands, and Omar, I am certain, will bring her back to us."

They pulled into the hotel for a rest and to wait for news of Sara.

While Mary, Maryam, and Jamal headed to Salem's room, Salem walked with Ahmed to his room to see if Omar might be back.

As he got closer to the room, he heard Omar's deep, distinctive chuckle. A familiar high-pitched sound—like so many tiny bells—soon drowned out his laughter. A sense of warm relief washed over Salem; he had missed his daughter's giggles.

He burst into the room, and Sara ran to him.

"Thank you for finding me," she said.

"I see you met your brother. He's entertaining, huh?" Salem studied Sara, relieved to see how healthy she appeared. There were no signs of the weight loss or tired-looking eyes that he and Mary had been told could point to a continuing addiction. "Are you okay?"

he asked her.

She burst into tears. "I'm so worried about Mum. And when I saw the papers with their bloody lies, I was so worried, Dad, about what they'd do to you."

He stroked his daughter's hair and kissed her forehead. "That's why I had to run, but I came back to get you just as soon as I was able."

"And Mum! We need to find my mum!"

Salem pulled his daughter close and winked at Ahmed, who stood next to him, smiling. "I believe your mother, Sara, is very, very close," he whispered to his daughter.

And he knew just the place where they would all be safe.

◆◆◆

Three weeks later, he and Mary watched quietly from a corner table at Interlude as Maryam smiled at customers and efficiently led them to their seats.

"It's just like you always said." Mary reached for

Salem's hand. "The palm groves are magnificent, and your parents, Salem? It's like they're already mine—the family I never had." They had just returned from a quick trip to Yemen so he could introduce his parents to Mary and his youngest children. Despite the language barrier, his parents adored Mary, and Mary adored them. When they had walked outside at night or sat out on the porch, Salem's mother often linked her arm through Mary's or sat close enough to pat Mary's hand.

Now, Mary took a sip of tea. "I expected all of that, but I did not expect my Maryam to be dizzy with new love. And a husband, Salem! It was a nice surprise, although I would have loved to see all of that begin." She looked a little wistful.

"You're here now. We all are." They would be back in England in time for Jamal and Sara to start the new school year in the fall. Once they had graduated, Mary and Salem would divide their time between Birmingham and Abu Dhabi, where both restaurants continued to do well.

At the hostess stand, Omar had appeared to confer with Maryam. He whispered something in his sister's ear that made her smile.

Mary followed Salem's eye. "He's so good with the customers and so smart, like his dad."

"Yeah. This place will be in good hands when I can't be here." Omar seemed to finally have the job that he was born to do.

Mary squeezed his hand. "That's what a parent wants, to see that their children have found their places in the world."

A peace washed over Salem. Jamal's anger had subsided now, and Sara laughed a lot, their relief having turned into thankfulness. For the first time in a long time, Salem felt a calm assurance that they all would be just fine.

Outside the window, the sun was setting over Abu Dhabi. He gazed across at Mary. His place in the world would always be with her.

She gazed out at the sunset. "So beautiful," she whispered.

He watched the fading light play against her hair. "Magnificent," he answered, but he kept his eyes on her. He knew that out the window, purples might be melting into gold and orange, but he'd rather look at Mary: his sun, his moon, his stars.

The End

About Author

I was born in Aden, South Arabia, in what is now the Yemen Republic. (Salem, one of the main characters you'll meet in my book, also hails from Yemen.) Professionally speaking, I am a translator and legal consultant with a varied background. This includes work as a Prosecution Attorney and Advocate before the Aden Supreme Court in the 1970s.

It was through my uncle, a longtime solicitor in Birmingham, England, that I became familiar with the experiences of the Yemeni community living in the U.K. Later, my uncle's stories and his descriptions of the expat life came to form the background of my book.

The novel tells the story of two couples, including Salem and an Irish beauty he meets in Birmingham. Their stories are a way to explore some topics that are important to me. This includes the need to find common ground despite the many issues that can divide conscientious thinkers. Matters of culture, religion, and philosophies of government are just a few examples.

There are lots of topics touched on in my book that I'd like to delve into further in my blog. The plight of young girls in undeveloped countries and their lack of hope for the future is only one such issue. In my book, I illustrate the problems that they face through the heartrending stories of some young women close to Salem.

The blog will also highlight symbols, events, and places in the book. In the first pages of the novel, you'll see two characters experience a transforming moment beneath the branches of a palm in Aden, South Arabia, in what is now the Yemen Republic. It's no coincidence that I had the two meet there. The palm is a sacred symbol with a history that is rich and meaningful—and well worth exploring. In the next post that you'll see from me, I'll tell you a lot more. So there's much to talk about! I hope that you'll join me often in my corner of the web. I'll be looking forward to some thought-provoking conversations.